MURDER
OF A
DEAD
MAN

A CHANCE INQUIRY NOVEL

HOLLY NEWMAN

CHAPTER 1

JUNE 1816, SUMMERWORTH PARK, KENT

Sir James Branstoke slowly laid the letter he'd just received onto his desk. He unconsciously pinched his lower lip with his thumb and forefinger as he considered the letter's contents. It was from Mrs. Lilias Montgomery. He remembered her from when he and his wife, Cecilia, were searching for young Christopher Sedgewick. She'd provided key information that led them to rescue the kidnapped child, the Earl of Soothcoor's nephew.

The short, obviously dashed-off letter, heavy with evidence of tear-blurred words, stated the Earl of Soothcoor sat in a gaol in Lincolnshire, charged with murder.

Murder? Soothcoor?

His brow furrowed. Soothcoor was being held over for the next county assizes. In the meantime, Soothcoor had directed her to contact them for help. Wise man.

She begged for James and Cecilia to prove Soothcoor's innocence before he must appear before a judge. She felt too shattered to explain the circumstances in a letter. When they came to London, she would explain everything.

He didn't like the idea of hieing off to London right now; however, Soothcoor was a good friend—and more than that—a good man. Of course, he would assist. That went without saying. But his concern was for his wife.

She'd succumbed to the influenza that had swept through their village last month with brute force. She'd been so sick for a time that the doctor warned she might lose their unborn child. By some miracle, she had not, though the illness lasted days, then weeks. It—along with its lingering cough—drained her strength and vitality away.

He frowned as he considered Cecilia's condition. She needed to regain her strength—for herself and for their child. Her cough lingered, depleting her energy. Worse, he thought, it sapped her of strength. That was not the Cecilia he loved, admired, and respected. She remained caught in the aftermath of her long illness. Could this news rouse her from the illness's lethargy?

Either way, she needed to know, and the sooner, the better.

He picked up the letter, rose from his seat, and left the library to find Cecilia.

"Daniel!" he called to the footman on duty in the hall as he came clattering swiftly down the marble stairs to the ground floor. "Might you know where to find Lady Branstoke?" he asked as he strode toward the footman stationed by the front door.

The footman sharply straightened. "Yes, sir, she is with Cook, taking baking lessons."

"Baking Lessons?" James repeated.

"Yes, sir," said the footman. "Do you wish me to advise her you wish to see her?"

"No, I'll go to the kitchen." His heart lifted at the news of his wife's activity. "I want to see what she is learning. This should be interesting."

He turned toward the back of the house and went through a door under the staircase that led to a ground-floor servants' wing of domestic-activity rooms. That Cecilia was doing *something* gave him hope for her continued recovery. Perhaps this letter—dire though it might be—would be the nostrum for her return to health and energy. He missed his wife's mischievous smiles, her tinkling laughter, and the way her dark blue eyes could shine when she was happy. Tiny in stature though she might be, she could be a determined woman when she had the bit between her teeth and off to solve a problem or take someone to task. Including him! He missed those moments—though they might sometimes rankle.

He stopped at the entrance to the warm kitchen; the fragrance of baking filled the room—yeast, cinnamon, vanilla, and almond smells made his mouth water. Cecilia, wearing an apron meant for a larger woman, stood before a long worktable, slowly rolling out dough —or attempting to, judging by the irregular shape of the dough. Some of her fine, white-blonde hair had escaped its pins and framed her face in tangled wisps. Flour streaked her cheek and nose.

He let out a snort of laughter as she tried to push wayward hair strands away from her eyes, only to succeed in increasing the amount of flour on her face. How he loved this woman, he thought as he stared at her.

Her head flew up at his laugh. "James!" she cried out. She ran toward him to hug him, but he caught her arms and held her away.

"You have enough flour on your person for a cake, but no need to share," he told her.

She looked down at herself. "Oh! I guess I do. I hadn't realized," she said, stepping back.

"Lady Branstoke be an enthusiastic baker," Cook said, coming up to them. She handed Cecilia a towel.

Cecilia wiped what flour she could from herself.

"Don't forget your face," James suggested.

"My face?!" Cecilia exclaimed, her beautiful blue eyes wide.

"Let me 'elp ye," Cook said, taking the towel to gently wipe the flour off Cecilia's face. "Now to get you out of that apron so Sir James might speak with ye," she said, pulling the apron strings and helping Cecilia to lift it off from around herself and over her head.

"But my shortbread biscuits!" Cecilia protested. "I wanted to have those with tea today."

"Hannah can finish 'em for ye," Cook advised, and on her words, a young scullery maid ran over to the table where Cecilia had been rolling dough and took up the task.

Cecilia looked over at the maid. "Oh, all right," she said doubtfully, her shoulders slumping. She held her hand against her face as she coughed slightly.

James took her arm. "Come with me. We have a letter from Mrs. Montgomery."

"The woman who helped us find Soothcoor's nephew when he'd been kidnapped?" Cecilia asked, looking back at the kitchen worktable one last time.

"She asks for our help," James explained as he led her back to the main part of the house.

"Help?" Cecilia repeated, looking up at him.

He saw interest flicker in her eyes and part of him relaxed. "Let's go to the morning room and I'll let you read it for yourself."

"It's serious?" Cecilia asked between coughs. She pulled a handkerchief out from where she'd tucked it in her sleeve. Grains of flour came with it.

James nodded. "Very."

He led her to the sofa before the fireplace and handed her the letter. He sat down next to her as she read the note from Mrs. Montgomery.

"What!..." Her left hand flew to her chest. *"Impossible!...No! No! No!"* she cried out as she read the letter. She looked up at James, shaking the letter she held in her other hand. "James, we must be off to London immediately!" She bounded off the couch. "I'll get Sarah to start packing!" Her enthusiasm set off a stronger coughing fit. She held her handkerchief to her face.

James grabbed her wrist before she could go running off. He repressed a smile at her enthusiasm yet worried for the continued strength of her cough. "Wait. We should discuss this first. And plan."

"But Soothcoor!" Cecilia protested, trying to pull away.

"Yes," James conceded. "He needs our help, but he is not in any immediate danger. Sit, please," he said, encouraging her to resume her seat next to him.

She did as he asked, wringing the handkerchief between her hands.

Inwardly, James felt excitement at Cecilia's reaction to this turn of events. This could be the event she needed to shake her out of the illness fatigue that plagued her, along with the lingering cough—so long as they could successfully rescue Soothcoor from this murder charge. He wondered who had been murdered, why, and why would Soothcoor be a suspect? Of all people to be a murder suspect, Soothcoor would be the last person he would consider.

"I can wish Mrs. Montgomery had provided more details in her letter, but by the tear stains, it appears she was highly distraught," he said.

"I believe she is the lost love we all surmised caused Soothcoor's confirmed bachelor status," Cecilia said.

"Truly?" James asked. "What led you to that belief?"

"Their careful formality with each other after we rescued Krishan," she explained, using the child's Indian nickname. She raised her handkerchief to her face and gently blew her nose.

"Hmm…I hadn't noted it at the time. Thinking back, you might be correct, my dear. She does state that Soothcoor is in a gaol in Lincolnshire. That is likely near where the murder occurred. In that case, we need to plan for an extended journey."

"The new fast, light carriage for us and the traveling carriage for Sarah, William, and the luggage?"

James nodded. "We'll send them—and a couple of outriders ahead to secure spare horses, meals, and lodgings—to an inn near the gaol, while we stop in London to meet with Mrs. Montgomery."

"You don't believe we shall need to begin our investigation in London and be there a few days?" she asked.

James shook his head. "No, not if the murder occurred elsewhere. We may need to return to London for another part of the investigation, but certainly not for the murder itself. We'll take Romley as our coachman and John Coachman for the traveling carriage."

Cecilia nodded. "Yes, Mr. Romley has proved himself a useful man in our other investigations. I'll get the household organized. Will you write to Mrs. Montgomery and inform her we will be to see her tomorrow morning?"

"Yes…And Cecilia, how are *you* doing?"

She cleared her throat and smiled faintly. "I believe an investigation will be more beneficial as an activity to speed my recovery than learning to bake proved to be."

He leaned forward to kiss her. "That's my dear delight," he said. He rose and helped her to her feet. "Let the adventure begin," he finished.

Cecilia smiled. A true smile, the first James had seen in weeks. He smiled back, a weight lifting from his chest.

CHAPTER 2

MRS. LILIAS MONTGOMERY

"*R*omley, change the cattle at our townhouse stable and tell Atticus he's to be our postillion when we leave. It will be his responsibility to see that our horses get returned to London tomorrow," James instructed as he handed Cecilia out of the carriage in front of Mrs. Montgomery's rented London townhouse. "Before you go, I have an errand for you."

"Aye, sar?" Romley said, making an adjustment to one of the horses' traces.

James pulled a note from his jacket pocket. "Take this to Dr. Nowlton at Malmsby House and await his reply."

Cecilia looked up at her husband in surprise. Dr. Merlin Nowlton was the youngest son of the Duke of Malmsby. Society gossip said the young man had chosen to become a doctor after his mother had passed away following a long, painful illness. His goal in life had become to help others in honor of his mother. Not at all the proper occupation for a duke's son, the wags whispered. Cecilia disagreed. She thought it quite fitting for a duke's son. More fitting than to think the church or the military were the only honorable occupations.

"When should I come fetch ya, sar?" Romley asked as he took the envelope from Sir James.

James shook his head. "We will walk home. It is but two blocks and we will be riding in a carriage for the rest of the day. The day is mild, and we could use the bit of exercise."

Cecilia nodded in agreement, though surprised to hear James encouraging exercise and not continuing to treat her as an invalid. She'd been sick too long.

"Mrs. Dunstan will be wantin' to hep," Romley warned, speaking of their London townhouse housekeeper.

James laughed. "Yes, set her to preparing a basket for us of food and beverage so we don't have to wait for a coaching inn's fare."

"Aye, sar," George Romley said, tugging at his forelock.

Lady Cecilia and Sir James Branstoke climbed the stairs before the Montgomery townhouse as Romley drove away.

"You do know," Cecilia said quietly, "the cook at Summerworth Park already provided victuals. The basket is under the seat."

"Yes, I know, but, as George said, Mrs. Dunstan likes to help."

Cecilia grinned at her husband. "You are thinking less mischief this way."

"We have a most earnest household," he observed.

She stilled his hand as he would raise the door knocker.

He looked down at her.

"Why contact Dr. Nowlton?" she asked.

"I am concerned for you," he said.

"James, I am well now."

"And so you appear to me as well, but with that continued cough, I need a doctor's assurance, Cecilia. Women rarely travel when carrying a child, and not two weeks ago, you were extremely sick. I am worried for you. The entire household is worried for you and our babe. Allow me to be the cautious husband," he said.

"For the impetuous wife," she said drily.

His small smile in response as he grabbed the door knocker had Cecilia smiling in turn.

A moment later, they were being escorted into the house and the butler was conducting them up the stairs to a small drawing room.

While the property lacked the paintings and other ornamentation found in an owned home, Cecilia thought the townhouse neat and well-maintained, the furniture had the high polish only attainable through carnauba wax, bees wax, and industrious polishing. Judging by what she saw as they followed the butler, the décor was done primarily in beige and cream with chocolate-brown accents. She preferred more color in her décor. How sad one couldn't be choosy in a rented property, she mused wryly.

Mrs. Montgomery, dressed in mourning black, rose from the sofa as her butler opened the drawing-room door. She rushed toward them. "You're here! Thank heavens, you're here!" she cried. She grabbed Cecilia's hands. Tears glistened in her blue-gray eyes.

"Yes," Cecilia said soothingly as she gently led the distraught woman back to the sofa and sat beside her, willing an incipient cough to subside. James pulled a chair closer to the sofa and sat down.

Mrs. Montgomery dabbed at her eyes with the handkerchief she'd kept grasped in her hand. "We were so happy," she said softly, "until this nightmare." Her eyes threatened to spill more tears. She looked up at Cecilia and then over at James.

Cecilia exchanged glances with James.

"Please give me a moment to settle my nerves now that you are here. I am not typically a woman given to emotional displays," Mrs. Montgomery said. "I left instructions with Curling, my butler, to see that tea and coffee were served when you arrived. He should be here soon."

"Take your time," James said in his calm manner. "We are here now, and rest assured, we will help."

She nodded. "Alastair said you would in the letter he wrote me." She smiled wanly.

Cecilia noted the use of the earl's first name. As she surmised, there was a relationship between this woman and the man all society referred to as *the dour earl* else she would not have addressed him by his first name. She patted her hand as she studied the woman. Her thick, dark mahogany-colored hair showed strands of gray at her temples, and faint lines bracketed her eyes, reflecting a person who typically smiled more than they cried in life.

"I'm not sure where to start, to be able to explain everything to you," she said helplessly.

"Perhaps if we said what we know, which isn't much, might that help?" Cecilia suggested.

"Yes, please," Mrs. Montgomery said, her breath coming out in a deep, painful sigh.

She paused as the door opened to admit a young maid with tea and coffee. After they'd been served and the maid had left, Cecilia continued.

"We understood from you when we met you at Lady Amblethorpe's musicale last December, and from what the Earl of Soothcoor has told us, you knew him from his childhood Scotland visits to Laird Murdoch Graeme, his maternal grandfather."

She nodded. "He came every summer. He was a good friend to Malcolm—that's my late husband's name. The two of them would be off fishing, hunting, and hiking together throughout the summer, and I was the little girl who chased after them. I so wanted to do what they did," she said, a gentle smile ghosting her lips.

"As we got older, my feelings for Alastair changed. I wanted him to see me as a young woman, not as the pesky girl who trailed after them. Finally, the last summer he came, I was of age. I wore my hair up and was looking forward to being introduced to Scottish society in the fall. And Alastair admitted he'd noticed me. Always had and had been waiting for me to grow up. I was afire for I'd loved him for years. He said he returned my feelings. We were so happy that summer," she said, smiling at her memories.

Then she grew serious. "But when Alastair approached my father, my father forbade the match. He would not allow any daughter of his to marry a *Sassenach*, even if he was only half-tainted by English blood. He said he had already arranged with Ewan Montgomery that I would marry his son, Malcolm."

She shook her head at the memory. "I was devastated. Yes, I liked Malcolm well enough as a friend, but to marry? *No!*"

Cecilia smiled. "You seem rather emphatic for a woman who has had three children from the man."

Mrs. Montgomery nodded slightly. "You see, though we were all friends, there was always something different about Malcolm," she said, her voice apologetic.

"Different?" Cecilia prompted.

She nodded. "Sometimes he could seem...different. It was why most people in the area only tolerated Malcolm. They were a bit afraid of him, I think. I didn't know why."

"But you weren't?" James said.

She shook her head. "Our families were close. It just seemed part of Malcolm, of who he was. And Alastair liked him, even if sometimes Malcolm did act differently."

Cecilia smiled and nodded. "Alastair would."

"But what about your father? Did he see anything odd in Malcolm?" James asked.

"My father was a good friend of Ewan Montgomery and only saw what he wanted to see: a fine Scottish match for our Montgomery and Fraser families."

James nodded his understanding. He crossed one leg over the other and leaned back in his chair. "Can you tell us more about Malcolm and his strangeness?"

She compressed her lips together for a moment, then took another sip of her tea, set her cup down, and folded her hands in her lap. "I suppose I must if you are to understand," Mrs. Montgomery said, "though it has long been carefully hidden and quietly denied," she explained softly.

Cecilia and James frowned. Cecilia set the cup she'd been about to drink from back in her saucer and leaned forward to listen.

Mrs. Montgomery's brow furrowed as she looked between Cecilia and James. "Malcolm was smart, yet he was ever a timid soul. Growing up, he was strictly tutor-educated and rarely traveled anywhere. He did not want to go away and resisted the efforts of his father to encourage a greater experience in life. And ultimately, when he did try, he couldn't handle boarding schools or, later, university."

"He was bullied," James suggested.

Mrs. Montgomery shook her head, denying this logical summation. "One would think so, but no. The headmaster at the first boarding school Malcolm had been sent to told Mr. Montgomery that Malcolm had an evil, violent streak in him."

"Evil and violent?" Cecilia asked incredulously.

She nodded. "It was a surprise to everyone and considered more the fault of the headmaster than Malcolm. When the Montgomerys brought him home, to us, and everyone else, he appeared the same pleasant boy who had gone off to school. After a time, they tried enrolling him in another boarding school. He didn't last long there either. No one could understand what these prestigious boarding schools were saying. Malcolm, evil? Violent?"

"Quite at odds with the timid soul you knew as a child," James suggested. He leaned forward in his chair, resting his elbows on his knees as he listened intently.

She sighed. "Yes. Malcolm angrily refused to try a third school, so tutors were hired instead. Malcolm had a keen intellect, and he liked learning. Ultimately, Vicar Douglas became his educator and Malcolm calmed down and felt happy."

"So, at a young age he was considered—in some way —defective," Cecilia said. She frowned. "That sounds harsher than I mean it to."

"But it is true, in its way," Mrs. Montgomery said. "Ewan Montgomery—quite unlike my own father— liked Alastair Sedgewick for Alastair did not mind Malcolm's occasional odd behaviors and strangeness, and he seemed able to pull Malcolm out of his timid self. Malcolm enjoyed the adventures Alastair suggested. Mr. Montgomery trusted that Alastair wouldn't lead either of them into mischief. They would simply enjoy the summer outdoors."

Mrs. Montgomery paused and plucked at the folds of her gown. "Alastair told me Malcolm felt damaged," she said softly, "splintered like a log with an ax embedded in it. He said sometimes they would talk for hours at a time about how Malcolm felt. Malcolm informed Alastair that he had blocks of time that he could not account for. He did not know where he'd been or what he'd done. It was like he'd been in a walking, waking sleep."

Cecilia and James again shared concerned glances.

"Abiding by my father's wishes, I married Malcolm." She smiled gently. "In the early years of our marriage, we were content. We did not have a love match. We were friends and that helped. Malcolm seldom displayed his strangeness. It was whispered that it was to be hoped he'd outgrown whatever malady occasionally afflicted him. He had only a few times of losing his sense of self and time and that pleased him, too."

She picked up her teacup but did not sip her tea. She stared into the cup as if it were a memory mirror. "Then, sometime after Sorcha, our second child, was born in 1800, he started changing."

"Changing?" James prompted.

Mrs. Montgomery compressed her lips for a moment. It was obvious she didn't quite know how to continue. She licked her lips. "He became more than one person," she said in a rush, a red blush rising in her cheeks.

"How do you mean?" Cecilia asked.

She lifted her hands helplessly, then let them fall back into her lap. "Just that. When I talked to Malcolm, sometimes it wouldn't be Malcolm I would be speaking to." She laughed brittlely. "Sometimes it would be Gregory, occasionally Archie—an evil, violent man, that one was." She visibly shivered at some memory only she could see.

"E'gad!" exclaimed James as Cecilia drew in a sharp breath, her eyes wide. She reached out to Mrs. Montgomery, laying her hand on hers in comfort for the memories.

"Sometimes it would be another altogether! Gregory was the nicest of the—of the—I don't know what to call them. People? Others? Ghosts? He kindly told me they all knew what Malcolm did and what each other did; however, he said Malcolm had little memory of what they did or said, just remnants of feelings. Gregory said no one liked Archie. Unfortunately, Archie was growing stronger, and he warned me that he might not be able to protect us from Archie!"

"The church would call him demon possessed," James said.

Mrs. Montgomery nodded. "Of a certainty they would, but it wasn't outside demons he warred with, not like they speak of from the pulpit. Malcolm reassured me that, contrary to what Gregory said, he was gaining more awareness. We had a very serious discussion. He knew he was ill—admitted he'd been ill since he was young—but he told me he could handle things. I wanted Malcolm to see a doctor. There are some brilliant doctors in Edinburgh who deal with illness of the mind. Malcolm said *no*. And for several years, it appeared Malcolm was correct, he could manage things. We lived happily, with only occasional instances of other persons taking him over at odd—sometimes humorous—times."

"But eventually, his demons won in the battle for control," James concluded for her.

"Yes, his personal demons that lived within him." Mrs. Montgomery visibly swallowed and stared across the room at another distant memory.

"Rather than demons, let's call them '*others*'," Cecilia gently suggested.

She smiled weakly at Cecilia. "Aileen, our eldest daughter, had just turned fifteen and stood on the precipice of leaving childhood behind. She was blossoming," she said quietly.

Cecilia and James nodded in understanding.

"One night, sometime after midnight, Malcolm stumbled into my room. He was shaken and crying. He'd *'woken'* if that is what to call it, back in control of his body and found himself bending over Aileen's bed. He felt lust thrumming through him. Lust for Aileen!"

"He thought he'd been possessed by one of the *'others'* within him, and they lusted for Aileen," James said.

"Yes. And at that point, it shook him so badly that he finally made the decision to seek help, to check himself into a sanatorium. If his *'others'* gained more control, he feared what he might do when one of them was in control. He said he couldn't take that risk for us. In consultation with various medical resources and the family solicitor, he first chose Autumnvale as the sanatorium, as it was only one hour away. It was a small, sunny, pleasant facility. Most of the patients in residence were older and suffered from dementia.

"That poor man," murmured Cecilia.

"He became terribly melancholy," Mrs. Montgomery said. "At first, I visited regularly. After six months, he asked that I not come anymore, that in consultation with his doctor, he'd decided to move to Camden House, a different sanatorium farther way, down in Lincolnshire." She looked away from them as she sighed deeply and dabbed her tearing eyes with her handkerchief.

Resolutely, she lowered her hand and turned back to face them again. "Two months after that, I was informed he'd died, that he'd taken his own life," she said matter-of-factly, "Which we know now was a lie," she ended with a long sigh.

James frowned. "How could he have arranged all that? For I gather he must have," he said.

She shook her head. "I don't know. I surmise it was with the help of his cousin. His cousin was Malcolm's father's estate executor and so I wrote to him—as I thought only proper—to inform him of my intent to marry Alastair. And it was he, in turn, who wrote to me to say I couldn't marry Alastair as Malcolm was alive."

"Is this cousin the estate executor and guardian of your son as well?"

She smiled a crooked, wry smile. "Yes, he is," she acknowledged. "But he has been fair, I really have no complaints other than he did not want me to bring the family to London for Aileen's come out. He certainly didn't agree due to any argument I presented! Aileen and Sorcha worked to wear him down until he laughingly agreed."

"And he knew all along that Malcolm lived?" James asked.

She nodded. "Three weeks ago, I received a long letter from him, full of apologies for the deception, as he admitted Malcolm was alive. He said the faked death was Malcolm's idea. He said for a while he feared Malcolm would take his own life, but once he'd faked his death, he seemed to relax and no longer talked of death, so his cousin took that to be a good thing."

"Did anyone else know Malcolm Montgomery was not dead?" James asked.

"In his letter, Boyd said only Malcolm's father, himself, the vicar, and my father knew. I am highly distraught to know my father and the vicar were knowledgeable and condoned the lies."

"I think it the height of impertinence for them not to consider you might wish to remarry," Cecilia said. "Typical male blindness."

James raised an eyebrow at her summation.

"Oh, don't look at me like that, you know what I mean," Cecilia said with a mild laugh.

"How is it that Alastair came to be arrested for his death?" James asked.

She shook her head. "When we discovered Malcolm was alive, Alastair decided to go see Malcolm. He said he would discuss paperwork for a divorce. He promised he would convince Malcolm it would be for the best. From what I gathered from Alastair's brief note, he must have been there when Malcolm died or had just left. I don't know," she said helplessly.

"Do you know Mr. Montgomery's cause of death?" Cecilia asked.

"No! It has not appeared in any of the correspondence I've received. Not even from Alastair!"

Cecilia frowned and turned her head to her husband. He returned her regard and shook his head. "It's late June; most likely, the quarterly assizes for that county are past, which is to our advantage," he said. "I don't know what the schedule would be before the next assizes in that area. We need to find out how he died, and we need to investigate before the trial."

"Yes," Cecilia agreed. "There would be too many who would love to see a peer found guilty. Best if we could absolve him *before* this goes to trial."

"My thought as well. Mrs. Montgomery, thank you for contacting us. Soothcoor is a great friend. We will do all we can to establish his innocence." James rose to his feet. Cecilia rose as well.

"Don't worry so," Cecilia said gently. "I know it is not in Soothcoor's nature to kill someone. We just need to find who did."

"Thank you, thank you so much," Mrs. Montgomery said as she stood and rang for her butler. "Can I get you any refreshments to take with you?"

"No, we prepared for this journey, and I know our cook will have more for us at our townhouse. Our servants made sure we were prepared!" Cecilia told her with a small laugh.

As the butler saw them out, Cecilia clung tightly to

James's arm. "I have never been so shocked by a tale. Have you heard of such an illness before?" she asked.

He shook his head. "Not directly, but if there are those who suffer from voices talking to them in their heads and others who see things that are not there, I fear there is much that those who study medicine today do not know about the mind, and these medicine scientists are only now beginning to learn."

"Poor man. I wonder if there was a cause of his affliction?"

"It would be hard to say. After seeing the types of illness of the mind that some of our veterans returned from the wars with, I would venture a guess that it was trauma related. Most likely—considering the early stages of perceptions of him as different—it was childhood related."

She nodded. "And how he must have loved his family if he concluded he needed to separate from them for their sake," she said. "Poor man. Poor, poor man."

James nodded and reached across his body to pat her arm.

CHAPTER 3

VISITORS WEIGH-IN

 $\mathcal{M}$ athers, their new London butler, met them in the entrance hall when they arrived at their London townhouse. "You have visitors. The Honorable Mr. and Mrs. Charles Sedgewick. They arrived not long ago and asked if they could wait. I have shown them into the parlor."

"Thank you, Mathers," James said with gravitas.

Mr. Sedgewick and Miss Rangeswamy met at their home near the end of their last adventure. Though Cecilia had thought to encourage a match between the boisterous Miss Rangeswamy and the Bow Street agent, Lewis Martin, the young Indian woman caught the eye and heart of a younger half-brother of the Earl of Soothcoor. After their wedding in April, they were to take a ship to India to settle the estate of another brother, Owen, Christopher's father. Cecilia was surprised Mr. And Mrs. Sedgewick yet remained in England.

"Well," Cecilia said with a laugh, "I had not expected we would be here long and not thought I'd remove my bonnet, instead I shall have to curb my impatience to be off," she declared as she removed her gloves and untied her bonnet ribbons.

"Yes. Though I thought they would be sailing for India by now."

"Such was my thought, as well," Cecilia said.

"I wonder if Soothcoor notified them or if Mrs. Montgomery sent a message to them as she did us. I am sure they are anxious for Soothcoor. Here, let me help you with your pelisse," James said, reaching out to ease the jacket off her shoulders. He handed it to the footman who held her bonnet and gloves. It had been an unusually cold spring, and now, at the beginning of summer, winter outer garments remained in use. At least on this day, it wasn't raining as it did so many others.

"I took the liberty of ensuring they had tea and coffee while they waited," Mathers said as they walked toward the parlor door.

"Excellent," Cecilia said. "Thank you. I became so involved in listening to Mrs. Montgomery that I didn't drink my tea. I could use some now, or perhaps coffee would be better."

"Yes, madam," replied Mathers as he opened the double doors to the gold parlor, the ground-floor parlor reserved for guests.

Inside, Charles and Rani rose to their feet. Rani ran toward Cecilia, taking her hands in hers. "You will help! Yes, yes!" she said. "I have been crying, oh so much crying, crying. Now you are here, and I know there is no need to cry. I can be happy."

Cecilia's eyes watered with memories of Rani and all she went through six months ago. Now she had to laugh at Rani's ebullience. She had almost forgotten the young woman's enthusiastic manner. She radiated sunshine.

"How is Christopher?" Cecilia asked as she sat down on the gold and Egyptian brown striped sofa.

"He is well. He has been staying at Appleton with my Charlie's mother, the Dowager Countess of Soothcoor," Rani said.

"Soothcoor wrote to say the three of you would be sailing to India after your wedding," James said.

"That was the plan," Charlie Sedgewick acknowledged wryly. "Only I came down with influenza right after the wedding. Sicker than a dog. Missed the sailing. Dashed nuisance all around," he said.

James gave a short laugh. "I can imagine it was! Cecilia has just recovered from the same illness."

Charlie looked at Cecilia. "Nasty stuff, ain't it?"

"Indeed, it is."

"Well, with all that, we'll leave in the fall, if everything is right and tight here. Didn't want to be sailing around Africa during the southern hemisphere winter, you know," Charlie said.

James drew out his snuffbox. "We met with Mrs. Montgomery this morning and learned that her husband had not been deceased as reported and Soothcoor went north to investigate."

Charlie nodded. "And somehow the news spread throughout society. Nothing in the press, but someone spread something somehow. Society has all taken to shunning Mrs. Montgomery, thinking the worst of her. That she led my brother on."

James frowned. "How could that get about? What would be the reason?"

Charlie shook his head. "I couldn't venture to guess. It's impacted Miss Montgomery—"

"Aileen," Rani provided, nodding.

"—and her engagement as well. Caught the eye of Benjamin Stackpoole. Steady sort. Not like me," Charlie said with a deprecating laugh. Rani playfully punched his arm. He grinned at her. "Baron Stackpoole wants his son to cry off," Charlie continued. "So far, the lad has stood firm."

"And what about the news of Mr. Montgomery's death?" Cecilia asked.

"We learned of that through Mrs. Montgomery. Sent round a note, she did. So far, that does not seem to be known," Charlie said.

James frowned. "Only a matter of time, I'm sure. Society will make a furor over that, particularly with Soothcoor arrested."

"There was a man who come around Mrs. Montgomery all the time," Rani said. "He was...what is word...*Rival?* Yes, yes, rival, I think, for Mrs. Montgomery. But she like Lord Soothcoor better."

Charlie snapped his fingers. "Yes, my sweet! Thank you. Nearly forgot about him. Cameron Ramsay. A widower from Scotland. He was courting Mrs. Montgomery, too—or seemed to be in a mighty weak manner. He was always about. He left London at the same time Alastair did. I thought that odd after all his attention to Mrs. Montgomery. I wouldn't put it past him to make trouble for my brother," he said sourly.

James nodded. "We'll keep watch for any news of him. His departure from London could be a coincidence. This is the time many people leave London for the country. It might be best if Mrs. Montgomery and her family left the city."

Rani turned to her new husband. "Appleton?" she asked, naming the Richmond estate of the Dowager Countess of Soothcoor.

Charlie cocked his head to the side. "Mama would probably agree with that, and Christopher would like more people around him, I'm sure." He looked at James. "We'll see what we can do."

"I think that would put Soothcoor's mind at ease as well," Cecilia said.

"Guess it was a good thing I got that plaguey influenza," Charlie said.

"If you will excuse us," James said, rising to his feet. "Lady Branstoke and I need to get heading north."

Charlie hurriedly got to his feet. "Thank you for seeing us and looking into this matter."

"No thanks are needed. Alastair is a good friend," James said as he walked them to the door.

"And the best of brothers," Charlie said. "The very best."

~

"Excuse me, sir," Mathers said after the door had closed behind the Honorable Mr. and Mrs. Sedgewick, "Dr. Nowlton has arrived. I have shown him to her ladyship's drawing room."

"Thank you, Mathers," James said, while next to him Cecilia made a face. James laughed. "Enough of that. Would you rather I went on horseback without you?"

Cecilia squirmed. "No, I just feel it is much ado about nothing."

"Perhaps, nonetheless, it will not hurt to see the doctor. You were gravely ill for almost two weeks, and you are carrying a child. As much as I like our village doctor, Dr. Patterson, a second opinion is not amiss."

She bobbed her head like Rani might, causing her husband to laugh again. He placed his hand lightly on her back. "Come, let's not keep Dr. Nowlton waiting any longer," he said, guiding her up the stairs toward the small drawing room.

Dr. Nowlton rose as they entered. The first thing Cecilia noticed was he did not resemble his elder twin siblings, Lord Lancelot and Lady Guinevere Nowlton. While the twins were both red-haired with tall, commanding presences, Dr. Nowlton was of average height with unfashionably long brown hair and unusual, thick-lensed glasses. He had a reputation for being an astute and highly competent physician, but Cecilia could not believe how young he looked—like he should still be in school.

She discreetly cleared her throat from a threatened cough.

"Dr. Nowlton, thank you for coming on such short notice," James said as they walked into the drawing room.

Dr. Nowlton nodded. "I was happy to. So, Lady Branstoke, tell me about this illness you suffered," he said in a low-keyed, empathetic manner.

Cecilia smiled as she took a seat across from him. She coughed into her handkerchief.

"There was an influenza in the village near our estate, Summerworth Park, in Kent." She frowned. "It seemed to burn through the area and affected women and children more than men."

"We've had a similar illness in the city," he acknowledged.

"We have just seen Mr. Sedgewick. He said he'd had the influenza."

Dr. Nowlton nodded. "In your village, was the severity the same for all?"

"No. For some it did not go beyond sniffles, for others, it was quite severe," she said.

"As it was for you," interjected James.

She nodded. "I was among those more severely impacted. It descended into my chest, and I coughed heavily. I still cough at times. As I coughed so hard, we were worried about the baby."

"That tisane Lady Aldrich recommended for you helped ease the cough and the light temperature you had," James said.

"What was in the tisane?"

"Peppermint, yarrow, and elderberry," James replied.

"Elderflower," Cecilia corrected.

"Yes, my mistake," James acknowledged, looking down at Cecilia. "Elderflower. Peppermint, yarrow, and elderflower. Sounds odious, but it helped her."

Cecilia laughed. "The elderflower gave it a bit of sweetness."

Dr. Nowlton nodded. "I'm familiar with that recipe."

"I thought you modern doctors frowned at herbal folk medicine," James said with a quirk of his lips.

Dr. Nowlton acknowledged his statement. "But not all do," he continued. "There is much we can learn from the traditional remedies. What I am interested in learning is why they work. From that information, we may formulate more powerful and better medicines," he told James. He looked at Cecilia. "I would suggest you continue to drink that tisane at least once per day so long as you have any vestige of a cough. You might also consider adding honey for its medicinal properties —after the beverage has cooled a bit. If the liquid is too hot when you add the honey, you lose the medicinal benefits from the honey. But let's look at you now. Sir James, would you be so kind as to call Lady Branstoke's maid?"

"She is not here. She has traveled ahead. I'll get Mrs. Dunstan, our housekeeper," James told him.

"Splendid," Dr. Nowlton said as James left the room to send someone to search out the housekeeper.

"Dr. Nowlton, our plan is to travel to Stamford to see if we can determine why the Earl of Soothcoor has been arrested for the murder of a man who was a patient at the Camden House Sanatorium," Cecilia said.

"Saw the news of that in the paper this morning. Unbelievable!"

"Today?" Cecilia exclaimed. "We hadn't thought it had made it into the news sources yet."

"I regret then to tell you, it has."

"It is unbelievable to us who know the earl. Do you know anything about this Camden House Sanatorium where the murder occurred?" she asked.

"I have never visited that facility. I do know its owner and director, Dr. Worcham, has an excellent reputation. It is not a facility for those who might be considered criminally mad or suffer dementia. From an article I read about the sanatorium a year or so ago, Dr. Worcham believes more people can be cured with peace and kindness than with harsh purges and other treatments practiced by some doctors."

"That is reassuring to know," Cecilia said as James slipped back into the room.

"Most of his patients suffer from migraines and nervous anxiety," Dr. Nowlton explained. "Not suffering severe mental issues, nonetheless requiring care for a time."

"I wonder why he accepted Mr. Montgomery as a patient?" Cecilia mused.

"And why he should be a party to his false death?" James commented archly.

"Yes," his wife agreed.

"Excuse me, I don't understand," interjected Dr. Nowton, looking from James to his wife and back.

"Oh, forgive us, Dr. Nowlton. Ah, here is Mrs. Dunstan now. After your examination of my wife, we can discuss the situation at Camden House and the illness that brought Mr. Montgomery to that facility."

"You do have me curious," the doctor said.

"I shall wait for you in the library. A word of warning," James said, looking down at Cecilia, "do not let my lovely wife try to talk you into approving this journey without an examination. I am trusting you to deliver an honest medical opinion."

"Humph! As if I would," protested Cecilia.

James raised an eyebrow as he looked down at her.

"Well, maybe a little," she amended with a grin.

"Precisely." He kissed the crown of her head.

JAMES HELD out a glass of ale for Dr. Nowlton when he joined him in the library twenty minutes later.

"I want to thank you again for coming on such short notice," he said.

Dr. Nowlton shrugged as he accepted the glass. "My family is away at the moment, and I'm not due at Mrs. Southerland's until this afternoon."

"Soothcoor pulled you into tending his charity house?" James asked.

"No, my sister did. There is a woman near her time who could have a breach birth. I promised my sister I would stay in town until after the birth of the baby. Afterward, I'll be going to the Cotswolds where my brother has a property. The area is without a surgeon or physician. I may settle there. I think it might prove to be a good place for me to pursue my further studies."

"Further studies?"

"Yes. As you noted, surgeons and physicians have not been interested in country medicines. I am interested. Especially in the work of the apothecaries. There is a well-known apothecary in the area that I wish to interview and see if we might work together."

"Are you aware that Soothcoor, through his late brother, has an interest in exploring the healing plants from India?"

"No, I did not. Interesting. I shall have to speak with him about his investment when he returns to London."

"Now, to the purpose of your visit. What is your opinion as to my wife's health?"

"Though a lingering cough occasionally nags her, she appears healthy and will be fine to take this journey. I gather it is important to her."

"But she seems so tired."

"She was bedridden for many days with her illness, was she not?"

"Yes, I insisted on it."

He smiled at James. "That was the right thing to do; however, it was also what tired her out."

"What do you mean?"

"The body quickly learns to relax. It does not as quickly relearn how to be active. I would suggest daily walks to rebuild her strength. It will also be the best activity she might do for the baby."

James frowned but nodded slowly.

"So, what can you tell me about the man murdered? I believe your wife called him Mr. Montgomery?"

James leaned back in his chair, taking in a large breath before he spoke. "Yes. Malcolm Montgomery from Scotland. From what Mrs. Montgomery explained to Lady Branstoke and me, Mr. Montgomery suffered from an illness of the mind, an illness that waxed and waned in severity."

Dr. Nowlton nodded. "Many such illnesses do. Go on."

"I'm uncertain how to explain it," James said slowly. "It sounds fantastical. According to Mrs. Montgomery, it was like he had multiple people all living within himself. They had distinct personalities and names. And different strengths. Different personalities could take him over and he, Malcolm, would have no memory of the incident. He lived with his family and with this condition until the night he came back to himself, only to discover he stood in his eldest daughter's bedroom with feelings of lust coursing through his body. It was one of his 'other' people. That this personality could come so close to violating his daughter, and he not being aware, deeply affected Mr. Montgomery and worried him. Shaken by the event, he decided he needed to be institutionalized so he did not, in any way, harm his family."

Dr. Nowlton nodded slowly, his brow furrowed. "I have read of a similar situation," he said. "I was incredulous as well. It read like some monstrous gothic tale my brother would write. In summary, a young woman had been raped by her father as a child on several occasions. To cope with the abuse, her mind splintered into different people."

"Was she placed in a sanatorium?"

He nodded. "For a time. When she appeared to be better and no longer suffered with other people splitting her mind, she returned to her home. Unfortunately, it wasn't long after that that her father attempted to bed her again, and she killed him and herself."

James shook his head. "What was the conclusion?"

"The article espoused that illnesses of the mind are not curable and such people with any kind of mental differences would be permanently institutionalized."

James's brows pulled together. "That seems to be rather a large generalization."

"It was, and it was the broad generalization that bothered me as well."

"I wonder why Mr. Montgomery thought he should fake his death and why Dr. Worcham should support that decision? And he must have done so."

Dr. Nowlton nodded. "If I weren't tied here in London to see to the woman at Mrs. Southerland's, I would be tempted to accompany you."

"Thank you for the sentiment. But, if you determine

Lady Branstoke is healthy enough for travel, we need to leave. My wish is to get to Cambridge today, weather permitting."

Dr. Nowlton nodded and stood up. "I will show myself out. I wish you safe travel and Godspeed in your efforts to clear Soothcoor of this murder charge."

CHAPTER 4

A FORTUNATE UNFORTUNATE ACCIDENT

"*Y*ou've been exceedingly quiet," James said to his wife.

They had been in their carriage driving north for two hours. They would stop soon for a change of horses and postillions and to walk about a bit. Since leaving London behind for open roads, Cecilia had remained quiet, just swaying with the motion of the carriage and staring out the carriage window.

The new carriage he'd ordered after the first of the year, beautifully appointed on the inside with blue velvet that matched his wife's eyes, also had the newest in metal springs and rode far more comfortably than their old carriage. It should make the long journey bearable.

"Are you feeling well?" he asked.

Cecilia turned toward him. A small, rueful smile graced her lips. "Yes, my love. While I own, I am not yet up to my past energy levels, I can sense a shift in feelings. As the coughing spells ease, the cloud that has hung over me is not so oppressive," she said, her smile widening.

"Then why that pensive, sad look I've been observing on your lovely face?" he asked.

She sighed and leaned back to nestle against him. He put his arm around her. "I've been thinking about Soothcoor and Mrs. Montgomery," she said. "—More so about Mrs. Montgomery and her marriage to Mr. Montgomery. By my reckoning, they lived together for sixteen years before he went into a sanatorium. What were those years like and did anyone else know about his peculiar affliction of the mind?"

"He might have been good at keeping those 'others'—I don't know what else we should call them—suppressed," James offered.

"*Hmm.* Yes. And if that was the case, what changed?"

"What do you mean?"

"I am thinking about cause and effect," she said. "My melancholy, we know, came from my long illness, and that it has been difficult for me—and you by extension, I am aware. I wonder if the issues he began to have with these 'others' didn't have a cause? I didn't think to ask Mrs. Montgomery anything of this nature."

"You mean you wonder what was going on in their lives that might have caused him to no longer control these 'others'?"

"Yes."

He nodded. "You may be correct. But what would that have to do with him being murdered now?"

She shook her head. "I do not know. Probably nothing," she admitted with a drawn-out sigh. "Do you think Soothcoor has worn the green willow for Mrs. Montgomery all this time?"

James cocked his head as he considered her question. "He has never fallen into the parson's trap with any woman, nor has he shown an interest in any of the ladies who regularly make an appearance in society."

"Except for Mrs. Montgomery," Cecilia said.

"Except for Mrs. Montgomery," he concurred. "He has been called *'the Dour Earl'* for as long as I have known him. Though he might smile and laugh, the light of laughter never reaches his eyes. Gossip, as it is in society, decided he'd suffered a disappointment of the heart."

"Which, we can now be confident, he had," said Cecilia.

"I assume so with the rapidity of his association with Mrs. Montgomery and her tale of their shared past."

"If she makes his smile reach his eyes, she has my gratitude. We will do whatever is needed to see him freed," she declared.

"That we will," concurred her husband. "That we will."

Their carriage rolled into the yard of the Taurus Stagecoach Inn and Tavern late that night—close to eight o'clock, due to the steady rain that began in the mid-afternoon. It made for sloppy roads and slow going. Thankfully, the booking request James had sent ahead had been received, and they had a bedroom reserved. Mr. Drupple, the innkeeper, wringing his callused hands against his dark blue waistcoat, asked if they wouldn't mind sharing the private parlor with a young man who'd suffered a carriage mishap. Said he was on his way to Stamford, as he understood they were.

James frowned. Cecilia laid a gentle hand on his arm. "What happened?" she asked the innkeeper. "Has he suffered any injury?"

"Sprained his wrist trying to ketch hisself when the carriage tipped. The missus wrapped it tight. Be jolly good again in a day or two. But wurst were to the gen'l-man's valise. Tumbled out it did, popped open. All his clothes landed in a muddy puddle. Got 'im wrapped in an ol' banyan sum gent left 'ere, sittin' by the fire in the parlor."

"The private parlor we reserved," James clarified.

The innkeeper had the grace to look down. "Yes, sir." He looked up again. "But I'll get his room warmed up good and move him there. Not to worry. Done in a tick."

"Has he had his dinner yet?" Cecilia asked.

"No, my lady. Not rite yet."

"Then he may eat with us while you prepare his room."

"Cecilia!" protested her husband.

"I want to know who he is, and why he is in such a hurry to get to Stamford that he should risk a carriage accident in the rain."

James laughed shortly. "Your impulsive curiosity has served us well in the past."

"Precisely." Cecilia turned to the innkeeper. "Please conduct us to the parlor."

"Yes, my lady, right this way." He turned to climb an inside stairway to the first floor. He knocked at a door at the back of the tavern, then pushed it open.

Inside, a young man with disheveled brown hair and round wire spectacles wearing a several-sizes-too-large tobacco-brown-edged-with-gold-braid banyan, sat slouched on a bench near the fireplace where a coal fire burned hot. He straightened and shot to his feet when he saw the innkeeper was not alone.

"These be the folks as reserved the parlor," the innkeeper told him as he escorted the Branstokes into the room.

"Oh! Yes—then I should go...," said the young man, trailing off uncertainly. "Where should I go?" he asked the innkeeper as he took a step toward the door.

"Nowhere," Cecilia put in. "We shall share the room with you through dinner," she declared. "Sit. We are the Branstokes. Sir James and Lady Branstoke."

The young man looked startled. He blinked owlishly

behind his glasses. "Aileen said her mother would write to you."

"Miss Aileen Montgomery?" James asked.

"Yes, my fiancée."

"And you are Mr. Stackpoole?" James confirmed.

"Yes, Benjamin Stackpoole, at your service, sir," the young man said, bowing.

James laughed. He looked down at his wife. "You were correct in your impulses, quite again."

She smiled cheekily up at him.

"I'll send the barmaid up to you directly," the innkeeper said as he sidled toward the door, looking bemused at the exchange between his guests.

"Just have her bring up a pitcher of your ale and mugs for all," James instructed.

"As you wish, sar. Your dinner will be ready in a thrice as well, that I promise," the innkeeper said. "And thank you, sar, fer yur understanding."

"I don't know many innkeepers who would cater to a young man who has met with an accident as you have. You are to be commended."

"Well, we've knowed Master Stackpoole since he were a tyke in short pants," the man said with a small laugh as he backed to the door. He bowed to them and left the room, closing the door softly behind him.

"You are local?" Cecilia asked as she untied the ribbons at the neck of her traveling cloak. James slid it from her shoulders. Cecilia murmured her thanks as she took the heavy, damp cloak from him.

"Yes," the young man said. "The Stackpooles have been in this area for three hundred years."

"So why did you come here and not to your family home?"

"It's complicated," he said, his shoulders slumping.

Cecilia sat down in a wing chair at right angles to his bench. "I understand from Mrs. Montgomery that your father wished you to call off your engagement," she gently said.

"Yes. But I will not," he said emphatically. "I love Aileen. She is the sweetest woman of my acquaintance and is not troubled by my poor eyesight or my desire to enter the diplomatic corps—which my father emphatically opposes."

"Why is that? Does he wish you to pay more attention to your patrimony?"

"No, he is one of those that believes England should only cater to England and not to other countries." He shook his head. "To hear him talk today, you'd not believe he made the grand tour in his youth. Visited places like Athens, Constantinople, and Medina, places I'd love to go to! And so would Aileen."

"She wishes to travel?"

"Oh, yes. Her grandfather traveled in his youth and used to tell her all manner of stories of exotic places. Not at all like my father who never talks about his travels and frowns on everyone and anything foreign."

"Did something happen on his travels that caused him to develop his dislike of foreigners?"

"I don't know, precisely. Something about a sweet he was given in Damascus that made him violently ill. He won't explain. I doubt he ever told my mother the details, either. Supposedly he was given something as a joke, but it made him violently ill. I don't know if that is what caused his attitude toward foreign countries or if it might have just been a contributor. He is anti any foreign investment or dealings. He was opposed to England going to war with Napoleon, certain he would never invade England. And he argued the country was raising taxes and wasting money by going to fight in other countries. Very insular is my father. Very loyal in his way, though insular."

He frowned, a petulant pout, which made him look

younger. "He was against Aileen as my choice for my wife as she is from Scotland," he admitted.

"He doesn't believe Scotland should be part of England?" James asked.

"Correct. But his disapproval of my wonderful Aileen did not become a major issue until he learned where her father was."

"That he was in a sanatorium?"

He snorted. "More than that, it was that he was in the Camden House Sanatorium."

"Why was that an issue?" Cecilia asked. "Did he know something about the institution?"

"In a way, yes. You see, that is where he has had my mother committed."

Cecilia and James exchanged glances. "Your mother!" Cecilia exclaimed.

"Yes, off and on since I was seventeen years old."

"Off and on?"

He sighed. "My poor mother suffers from excessive nerves. She does not handle disruption well, and my father is nothing but a disruptive man. Theirs was an arranged marriage and as such, to my mind, is a major argument against that societal marriage arrangement. At the sanatorium, my mother is calmer and happier. She only returns to our estate around the holidays, as that is her favorite time of year. She loves to decorate the old house with pine garlands, wreaths and mistletoe. She is happy, she laughs and is relaxed. Then, after twelfth night, she once again sinks to a mere shadow of herself, crying all the time, begging my father to let her return to Camden. And he does readily. Neither of them enjoys the other's company, and her residing at the sanatorium allows them to live apart without scandal."

"But what a life!" Cecilia exclaimed. "Locked in an asylum!"

"Camden House is not like most sanatoriums. Certainly not like Bedlam," the young man hastened to assure her. "It looks more austere than it is, being a large gray-stone-and-brick former monastery situated on the edge of fens with marshy swamps around it."

"That does not sound appealing."

"It's built on a small knoll with the drainage canals surrounding it, there is only one approach to the property."

"Rather like a moat, I would imagine," James said.

Stackpoole laughed. "Almost! Inside there are private rooms for those with the funds to pay for private accommodation. For others, there are small dormitories. The men and women are kept in separate parts of the main building. There are some common areas allowed for those deemed not a danger to others: a dining room, a large, combined library and card room, and an outdoor area—all properly chaperoned, of course."

"It sounds like you are quite familiar with the sanatorium."

He nodded. "I try to visit my mother quarterly. There is an inn close by where I can stay. It caters to the families of those in the sanatorium."

"The New Bell Inn?" James asked.

"Yes."

"That is, fortuitously, where we have booked accommodations," James said. "Can you tell us more about the sanatorium over all?"

"Like what?"

"The staff, the atmosphere, how available it is for visitors, that sort of things."

Mr. Stackpoole blinked rapidly as he thought. It gave him an owl appearance. "The sanatorium is owned by Dr. Thaddeus Worcham, and he does live on the property with his wife. He generally has young doctors from medical schools on visitation for six months to a year at a time, those that wish to learn more about afflictions of the mind." He frowned. "And about eight months ago, he hired a superintendent to assist with the functional aspects of the sanatorium."

"I take it you do not like him," James observed.

Mr. Stackpoole's mouth twisted as he considered his feelings. "I don't know if I do or don't. He strikes me as not as affable as he appears to visitors, and from the few things my mother has let drop when I visit, I gather it is a carefully crafted façade. In truth, I have been wondering if I should investigate other accommodations for my mother."

"Interesting," James murmured, exchanging a glance with Cecilia.

"It is easy to gain entrance to the building, though a staff member must unlock a broad set of double doors to get beyond the entrance hall. Most of the time, they have been ready to do so without questions."

"Would you say their intent is to keep the patients in, not keep others out?"

"Yes. Especially after the accident last year."

"Accident?"

He nodded. "Tragic story. One of the young female patients," his brow furrowed, "at least I believe she was a patient—in truth, I cannot say if she was or wasn't—wandered out at night. She was found the next morning drowned in the canal in front of the manor. That is what made Dr. Worcham decide he needed a superintendent to take care of the facilities and to put policies in place to prevent anything like that from happening again. My mother told me the doctor was quite distraught over the young woman's death."

"Do you know the identity of the woman who drowned?"

"No, I'm sorry I don't. I'm afraid I didn't think to

ask my mother her name. I do know she hadn't been there long. Leastwise, that is what my mother told me at the time. I assume she was a patient, but now that I think about it, Mother didn't say that directly, either. The woman's death so upset her that she briefly thought of returning home! That is what we talked about the most, the possibility of her coming home again."

"If I might, I'd like to return to your father. You said his disapproval of your fiancée increased when he learned Miss Montgomery's father was in the sanatorium. Why?"

"He feared she could become unstable in the future."

"Some inheritance from her father?"

"Exactly. I told him that was nonsense, but he was adamant. So adamant he did something I have not known him to do in all the years mother has resided at Camden House. He went up there to visit and to find out for himself about Aileen's father."

"When did he do this?"

"About the same time as Lord Soothcoor went up north to visit Mr. Montgomery—I can't see Lord Soothcoor as killing Mr. Montgomery, no matter what others believe," the young man said earnestly.

"Neither can we, which is why we are going up to the sanatorium to investigate."

"Might I accompany you as my carriage is a loss? I am only an indifferent rider, so I don't wish to ride there. Mayhap I can assist you!" he said earnestly.

"Maybe you can," Cecilia said, cocking her head to the side as she considered him.

"Cecilia, I can see you are planning something," her husband said.

"Perhaps. I need to think about it more before we discuss it."

"But we will discuss it," James said forcefully.

Her laughter brightened the room. "Of a certainty, my love."

Mr. Stackpoole frowned as he looked from the husband to the wife.

James and Cecilia looked at each other and grinned.

A knock on the parlor door brought with it the fragrant smell of an enticing roast. By the appearance of the number of platters, the inn staff brought in a hearty dinner.

Cecilia clapped her hands together. "Wonderful! I vow I am famished."

"Best you pile your plate high, Mr. Stackpoole," warned James. "Lady Branstoke has a hearty appetite for all her small stature. You won't get a chance for second helpings," he warned.

Cecilia playfully glared at him.

An hour later, the maid came to the parlor to remove the remains—such as were left—of the hearty repast. She was followed by the innkeeper.

"Mrs. Drupple has most of yur clothes cleaned and dried now, Mr. Stackpoole. They be in yur room," the innkeeper said as he glanced about the room.

"Thank you, Mr. Drupple." Mr. Stackpoole turned to the Branstokes. "So, might I accompany you in the morning?" he asked, his expression open and earnest below the straggly waves of brown hair that lay over the edges of his glasses.

James nodded. "Yes. I hope to leave by eight." He looked at the innkeeper. "Might we have breakfast before then?"

"Yes, sar. I'll tell the missus to plan fer seven."

"Excellent. Until the morning, Mr. Stackpoole," James said, inclining his head, dismissing the young man. He turned to their innkeeper. "Mr. Drupple, if I might have a brandy before bed?"

"Yes, sar, immediately." He scurried away.

James gathered Cecilia into his arms and pulled her onto his lap as he sat in the corner of a tall-backed settle near the hearth.

She snuggled against him.

"Now about this plan you have…"

CHAPTER 5

THE PLAN

"How is your wrist this morning, Mr. Stackpoole?" Cecilia asked when she saw him awaiting them the next morning at the base of the inn stairs. James followed behind her as they descended to the taproom floor.

Stackpoole glanced down at his arm in a sling, his hand wrapped to keep it still. "Much better, thank you," he said. His clothing looked a little rumpled, but otherwise clean. He brushed a lock of brown hair away from his glasses with his good hand.

"Glad to hear that," James said gruffly as he and Cecilia attained the ground floor. "Are we ready to leave?" he asked curtly.

Mr. Stackpoole drew back at James's tone.

Cecilia laughed. "Don't mind my husband," she said, leaning forward confidentially. She straightened and tucked her arm through James's arm. "He is quite put out with me and has been like a grouchy old bear since last night after you left, and I told him my scheme for helping Lord Soothcoor."

"I don't like it," James said as they left the inn and walked to their waiting carriage.

"What plan is this?" Mr. Stackpoole asked as he

47

trailed behind them then hurried forward to hear what was said.

"For James to check me into Camden House," she said as she ducked into the carriage.

"What!" exclaimed Mr. Stackpoole.

"Those are my sentiments, precisely," James said. He followed his wife into the carriage and sat next to her on the forward-facing seat.

Mr. Stackpoole climbed in after them, tripping on the carriage edge.

James reached out a hand to help him catch himself.

Mr. Stackpoole blushed bright red as he got both feet into the carriage and sat facing them. "Thank you, Sir James," he said.

James tapped the roof of the carriage to signal Mr. Romley they were ready to leave. The carriage started out briskly, without rain to impede them.

"I don't think Camden House would admit you, Lady Cecilia," Mr. Stackpoole said, as they rocked to the motion of the carriage. "Dr. Worcham says he must see evidence of issues."

"I am recovering from a severe influenza," Cecilia explained.

"Lady Cecilia was sick in bed for over two weeks. We were worried for her and the child she carries...," James said softly. He looked down at Cecilia and gently squeezed her hand.

Cecilia nodded. "There was worry for the health of the babe," she said, "I've suffered terribly with fatigue and lack of energy. It is only the news that Lord Sooth-coor needs us that has dragged me out of that affliction."

"For which I am grateful, not that I wish that it be in this manner!" James stated.

She looked over at Mr. Stackpoole. "I clearly re-member the worst of those feelings. I am certain I can bring them forward such they will convince the good doctor. How is it your mother seems to come and go from Camden House?"

"The doctor claims her condition is rooted in seasonality and the weather that comes with the seasons. And she and the doctor's wife have become good friends.Do not mistake me, after the holidays her mien *is* quite distraught. There is only so much of my father she can handle for any length of time, and the weather this year has been especially troublesome."

Cecilia nodded. "I sometimes wonder if we'd had spring sun and spring warmth on more days, I would have improved faster. The rain and cold has been hard on everyone."

"How might I help with your investigation? I had intended to do some investigation on my own, anyway. I don't wish to be acting in cross purposes to what you do," Mr. Stackpoole said earnestly while grabbing the leather strap and swaying with the carriage as it crossed a particularly bad patch of road.

With one hand James grabbed the strap at his side and, with his other, he anchored Cecilia to his side.

"You can serve as our referral to Dr. Worcham and the sanatorium."

"Easily!"

"And I should like an introduction to your mother," Cecilia said. "She knows the people and attitudes of those within the sanatorium now. She could be invaluable to my investigation."

Mr. Stackpoole nodded. "I can do that. I think she would be supremely amenable to assisting in your inquiry. I have heard her mention a Mr. Montgomery in the past. The library is one of the common areas for men and women, and I believe she used to discuss books with Mr. Montgomery in that room—I just never connected the Montgomery she mentioned with my Aileen's father!"

"There is no reason you should have as Miss Montgomery's father was supposedly deceased," James observed.

Mr. Stackpoole's brows drew together, and his lips compressed.

"What is it, Mr. Stackpoole? I can see something has you bothered," Cecilia asked.

"I don't understand Dr. Worcham. I've always known him to be an upright gentleman. He had to have agreed to this farce."

"Farce?" James said.

"Yes! Mr. Montgomery faking his death. He probably has no idea the depths to which it has affected his family."

"He may not know he has any family other than his cousin who helped him enter the sanatorium."

"I suppose there could be truth in what you say. Aileen told me he has lived with his affliction for years. She could not understand what changed to make him decide to enter a sanatorium."

James and Cecilia exchanged glances.

"I'm sure he felt he had a good reason. Perhaps he felt he was getting worse and wanted to go away to protect the family," James suggested.

"And to preserve blessed family memories," Cecilia offered.

James nodded.

"But fake his death?"

"From some things Mrs. Montgomery told us, I gathered he did not want them to visit him while he was in the sanatorium, and he didn't want them holding false hopes that one day he might be cured. They needed to get on with their lives."

Mr. Stackpoole snorted. "Which Mrs. Montgomery

was trying to do. He didn't think through the ramifications of his *'death.'* Did he honestly think she would never want to remarry? That is cruel and disrespectful," he declared.

"We cannot know what was in the man's mind and heart," Cecilia said with a sad sigh.

Mr. Stackpoole leaned back against the carriage squabs. "I could never believe Lord Soothcoor to be a murderer. Do you think it is possible Mr. Montgomery could have taken his own life?" he asked.

"We don't know," James said resignedly. "We have much to learn."

The Branstoke's carriage rolled into the courtyard of The New Bell Inn as sunset colors brushed the sky with faint pinks and oranges, muted by the persistent overcast weather. Cecilia thought in any other year than the miserable cold year they'd had, the colors would appear as a vivid blaze across the fenlands.

James took her arm to lead her into the sprawling redbrick inn. She was surprised at the Georgian styling of the building, obviously a newer construction than many inns where they stayed.

"Mr. Price is the innkeeper," Mr. Stackpoole said, hurrying to come alongside them. He pushed his round glasses frames higher on his nose.

A tall, angular man came out of the inn. He looked all legs and arms. "Sir James Branstoke?" he said, his voice higher pitched than Cecilia would have guessed from looking at him.

"Yes. Has my staff arrived?" James asked.

"Two hours ago, sir."

"Excellent. We have added one more to our party, Mr. Stackpoole, here. Might you have a room for him as well?"

The man bobbed his head at Mr. Stackpoole. "I

knows him from other times. We can accommodate him on the floor above yours. Small room, though."

"That's fine," Mr. Stackpoole said hurriedly.

"This way then," the man said. At the top of the stairs, he pointed to a room on the right. "This be yer parlor, and right down here a pace be your bedroom." He ushered them into a room at the back of the inn away from the sounds of the comings and goings of the travelers in the courtyard.

"Dinner in one hour in the parlor?" he asked.

"That should be fine," James said.

The innkeeper nodded. He turned to Mr. Stackpoole. "I'll show you to your room now."

"Thank you."

"We'll see you at supper then," James told Mr. Stackpoole.

~

"WHAT DO YOU THINK?" Cecilia murmured to James as Mr. Price led them to their room.

He shrugged, nodding toward their host who led the way before them.

Sarah, Cecilia's lady's maid, and William, James's valet, met them in the hall before their room. William wore his austere mien, Sarah stood with her eyes downcast, her hands folded before her.

Cecilia and James exchanged glances.

"Is everything all right?" Mr. Price asked William.

William nodded curtly. "All is in readiness," he said, his gaze flicking over to James and Lady Cecilia.

"An hour, then, in the parlor," James said to the innkeeper.

"Yes, everything will be to your liking, I assure you," Mr. Price said as he bowed and turned away to return the way they came.

There was silence in the group gathered before the door to the room as they watched the man leave.

Cecilia raised a brow in mute inquiry to her maid. Sarah nodded and opened the door to their chamber to lead them inside.

"What is it?" Cecilia asked, once they were all in the bedchamber and the door closed after them. Though the room was large by inn standards, with the four of them standing beside the bed, it seemed tight.

"Strange doings with the sanatorium," Williams said heavily.

"What do you mean?" James asked.

"It has always been a good neighbor in the area, for years and years, the staff here says."

"By the way you say that, I gather that is no longer the situation," James said as he removed his hat and pulled off his gloves.

Williams hurried to take them from him and assist him out of his greatcoat. Sarah assisted Cecilia, hanging her cloak on a hook near the door.

"Rumors differ. Some say it changed after the new superintendent was hired. Others think the changed happened after a woman, a resident of the sanatorium, was found drowned in the canal that runs around the property. The events were near to each other. I couldn't get a clear answer as to which came first. I was loath to press too hard."

"Understood," James said, nodding approval at his man.

"A woman drowned?" Cecilia asked? "A patient of the sanatorium? Not a maid or matron?"

William turned toward her. "Yes, my lady," he said differentially. "Now, they claim her ghost walks along the edge of the canal at night."

Sarah appeared to shiver at the thought while Cecilia giggled, then broke into a full laugh. "I'm sure they do! It's a perfect story for a drowning—and a sanatorium."

Sarah smiled thinly. "I suppose it would be at that," she said.

"Don't let the waves of imagination and stories sway you," Cecilia told Sarah. "Seeing would be my belief."

"I suspect I'm too timid to want to see any specters," Sarah ruefully admitted.

The others laughed.

"You shan't. Not here at any time with us. They should most likely run before us."

"Careful, Cecilia, that you do not rile the dead into thinking you have issued a challenge," James said.

"Not you, too!" protested Cecilia.

"No, but, I learned long ago not to doubt too loudly. There is much in the world we don't know."

Cecilia screwed up her face in conflicted doubt. "I should wish to hold my monsters at bay. I fear your tales might make my thoughts and imagination run rampant."

James shook his head. "You are much too pragmatic, for all your feigned fragility—I am curious why you did not adopt the fragile wife mien when we arrived."

"You mean, start as I mean to go on?"

"Yes."

She shrugged. "We were so comfortable with Mr. Stackpoole that I didn't think of it. You think I should have?"

"If you are determined on your course of action to become a patient at the sanatorium, then, yes, I think so. We don't know who here might know someone who works at the sanatorium."

Sarah turned back from setting out Cecilia's night things. "You want to be a patient there? Even after what I told you about that woman's death?"

"Mr. Stackpoole told us of the young woman's

drowning during our journey here, without the added embellishment of the ghost story. I am not concerned. Her death was a year ago."

"Mr. Stackpoole?" William asked.

"Ah, yes. You would not know of the travel companion we acquired yesterday. He is on his way to Camden House as we are. He knows the Earl of Soothcoor, and like those who do know him, he finds it hard to believe him to be a murderer. His mother is a patient in the sanatorium so he thought he would talk to her about Mr. Montgomery's death."

A knock at the door ended their discussion. William opened the door to admit a maid with hot water for the Branstokes to freshen up with before dinner. Cecilia immediately slumped against James.

"How lovely," Cecilia said faintly. "I should love to clean my face and hands. Sarah, can you find my lavender water? I need it, I fear."

Sarah's eyes widened, but she quickly recovered. "Right away, my lady," she said, turning to a valise set next to the window.

"Is there anything else you need?" asked the maid, staring at Cecilia as she leaned on James.

"No, no. My wife is recovering from a long illness," James said. "Come, why don't you lay down for a few minutes before dinner," he said to Cecilia as he led her to the bedstead.

William crossed to the door and opened it. "Thank you. Sarah or I will let the proprietor know if James and Lady Branstoke have additional requirements."

The maid nodded and curtsied, then scurried out of the room.

After washing up and changing his neckcloth, James dismissed his valet for the evening and told Cecilia he would go on the parlor while she washed.

"I should also like to change my dress," she said. "I

need to proceed in my weakened role and clothing can be part of that role."

James shook his head. "I don't like it when you play the weak, unwell female though I'll own it has served us well in the past. That duality of consideration makes me a hypocrite, and I don't like that, either." He ran a hand through his hair.

She grinned at him. "My height and coloring play so well with the role," she said, waving her hand from her head to her toes in reference to her short and slight stature as well as her pale skin and almost white-blonde, flyaway hair. Sometimes James referred to her as his fae nymph.

James shook his head and left the room, leaving Sarah with Cecilia.

JAMES HAD the private parlor to himself. He'd sent a barmaid for a mug of ale before he'd entered the room and now sat in one of the brown, jacquard-covered wingback chairs that flanked the large fireplace, with the ale mug clasped loosely between his hands. The room had more the look of a gentleman's library than a parlor. Warm, golden oak paneling covered the walls, a material not common in this part of the country. He stared into the cold stone fireplace. He considered asking for a fire to be laid as rooms chilled with the coming night. Cecilia chilled easily.

He looked up when he heard rain against the already wind-rattled windows. Though approaching summer, the weather stubbornly held onto winter. A fire would be welcome for all. He rang the bell.

While a servant coaxed fen-sourced peat bricks into a fire, James thought about Malcolm Montgomery.

Had he killed himself? It was not outside the realm

of imagination. If he loved his family, as he appeared to, the sacrifice he made to leave them and enter a sanatorium attested to his love. If he'd learned his wife wished to remarry, might he have chosen suicide to clear the way for her legally? He wished he knew his manner of death, that would inform their investigation. He wondered why Mrs. Montgomery had not been told. And why was Soothcoor so quickly a suspect?

He didn't like Cecilia doing covert investigation as a patient. His delightful wife was intelligent. —She could also be impulsive. He counted her and himself lucky that nothing had yet happened to her due to her impetuous nature. She cared deeply and that, he knew, was the root of her behavior.

The servant kneeling in front of the fireplace rose to his feet. "There you go, sar," he said. "Don't know what experience yous had with a peat fyr 'afore, but a peat fyr don't burn hot likes a wood fyr, but 'tis more even-like heat. It'll warm this room up, you'll see."

"Thank you," James said, rising to his feet. He slipped the man a coin.

When the man left, he almost ran into Mr. Stackpoole, who stumbled backward, then recovered and slid past him into the room. He came toward the fireplace and its heat.

James passed a mug of ale toward Mr. Stackpoole when he sat opposite him before the fire. "The inn is quite modern. Do you know anything of its history?" James asked.

Mr. Stackpoole nodded as he took a sip of ale. "It was built right before John Rennie became the engineer involved with building canals for more fen drainage," he said, "an investment by the Marquis of Widmirth."

"The inn or the canal project?" James asked.

"What—? Oh, both!" he said. "He organized a new group of *Gentlemen Adventurers*—much like the Earl of

Bedford did in the 17th century—for investment in both projects."

"You seem to know a great deal about the area," James observed.

He shrugged. "I read history at the university and I'm curious. I like to know things, so I ask questions." He frowned. "My father says I ask too many questions."

"I imagine the ability to ask the right questions would be an advantage in diplomatic work," James observed.

"Yes! Exactly my thought!" Mr. Stackpoole said excitedly.

James swirled the ale in his mug. Mr. Stackpoole's curiosity could be a benefit or a hindrance to their investigation.

"Mr. Stackpoole," he said carefully, "I would caution against your natural curiosity at Camden House."

"I beg your pardon? Caution me, why?" the young man bristled.

"Sometimes one learns more by silence," he said. He raised his eyes from contemplating his ale. "And patience. Silence and patience—though I'll own those are not habits of Lady Branstoke," he said ruefully as the door to the parlor opened.

"What are not my habits?" Cecilia asked as she entered the parlor, then, looking over her shoulder, louder, "You were right to encourage me to rest, James," she said in a plaintive voice. "Sarah rubbed some lavender water into my temples and that helped as well. Oh, that this melancholy might lift!" she whined, crossing to the bench before the fireplace.

A maid walked into the room behind her carrying a large tray. She set it down on the round table in the center of the room. "Mr. Price says as how you'd like sum brandy now after your travels, along with hot tea, and the mistress said as how my lady should like a soothing tisane as she's feeling peaked."

"Did you bring enough for me as well?" Mr. Stackpoole asked. "I like Mrs. Price's tisane after a day of traveling. I've had it many times over the years. I've tried to get the recipe from her; but she rebuffs me with a laugh," he told the Branstokes.

"There is plenty, Mr. Stackpoole. Mrs. Price knew as how you'd like some, too. She even had me bring honey as she knows you like it with honey. It's a jar Baron Stackpoole left here."

"My father left a jar of honey here?" He laughed. "He must have received it as a gift. He hates honey. Or at least claims to," he explained to the Branstokes.

"That is very kind of Mrs. Price. Please tell her so," James said.

"Aye, sar," the maid said. She bobbed a curtsy then left the room, closing the door carefully, though not completely, behind her.

James frowned and rose to quietly push the door until it latched.

Lady Cecilia's lips quirked up on the side as she saw his action. She straightened on the bench. "While I appreciate Mrs. Price's thoughtfulness, I should rather have a watered ale," she declared.

James laughed and crossed to the table to pour her a mug of ale and add water. She did like an occasional mug of watered ale for her digestion.

"If you do not mind then, I'm for the tisane. It is wonderfully relaxing for me," Mr. Stackpoole said. "I'm still feeling chilled on the inside, and my room lacks a fire." He poured himself a cup and sat in a chair at the table.

"Why don't you request a fire be laid in your room?" Lady Cecilia asked as she accepted her brandy from James.

"Too tired."

"Nonsense," Cecilia said. "We shall engage the staff to build a fire for you when they come with our food. The room can then be warm when you retire."

"I don't—"

James interrupted him. "It is a waste of words to argue with Lady Branstoke," he said laconically. "I have had to devise other means of persuasion," James said, smiling down at his wife.

She cuddled closer to him. "Odious creature," she said playfully.

"A toast then, to my odious nature," he said, raising his glass. They clinked their glasses as they stared into each other's eyes for a moment, then Cecilia closed her eyes and relaxed against him.

James squeezed her closer, relaxing for the first time since he'd received Mrs. Montgomery's letter. He rested his chin on her head as he watched the peat fire burn.

His Cecilia was back, and James felt his heart ready to burst from his chest. He loved this tiny, slight, fae, intelligent, impetuous, determined, and willful woman. He allowed that his role in their marriage was to cherish her and protect her—sometimes from herself. Woe be to anyone who tried to hurt her or come between them.

The fire crackled and hissed as they contentedly sipped their drinks. A clock on the mantle ticked the quiet minutes by.

A low moaning groan came from behind them.

Cecilia raised her head as James turned toward the sound.

Mr. Stackpoole did not look well. He tried to rise to his feet. "My apologies. I fear I am to be sick," he said, stumbling against the table. He held a hand against his stomach, his face an unnatural white. His body convulsed as he tried to move toward the door.

Cecilia quickly rose from the bench and grabbed a large bowl underneath a pitcher of water available for guests to wash their hands. She thrust it at him just as his body heaved again and released the contents of his stomach. She squeezed her eyes shut and turned her head away from the foul stench of regurgitated matter.

"So sorry," he whispered before his body heaved again.

James took the bowl from her and set it on the table. Cecilia pulled out the handkerchief she'd stuffed into the end of the long sleeves of her dress and held it to her nose.

"I think that is all," Mr. Stackpoole said weakly. He sank back down in his chair, sweat now beading on his brow. He closed his eyes, rocking back, his expression contorted.

James opened the door to call for a servant.

A burly waiter came to James's call. He reeled back at the awful sink in the room.

"Oi best fetch da missus," he said, backing out of the room.

James grabbed him by the shoulder. "No, you stay here with Mr. Stackpoole. Lady Branstoke and I will notify the innkeeper of this occurrence," he said.

He pulled Cecilia to her feet and hurried her from the room.

"Thank you," Cecilia said. "Though I may feign illness at times, I cannot stand illness. It turns me from a spectator to a real patient," she whispered.

James nodded. "I understand. For me, after the smells coming from the battlefields in Spain with their sick, dead, and dying, noxious smells no longer traumatize me."

He led her down the stairs, only stopping once to

call out to a passing servant to notify the Prices of a sick guest.

James led Cecilia toward the large hearth in the pub room. A young man seated by the fire saw their approach and jumped to his feet. "Here yar, please to give da lai-dy my seat," he said, quickly doffing his brown plaid cap.

"Thank you," James said as he led Cecilia to sit down. "Will you be all right while I speak with Mr. Price about Mr. Stackpoole?" he asked her.

She smiled up at him. "Yes, I shall be fine."

"We'll watch after da lai-dy," the man said as he stuffed his cap in his coat pocket.

The other men heartily agreed.

"Now go, go," Cecilia encouraged. "I have work to do," she whispered as he leaned over her.

James straightened and raised his eyebrows as he looked down at her. "That is what I'm afraid of."

CHAPTER 6

THE PUB

Cecilia looked about the inn's pub room. It was airy in feeling and appearance, though it smelled of burning peat and pipe tobacco. Wainscoting covered the lower half of the walls to elbow height, topped with a shelf all around wide enough for setting down mugs of ale and pipe ashtrays and an elbow or two. The wall to the ceiling, originally white-washed, now appeared a creamy gray color. A few prints hung on the walls in a nod to décor.

The room was not inordinately crowded; however, those here seemed to know each other. Cecilia wondered if her party were the only travelers at the inn. Most of the patrons were men, though there was a woman seated in a corner, knitting. Her smooth, worn, wooden needles were held in hands with enlarged arthritic knuckles. The needles clicked in a rhythmic manner. While the woman sat to the side, she obviously listened, for she raised her head now and again, her nimble facial movements betraying her keen attention to the conversations in the room.

She appeared old—perhaps the oldest in the room —but Cecilia knew that appearances could be deceptive as life's circumstances often wrote largely upon a person's countenance. She wore a plain white cap on her head. Coarse gray hair strands escaped from under it. A dirt-streaked apron covered her dress made of a rough brown wool. Around her shoulders and over her chest she wore a dark blue serviceable shawl crossed in front and tied behind her to keep it in place.

She caught Cecilia's regard, smiled a gap-toothed smile, and then winked. Her face might have been a map of care and hardship, yet her rheumy gray eyes twinkled in the lantern light when she looked up.

Cecilia decided this would be the person for her to get to know. She motioned the woman to come over and sit with her, patting the bench space beside her.

The woman jerked her head back in surprise, her face registering questions. Cecilia nodded.

The woman stuffed her knitting into a worn canvas satchel at her feet and rose to walk over to Cecilia. She rocked left to right in a duck's waddle as she came, but she stood and walked upright, without the stoop of infirmity. Judging by her walk and her clothing, Cecilia thought the woman might have been in service.

But just as she was studying the woman as she approached, Cecilia realized the woman was studying her. Cecilia rounded her shoulders a little and looked about the room again, this time with what she hoped was an apprehensive expression. She turned back to the woman and patted the bench beside her again.

"Please?" she said, her voice faint—and she hoped—frail. "I am Lady Branstoke. When our traveling companion became ill, my husband brought me down here while he searches out Mr. Price." She looked about the room, her eyes wide. "I told him I would be fine. But..."

"You're a mite fearful," the woman said.

Cecilia nodded. "Yes," she said, her voice a thread of sound, then stronger, "I saw you and thought, well, I thought if I was by another woman I wouldn't be so fearful," she said.

The woman nodded slowly and reached over to pat Cecilia's hand. "I'm that happy to be of service."

"Your voice. It sounds like you are in service?" Cecilia asked.

The woman laughed, then nodded again. "I was. For more than forty years. My name's Janet Hammond."

"I'm glad to meet you, Mrs. Hammond."

The woman shook her head. "Not Mrs. Hammond, Miss Hammond. Never found a man who could put up with me," she said with a cackling laugh.

"Would you join me in a mug of ale?" Cecilia waved to the barmaid. The young woman hurried over and Cecilia requested watered ale for herself and a large mug of ale for the old woman. When the barmaid left to get their drinks, Cecilia turned back to her companion.

"My stomach is a bit queasy from traveling and with Mr. Stackpoole's sudden illness up in the private parlor, it is a bit worse. Sometimes an ale can settle a stomach."

"That it can, and I would be honored, Lady Branstoke. Excuse me, did you say Mr. Stackpoole?"

"Yes. Do you know him?"

"Some. I've talked to him a time or two. His mother introduced us."

Cecilia's attention sparked, then a cough interrupted her eager words. She cleared her throat. "You worked at the sanatorium? At Camden House?" she asked.

Miss Hammond nodded. "I was matron for the women that had private rooms. A bit of a housekeeper, bit of a nurse, and bit of a friend when they needed one," she said, tilting her head to the side. Cecilia could tell the woman's smile was for her memories.

"You retired?"

Miss Hammond looked quickly over at Cecilia, her expression collapsing into a bitter frown. "Hardly. I was let go—would have been let go with nothing if it hadn't been for Mrs. Worcham. She insisted I have a pension for all me years."

The maid came up with their ale. Cecilia couldn't believe her good fortune to actually meet someone who worked at the sanatorium. It was all she could do to keep her manner fragile and ill.

"What do you mean?" Cecilia asked, clearing her throat again. She took a sip of her watered ale.

Miss Hammond compressed her lips together. "That new superintendent the doctor hired set down rules when he came, and one said staff were not to socialize with patients. I didn't think that meant me, as Dr. Worcham always told me what I did was a benefit to the ladies and their well-being." She frowned. "Two months later, I was let go for not following his new rules, for being too friendly with my ladies. He called it insubordination, and he was going to make an example with me so the rest of the staff would know he was serious."

Cecilia sipped her ale. "But if Dr. Worcham approved of your work, how did he allow you to be let go?" she asked.

"It was in the contract," she said bitterly. She took a drink of ale. "The man told Dr. Worcham he would only take the position if he would have complete say as to the working of the sanatorium, like the rules, the facility staff, the provisioning, leaving all the medical to Dr. Worcham."

"But wouldn't your care be under the medical work done by the sanatorium?"

"That's what Dr. Worcham said to Mr. Turnbull-Minchin, unfortunately in the staff ledger, I'm listed as a housekeeper. Dr. Worcham told me afterward he should have changed my title to nurse long ago, but never got around to it. That's when Mrs. Worcham said they needed to give me a pension. Mr. Turnbull-Minchin reluctantly agreed."

"A compromise," Cecilia said. "He still got rid of you and still maintained control. The pension was a way to appease his employer without them coming to odds as to what he did—Or, I would imagine, looking too closely at the books."

Miss Hammond snorted. "That's the truth. But I have to admit, some of the changes he made were right ones."

"Like what?"

"Where the provisions come from. Dr. Worcham got one supplier and never checked to see if anyone might cost less. Mr. Turnbull-Minchin, he switched the greengrocer without losing quality, maybe even improving it a mite," she reluctantly admitted, her face scrunching.

Cecilia grinned at Miss Hammond's reluctant admittance. It spoke to the woman's honesty and character.

"But some of them new rules!" Miss Hammond rolled her eyes. "What, I say, is the reason to stop all staff from eating together?" She scratched her head through her cap.

"What do you mean?" Cecilia asked.

"Those that cared for the women's side and those that cared for the men's side."

"So, the male and female servants couldn't eat together," Cecilia stated. There was some sense to that, she supposed.

The woman shook her head. "There's men and women that work on both sides. No. Just the two groups couldn't eat together. I can see why he said housekeeping staff and medical staff should be apart to separate those who report to Dr. Worcham from those that report to him."

"That would be part of his control issues," Cecilia suggested.

She nodded. "But why the separation within the housekeeping staff? Made no sense to me."

Cecilia nodded. "I'm sure he had his reasons," she temporized, holding her handkerchief against her lips to ward off another cough.

"I know, he didn't see that sometimes it's good to talk amongst us. But if he wanted us to not talk together, he'd have to stop them mingling in the garden or the library."

"But to do that," Cecilia suggested, "the patients would need to be separated as well."

The woman nodded, smiling at Cecilia for understanding the crux of that issue. "Yes, my lady and that is something Dr. Worcham won't do as he believes it is advantageous for the men and women patients to meet socially, as they might in society."

"This Mr. Turnbull-Minchin sounds like an unusual superintendent. Do you know where he came from?"

She shook her head. "Just that he come from London."

"Are there many patients who are long-term patients at the sanatorium like Lady Stackpoole?"

"A few, five I think, last I knew. Most patients only stay for six months to a year at most. Dr. Worcham does not want patients, or their families, to treat Camden House like a permanent residence. The doctor wants to cure people or make them better. He always said there are other institutions for life care."

"There is a man I know of—" Cecilia began carefully.

"There you are!" they heard Mr. Price behind them.

They turned to see him coming toward them, followed by James.

"Miss Hammond," Mr. Price said, "we have a gentleman who's taken sick upstairs. Might I prevail upon you to take a look in on him?"

"Yes. I assume the gentleman is Mr. Stackpoole?" Miss Hammond said. "Lady Branstoke said he had taken sick."

"Yes, please," Mr. Price said, wringing his hands together. The one thing a publican might worry about is a sick guest who could pass on an illness to another at the inn—or worse spread rumors the establishment was one where guests took ill.

Miss Hammond nodded and stood up, gathering her knitting bag as she rose.

Cecilia looked at the woman beside her in surprise. Miss Hammond shrugged. "I learned a bit from Dr. Worcham and now help out in the village as I can."

She followed Mr. Price upstairs to their parlor.

James came up beside his wife, shaking his head. "How do you do it?" he asked. "Mr. Price said there was a woman in the pub room who had some nursing skills who used to work at the sanatorium, and I returned to find you chatting with that very person."

Cecilia took his arm and let him lead her to the stairs. She didn't bother to pretend she didn't know what he meant. Of all the people at the inn, she'd discovered a person who could provide them with information about the inner workings of the sanatorium.

"A gift?" she asked. "Seriously, she was the only woman in the room and though she sat apart from everyone, I could tell she listened to all that went on. I thought a listener might have the information we need. It was a surprise to discover she formerly worked at the sanatorium!"

"Did she know Mr. Montgomery?"

"I didn't get a chance to ask her before Mr. Price and you came up to us. She does know Lady Stackpoole. She'd been the matron for the floor where Lady Stackpoole resides."

"Why is she not yet working at the sanatorium?"

"According to her, she was part of the housekeeping staff and supposed to know her place. She became quite friendly with her 'ladies' as she called them, so she was let go as that was against the new superintendent's rules."

"Hmm," James said thoughtfully.

At the top of the stairs, they stopped and looked in the direction of the parlor. The door stood partly ajar, and from within, they heard the muffled sounds of talking. They turned away from the parlor and returned to their room.

A trimmed lantern sat on a bedside table casting a glow across the bed where Sarah had laid out Cecilia's night rail. The fire in the hearth burned steadily, pushing warm air into the room.

"I saw Sarah when I went looking for Mr. Price. I told her you wouldn't need her anymore this evening," James said. He pulled pins out of her hair.

Cecilia turned her head to look at him. "That was forward of you."

"Hmm."

"That's the second time you've used that response. What is going on in that magnificent brain of yours?" she asked, turning into his arms.

He smiled down at her. "Thoughts of my amazing wife."

She wrapped her arms around his neck. "I think it is time we rediscover just how amazing we are together."

His lips hovered over her lips. "Beyond time," he whispered before his lips touched hers and mutual sighs stirred the air.

CHAPTER 7

THE GAOL

"How is Mr. Stackpoole this morning?" James asked Mr. Price the next morning when he descended the stairs. He and Cecilia had agreed that she would break her fast in their room to perpetuate her impression of delicate health.

"Still sickly. Miss Hammond says it looks like stomach influenza. She said she would be back later this morning to check on him. He's not to eat. He's to rest his stomach, she said. We're to give him plenty to drink. Mrs. Price has made up a big pot of her special tisane as he is partial to it."

"That is a trifle worrisome as we spent all day yesterday in a closed carriage with him," James said. "My wife has a delicate constitution," he explained, unabashedly lying.

Typically, Cecilia was quite hardy, for all her dissimulation of illness. However, she had been frighteningly ill with influenza, and he did not know if she had yet regained all her strength. He would not take chances with her health. While he did not like Cecilia's idea of becoming a patient at Camden House, if she were to come down with Mr. Stackpoole's illness, it would be the best place for her to be.

"How far is it to Stamford?" he asked.

"Five miles."

"And to the gaol?"

"The gaol!" Mr. Price exclaimed.

"Yes," James said, not offering any other information.

Mr. Price frowned. "Not more than another mile."

"Thank you." James turned to go back upstairs.

"Should you like some breakfast, sir?" Mr. Price asked.

"Yes. In the private parlor in, say, thirty minutes?"

"Yes, sir. And the missus?"

"No, Lady Branstoke will break her fast in our room."

"Very good, sir."

"And please let me know if Miss Hammond returns while I am still here."

"Yes, sir."

James nodded and turned to go back up the stairs.

He returned to their room to find Cecilia sitting up in bed reading a novel. She set it aside as he entered.

"You should read this novel," she said. "It's the new one by *Anonymous* from the Merriman publisher."

"Is that the new gothic one touted in the papers?"

"Yes."

He shook his head. "I am not a gothic reader."

"This one is different. You should at least try it."

He snorted. "Perhaps."

"Oh you, that means you won't," she accused.

He laughed. "No," he contradicted, "it means perhaps."

She frowned at him, then laughed. "All right. So, what have you learned of Mr. Stackpoole?"

"Mr. Price says he is still sick, and Miss Hammond believes it to be a stomach influenza."

She wrinkled her nose. "And we spent all yesterday in his company."

"Yes, which is why I'd like you to rest here this morning while I visit Soothcoor. We will go to Camden House on my return."

"But I wanted to see the earl!" she complained. "I have so much to ask him!"

"That wouldn't be in keeping with the ruse you intend to play."

She made a face at him. "No, you are correct. Though sometimes it doesn't feel like a ruse with this plaguey cough."

He touched her head. "I know. Do you not trust me to question Soothcoor adequately?"

"Of course I do. Probably better than I should. It's just…" she trailed off.

The corner of James's lips kicked up in a faint smile. "Consider you will be conversing with people at the sanatorium when I am not present to hear. We shall have to trust each other."

She laughed and nuzzled his hand as he slid it down the side of her face. "And we do," she said.

"Yes, we do. I have requested breakfast for myself in the private parlor after which I will be on my way to the gaol. Mr. Price says it is about six miles away. I shall see about renting a horse so I may ride. It will be quicker and easier. He will see that food is sent here for you."

She nodded. "I shall be ready to go to the sanatorium on your return."

"Excellent," he said. He leaned over to give her a quick kiss. She pulled his head down for a deeper kiss.

"Be careful, my love," she said when he stood again.

"Always."

~

THE STAMFORD BOROUGH Gaol was a four-story, free-standing stone building at the back of the town hall. James rode up to the gatehouse and asked to enter.

"Visitors on'y on Saturdays," the turnkey declared. He looked askance at James. "What dealin's would you be havin' with the likes of these people? We gets the scum here," he shook his head, his lips compressed tightly.

"I should like to see the Earl of Soothcoor," James told him, his voice measured and quiet, but with a honed edge of steel he'd developed in his military days.

"Oh, he's not in the bridewell proper. He ain't been tried and him being a peer and all—at least until the trial."

"Then where is he?" James asked.

"He's in a room in the warden's house. Normally, that's where we put the debtors, but we don't have any now, and he being a peer and all...," he repeated and trailed off.

James nodded. "I need to speak with him about the charges against him."

"He kilt that man! What's to know?"

"Has the trial occurred yet?"

"No. Be 'nother three weeks 'afore the next assizes, I'm thinkin'."

"Then he is not guilty yet," James said evenly.

The turnkey scowled and scratched his head. "I guess."

"Where might I find the warden?"

"In his office."

"And where might that be?" James continued patiently.

The man's expression cleared. "Oh, that door over there," he said pointing to the left.

"I shall speak to him then. Thank you," James said, walking past the turnkey.

The turnkey frowned but didn't stop him.

James knocked on the heavy oak door. There was an opening covered with iron bars over a small door set eye height on the larger door. When the small door opened, all James could see were pudgy, filmy gray eyes peering through the opening.

"Visitin' hours t'aint till Saturday. Didn't that fool-headed turnkey tell ye that?"

"I am here to see the Earl of Soothcoor," James said evenly. He didn't say anything more and passively stared at the gaol warden.

The man behind the door squinted his eyes. "And who be you?"

"Sir James Branstoke."

He harrumphed, stepped back and closed the little door. James heard a key scrap against metal, then the door opened.

A large man with rolls of fat beneath his chin filled the door frame. He frowned. It looked habitual. Fuzzy hair came to a forward V shape on his forehead, the edges receding steeply at the sides of his head, the skin polished pink. His full cheeks resembled a squirrel's cheeks after discovering a hoard of nuts.

"Sir James," he said.

"Yes."

The man's nose scrunched up. "Battle honor?"

James allowed a smile to ghost his lips. "Peninsular battles," James said.

The man nodded. "Name's Harvey. Henry Harvey. I'm the warden here. Come in," Warden Harvey said, stepping away from the door. He waddled to a desk in the middle of the room and stood by the large chair behind it. He waved his hand, indicating James should take a seat, then sat as well.

"Me older brother were a Chosen Man with the 95th Rifles," the warden said, pride in his tone.

James knew the 95th Rifles was a regiment organized in 1800. The rifles regiment took the best and brightest men from different regiments to form a radically different corps of men, trained to be sharpshooters using the new Baker rifle; men who could think for themselves and be skirmishers instead of line and square fighters. They even had different uniforms: dark green with black leather trim to provide camouflage.

"Congratulations," James said. If talking about the Peninsular War and this man's brother would get him to talk to Soothcoor, it was worth the time. He relaxed back in his chair.

"My main experience with the 95th was during the Siege of Badajoz," he told the warden. "They did a fine job of eliminating the French artillery crews there."

The man compressed his lips and nodded. "He told us about that battle." Then he shook his head. "Unfortunately, he got injured durin' The Battle of Tarbes, so he missed Waterloo."

"He was discharged?" James said.

"Aye. Injured his shootin' arm, couldn't hold a rifle fer a long while." He laughed. "Got it good now, though. Gamekeeper on the Marquis of Keirsmyth's estate."

Then his expression dropped, and he rested his head on his chins as he looked at James.

He leaned forward. "So why do you want to visit a murderer?"

"I don't believe it is possible for Alastair Sedgewick, the Earl of Soothcoor, to kill a man."

The warden's eyes narrowed. "Any man can kill another. Been the same forever. We's taught that in the Bible when Cain kills Abel."

"I do not argue with you. But not Soothcoor."

The Warden snorted. "Ya think the man's a saint?"

James shook his head. "No. Then again, I have never met a saint, so I don't know what one would do or not do."

The Warden smiled at that. "I like that. So, tell me about my prisoner."

"The Earl of Soothcoor is well known. His holdings are in Northumberland; however, he spends most of his days in London. In society they refer him to as 'The Dour Earl' for he rarely smiles. He has never been married. He is well-liked and invited everywhere. He is also a private person. Few in society know that his hobby is building and fixing musical automatons or that his passion is helping women and children from the worst parts of London, like Seven Dials, get chances to rise above their circumstances."

The warden nodded. "He is a quiet man. Paid fer things he's asked fer, but he don't ask fer much. Only thing he's asked fer is books to read, and blankets fer all prisoners."

James laughed. "That sounds like Soothcoor."

The Warden reached up to scratch his ear. "Me and the wife were away that night he were brought in." He grunted. "Left the Turnkey in charge," he said, shaking his head. "The magistrate had the earl sent to the general prison first night they brung him here. The turnkey on duty didn't know he were sum titled bloke so didn't think to question the magistrate, not that he would have even if he had two thoughts in his brain, which he don't. Magistrate jus' gave 'is given name when 'e brought him in."

"And the earl noticed the state of the blankets right away," James suggested, "because the one given to him was thin and moth-eaten."

The Warden nodded. "Aye. When I got back the next day and found out where 'e'd put the earl, I wasted no time in getting him to a proper cell. Put 'im in an empty debtor's room attached to my 'ouse. My wife sees to him. 'e's always soft-spoken and nice 'cept when he brought up the matter of the blankets. Demanded I get new ones immediately. He pulls a yella boy outta 'is waistcoat pocket and slaps it down in front of me. Said that should cover it, and it did. Quite passionate 'e got about them blankets."

"I believe you," James said. "He is accused of murdering Malcolm Montgomery."

The Warden nodded.

"Who accused him? How did it come about?"

"The magistrate says I don't need to know," he said, sneering.

James frowned. "I would consider that suspicious."

The Warden nodded, his lips still flicking upward at the corner.

"How did Mr. Montgomery die?"

"Drowned."

"Drowned? Where? And didn't something else like that happen there a year or so ago?"

With lips compressed, the Warden nodded and pointed his finger at James for being right.

James's frown turned to a deep scowl.

"How?"

The Warden shook his head. "No one is sayin', which is jus' not normal fer a murder."

"You don't think Soothcoor killed Mr. Montgomery, do you?"

The warden shifted his bulk in his chair, the chair's wood joints groaning. "Not fer me to say." He inhaled deeply. "But someone wants him to 'ang."

"May I speak with him?"

"Why?"

"I want to talk to him about his meeting with Mr.

Montgomery. Soothcoor is not a murderer. I'd like to find out who is."

The Warden nodded, then turned to pull a ring of keys off an iron hook embedded in the wall beside him. "Let's go," he said, rising to his feet. He lumbered to the door.

The warden led James out of the gaol and around to the back of the building to a brick house, separated from the prison by a narrow road. The house had two doors. The door on the right had a small plot of herbs growing on either side. The one on the left did not. The warden led him to the door on the left and selected a key from his ring to unlock the door. It swung open without a screech, indicating it was well maintained, unlike what he'd seen in the prison. They stepped into a narrow hall. Before them were two more doors, each with small openings covered with iron bars, a little larger than the warden's office door and without the ability to close off the rooms beyond from view.

The warden peered into one of the rooms. "My lord, I brung ya a visitor," he said. He turned the ring of keys around until he found the one for the cell, unlocked it, and pushed open the door.

Soothcoor had been sitting on a low bed, leaning against the wall, reading. He slowly stood when the door opened. His clothing appeared dirty and torn, his hair, a lanky tangle of gray-and-black strands. He hadn't shaved in a week. His features appeared sharper than normal.

"Visitor," the warden declared. He looked about the room, nodded, then moved out of James's way so he could enter.

"James!" Soothcoor exclaimed, limping toward him. They grasped their arms. "I am delighted to see you! Thank you, Mr. Harvey, for allowing James to visit," he said, in typical polite Soothcoor fashion. He put a hand down on the table then hobbled around it to sit back on the bed. "Please sit down," he said, waving his hand at the only chair in the room tucked under the table.

"Why are you limping?" James frowned, looking from Soothcoor to the warden and back.

Soothcoor waved his hand dismissively. "A slight misunderstanding."

The warden harrumphed. "Right of passage in the prison. 'e wouldn't defend 'isself. Got a chair whacked across 'is leg."

"Has a doctor seen to it?" James asked the warden.

"No funds fer a doctor," the man said, crossing his arms over his chest.

James scowled at the warden, then turned his head to look at his friend. "You used the money you had on you to purchase blankets, didn't you?"

Soothcoor shrugged.

James shook his head dolefully at his selfless friend. "Mr. Harvey," he said, turning back to the warden. "Have a doctor see to Soothcoor and send the bill to me at The New Bell Inn—At the least he could do with a crutch to keep weight off the leg." He looked back at Soothcoor. "Did it bleed?"

Soothcoor nodded silently.

James stared at him, wanting more.

"A little," Soothcoor finally said. "I used my cravat to wrap around it to stop the bleeding."

"Which hasn't been changed in the week you've been here, has it?" James said, leaning across the table.

Soothcoor looked down at his hands, but not before James caught the faint smile pulling on his friend's lips.

"Yes, I'm taking charge," James said, fighting against an answering smile for he knew what caused Soothcoor's humor. James maintained a phlegmatic manner in society, unless his friends or family were in distress or danger, then the commanding Peninsular War army colonel returned.

The warden walked back to the door. "I be breakin' me own rules as it is to 'ave you here. I'll give you one 'our," he said. He closed the door behind him.

James heard the key turning in the lock, securing him inside. He wouldn't be able to leave until the warden returned.

CHAPTER 8

ILLNESS SPREADS

"You look the healthiest I have seen you look in over a month," Sarah critically told Cecilia as she removed her breakfast tray from Cecilia's lap.

"Two days ago, I would have celebrated that observation," Cecilia said with a wry smile.

"I remember how pale you looked and the circles under your eyes. Perhaps…" Her words trailed off. She set the tray on the table beside the bed and went to the small coal stove. She swiped her fingertips in the hearth where the stove sat. Bits of coal and ash dust colored her fingertips. She wiped the heaviest off on the underside of her apron then crossed back to the bed.

Cecilia nodded appreciatively and tilted her face toward her maid.

Sarah lightly wiped the gray residue on her fingers below Cecilia's eyes and a little on her eyelids. Using a handkerchief, she gently blended the gray in. "Too dark would be suspect," she said to Cecilia. "You want just a bit of a wan look."

"It is too bad we don't have any rice powder for my

complexion," Cecilia murmured as she stayed still beneath Sarah's ministrations.

"Yes, but I think this will do. You are supposedly over being sick, just slow to recover, right?"

"I have been slow to recover," Cecilia agreed. She turned her head away a moment to cough.

"As sick as you were, the staff thinks you are doing well since you rose from your sick bed. And you do still have that cough," Sarah pointed out.

"That is the only thing, and Dr. Patterson said that is what lingers with everyone who's come down with this wretched illness."

"That is the reminder you are not totally well yet and to take it easy. Let me fetch the hand mirror so you may see what I've done." She brought back the mirror and handed it to Cecilia.

Cecilia looked at her face from one angle and then another. She smiled at what she saw, then quickly dropped the smile. "It looks convincing, I think, so long as I don't smile. Smiling destroys the image."

"Well, as you are supposed to be sick still, you wouldn't be smiling."

"True...Maybe a small weak smile for effect."

Sarah laughed. "Yes."

"Please get me my clothes out. I should like to visit Mr. Stackpoole."

Sarah had crossed the room to fetch clean linens when someone knocked on the door.

Cecilia waved at Sarah to answer.

"One moment," Sarah called out. She set the linens on the bed and crossed to the door. She pressed on the latch and pulled open the door a few inches. When she saw who stood on the other side, she opened it all the way.

"Who is it?" Cecilia asked.

"Miss Hammond, ma'am."

"Have her come in. I am anxious for news of Mr. Stackpoole," Cecilia said. She grabbed her robe from beside the bed and slipped it on.

"Beg pardon, my lady," Miss Hammond said as she entered.

"Nonsense. Please come in. Tell me of Mr. Stackpoole."

Miss Hammond shook her head. "Not well, madam. He was better last night when I left, but when I arrived, I found him very sick again. Like it came back around again, just as 'afore."

Cecilia frowned. "That is worrisome. Is he in danger of dying?"

"That I can't be saying, I've never seen the like of this. It be almost like he's poisoned, but he don't die. I told Mrs. Price he is not to have anything to eat or drink save water, and that sparingly, to keep his mouth wet. She didn't like that none as she believes her tisane is the best for what ails a body."

"Had he had anything to eat earlier today?"

"Mrs. Price had a tray taken to him his morning as he was so much better last night. I don't know all he ate or drank. Didn't appear to be much to eat.

"He said he took only a few bites, then pushed it away as it made his stomach queasy like. He did drink the tisane Mrs. Price made for him, and I thought that good...Pardon, madam, you don't look so good yourself this morning. You feeling queasy?"

"No, I'm just still tired after my illness and James and the staff having to take care of me," Cecilia said distractedly as she thought about Mr. Stackpoole.

A heavy pounding on the door startled the women.

"Miss Hammond, be you here?" They heard from the other side of the door. It was Mrs. Price. "We have need of you. Please."

Sarah opened the door. Mrs. Price peered around

her to see Miss Hammond then pushed past her to hurry toward Miss Hammond.

"It's Susan Divers. She has taken sick just like that Mr. Stackpoole. Maybe worse."

"Susan!" exclaimed Sarah from by the door. "We just spoke this morning. Her voice was a little hoarse, and she said her throat felt scratchy, but she didn't appear terribly unwell."

Mrs. Price turned toward Sarah. "And she wasn't that sick. We both thought a cup of my tisane would make everything fine. And she was one moment, and the next not!" She turned back to Miss Hammond. "Can you come to see her, please?"

"Yes, immediately. This is all highly curious. Your pardon, my lady," Miss Hammond said, turning to curtsy to Cecilia and then following Mrs. Price out of the room.

"Help me get dressed," Cecilia said as she slipped off her robe. "I should see if I can help."

"You can't do that!" Sarah protested.

"Why ever not?"

"It wouldn't be in keeping with your sickliness."

"Blast. You are correct. I have painted myself into a corner. Bother."

Sarah laughed. "Yes, ma'am, but you wouldn't want to risk the babe either, not after you just recovering from being unwell for so long yourself," she said as she helped Cecilia remove her nightgown.

Cecelia made a face and nodded. "Perhaps I can sit quietly in the taproom and eavesdrop on conversations. I'd wager all will be talking about the illness and most particularly speculating on its cause."

Sarah gathered up Cecilia's dress to help her into it. "Aren't many here this early in the morning."

"True, there wouldn't be. Then where might be a good place to hear the local gossip?" she wondered.

"Maybe a slow constitutional walk to the linen drapers?"

"That be a good idea," Sarah said, securing the fastenings at the back of the dress. "Always good gossip at the drapers."

"Well, let's get me put together and see if we need any more ash for my weak persona." She picked up her silver-backed hand mirror from where she'd laid it on the bed and studied her complexion. "Suitably weak looking, now it only needs the resolution to maintain the ruse."

"Yes, ma'am"

CHAPTER 9

ALASTAIR

James took his beaver hat off and laid it on the table in Soothcoor's cell. He sat down.

"You told Mrs. Montgomery to contact Cecilia and me, which she did. She told us about you knowing each other growing up." He summarized their conversation with Mrs. Montgomery. Then he leaned forward and clasped his hands on the table.

"Now, *you* tell me everything."

Soothcoor carefully lifted his bad leg off the floor onto the bed and pressed his back up against the wall. He pushed greasy strands of black-and-gray hair away from his eyes. "Lilias was distraught at learning Malcolm was not dead," he began slowly, "More for their children's sake than for herself—though I should wish she gave more thought to herself and her own happiness. She was relieved to learn he had not committed suicide. That had weighed heavily on her soul."

"She wondered what she might have done to prevent that?"

"Precisely. I did not know the extent of Malcolm's illness until Lilias and I spoke of it. I suspected much when we were young men, but I lacked the life experience at that time to appreciate what he told me."

"Why did you journey here to see him?"

"Lilias wanted to come; however, her youngest, Hugh, was just home from school, Aileen was engaged with a wedding looming, and Sorcha was distraught. She always felt jealous that Aileen had more of an opportunity to know their father than she did, and to learn he was alive and that she might have had time to visit him still distressed her. Lilias knew Malcolm would not have allowed that, afterall, how can you tell a young girl—a young woman—that she couldn't see her beloved father?"

"So, you volunteered to come."

"Of course. Malcolm had been my friend for years. We had grown apart when he married Lilias. That was my issue. I couldn't visit them; my heart was too heavy to accept her marriage to Malcolm; it was best I stayed away, so our friendship faded. He did write to tell me there would be no more correspondence from him. This was when he first went into an asylum. I didn't know that at the time and was perturbed. Nonetheless, that was Malcolm's choice, and I honored it."

"When did you arrive here?"

"Nine days ago, and immediately after leaving my bags at The New Bell Inn I went to Camden House.

"That first day was a day of reminiscences. I didn't push him for an answer for why he put it about that he was dead. He had been genuinely happy to see me. And truthfully, I, to see him, too. We laughed and traded tales. I told him of what I do in London, and I told him about his children and Aileen's engagement. He was happy. He promised not to say anything to Lady Stackpoole until her son did. That first day we didn't discuss why he faked his death. It was a strange day.

"The next day, I walked around the village, thinking. Then, I rode into Stamford for a while. I was not doing anything that day except, maybe, avoiding what I had really come here to talk to Malcolm about. We both had been avoiding what we both knew we should discuss. Finally, I decided I had to see Malcolm again. My mind had been so fraught with ideas as to why Malcolm did what he did that I had to see him...The drive to see him became of great urgency, a need to begin to put a structure around the events of the past. To rationalize his actions. I rode from Stamford to Camden House. It was near the end of the day, and the sanatorium staff at first weren't going to let me in, but I persuaded them otherwise."

"What was his reaction on first seeing you again?" James asked.

Soothcoor sighed. "Sadness."

"Sadness?"

He nodded. "He knew we had not discussed the reason for my visit the day before and that we needed to. He said he never wanted to hurt Lilias or their children. He felt that the knowledge of him residing in an institution would hang over them. He convinced Dr. Worcham that if he didn't help him with his faked death scheme, he would, in truth, kill himself. Dr. Worcham said his father had to know the truth, or else he would not agree, and they would instead have to keep him in restraints to prevent him from killing himself— If for no other reason than to have someone continue to pay the bills. He sent a letter to Malcolm's father, unfortunately, the elder Mr. Montgomery was very frail by this time. It was his cousin, Boyd Ratcliffe, who read the correspondence."

"Why did a cousin read the correspondence?"

"Some months earlier, in the absence of Malcolm, his father had named Boyd, his older sister's son, estate manager and let it be known he would be the executor for the Montgomery estate when he died. Ratcliffe had control over the Montgomery estate as long as Malcolm stayed in the sanatorium. This angered Malcolm, but, he conceded he'd set the path."

"Why? He has to know someone had to take the reins of the estate, and he would not be allowed to do so while in an asylum. Did Malcolm think Boyd was too young for the responsibility or worried he would snatch up Mrs. Montgomery's affections?"

"Yes, and he has, but not the Mrs. Montgomery you are thinking of. He married Malcolm's mother on the anniversary of Malcolm's father's death."

"Malcolm's mother?"

"Yes, though it is not as scandalous as you might think. His cousin is nearer Malcolm's father's age than Malcolm's age. Malcolm said he was furious. He said none of *them* liked Boyd Ratcliffe."

"You mean these 'other' personalities?"

His brow furrowed. "Yes, at least that is what I inferred to be his meaning."

James nodded in understanding. "Do you personally know Boyd Ratcliffe?"

One corner of Soothcoor's lip kicked up. "I have that misfortune."

James raised a brow.

He sighed and leaned back, propping his weight up with his arms. "He owns Lincolnton Bank and calls himself a banker. I find him more akin to a usurer."

"And now Mrs. Montgomery—Malcolm's mother— is Mrs. Ratcliffe."

"Yes."

"He's in England, not Scotland?"

"Yes. His sister's husband was English, and they live not far from the sanatorium."

"Tell me about this second visit with Mr. Montgomery."

"I arrived at the sanatorium during the dinner hour. The sanatorium keeps early country hours. After their dinner, one of the matrons went to tell Malcolm I was in the receiving hall. He came out there to meet me." He frowned a moment. "From what I learned talking to staff as I waited on Malcolm, visitors used to be welcomed anywhere on the ground floor. One of the changes made by Mr. Turnbull-Minchin, when he became superintendent, was to limit visits to the great hall, which they call the receiving room, and outside on the grounds. Malcolm suggested we go outside to talk, away from listening ears.

"The sun was starting to go down, and to the east, clouds were gathering, foretelling more rain in the night. The wind had started to increase, bringing a nip in the air. It was actually a wonder it hadn't rained that day. We walked nearly around the building then back again. Have you been out there yet?"

"No, we only arrived yesterday. I wanted to speak to you first."

Alastair nodded. "Camden House is situated on an island of land created in the last century when canals were dug for drainage."

"Mr. Stackpoole mentioned something to that effect."

"You've met Aileen's fiancé? Benjamin?"

"Yes. He was on his way to Camden House when his coach broke down. We invited him to travel with us."

"He was going to Camden House?"

"His mother is a resident at the sanatorium. I think he has some notion of discussing Mr. Montgomery's death with this mother and learning something useful."

"I knew Lady Stackpoole resided in a sanatorium; I had not realized it was Camden House."

"Unfortunately, Mr. Stackpoole has taken ill," James said.

"Nothing serious, I trust. Aileen is deeply in love with the young man and he her, in turn."

"But his father is against the marriage.."

"So, I understood from things Mr. Stackpoole said when he asked Mrs. Montgomery for Aileen's hand in marriage. He has attained his majority, has a modest income inherited from his paternal grandmother—much to his father's annoyance—and has the promise of a position with the Foreign Office, another choice his father condemns."

James nodded. "From our discussions, it did not appear his father had any leverage to force Mr. Stackpoole to follow his orders."

"Quite the reverse, with Baron Stackpoole's treatment of Lady Stackpoole at the top of the contention list." Soothcoor laughed. "With his glasses and perpetually messed hair, he does not appear like a determined young man; however, I assure you, he is. There is a rod of steel hidden within his polite gentleman appearance."

James smiled. "I am delighted to hear that. But continue with your visit with Mr. Montgomery."

"Ah, yes. Malcolm was delighted that I wished to marry Lilias but distressed that the fact he was alive had become known. He would have preferred to go on being considered dead."

"The fact that he wasn't dead meant if you had married Mrs. Montgomery, there would have been immense problems for all involved."

"Yes, but Malcolm didn't think it needed to be of concern. I reminded him that so long as 'someone' was paying for him to live at Camden House, his supposed death could never be believed. It was only a matter of time before it became known. He seemed depressed at that reality."

"Depressed enough to commit suicide?" James asked.

Soothcoor shook his head. "I don't believe so. He

admitted he had considered suicide a couple of years ago. Luckily, those others in his head would not let him because that would be killing them as well."

"They are that powerful?"

"Apparently. It is beyond my comprehension, so I simply took what I was told. At one point Malcolm stopped and stared out across the canal to the fenlands. I could tell he was furiously thinking. I wondered if he was having a conversation with the others within him. I don't know if that is possible or not, but his stillness as he stood there had that feeling. Finally, he shifted position, stood straighter, taller somehow, and said the day before I arrived, *they* had requested a solicitor journey to Scotland to submit divorce papers. It is easier in Scotland to obtain a divorce than in England. He asked me to support them in their endeavor. At that moment, I knew I was talking to one of the other people who lived in Malcolm. He told me Malcolm loved Lilias and, for that reason, knew Malcolm needed to free her for, as he said, *we* can never leave Camden House. He told me—with an eerie earnestness—that it would be too dangerous for others. He had been aware that I wished to marry her in our youth and knew I would take good care of her and Malcolm's children."

"I can't imagine participating in a conversation like that. And you are sure it was not Malcolm playacting?" James asked, leaning forward.

Soothcoor sighed deeply, compressed his lips and nodded. "Yes, I am certain. You'd have to have witnessed it to believe it."

"What did you tell him?"

"I told him I would make inquiries, but I thought he should contact his cousin who stood as executor. It was odd. When I said his cousin's name to Malcolm, there was no reaction. Mentioning Boyd Ratcliffe to this person had the result of anger at even voicing the name, let alone saying something about him being Malcolm's de facto guardian. He claimed the man did not have Malcolm's best interests in mind and implied that he was somehow responsible for the state they found themselves."

"Interesting. I spoke to Dr. Nowlton before I left London. Do you know him?"

"Yes, we have met. His sister *volunteered* him to work at Mrs. Southerland's, one of my charities."

James nodded. "I had him examine Cecilia before I allowed her to journey north. We spoke about Mr. Montgomery and the condition Mrs. Montgomery described to us. He said he had no personal experience with a similar case. However, he had read about a young woman who appeared to be different people at different times. She was fine in the sanatorium where she'd been placed, but when she returned home, she killed her father and then herself."

"Why? Do they know why she would suddenly do that?"

"Evidently, the father had raped her repeatedly as she was growing up. Being back home, he thought he would go to her bed one more time. She killed him and then killed herself."

Soothcoor shook his head dolefully. "I wonder if Malcolm ever had any traumatic experience with his father in life?"

"Or with this cousin."

Soothcoor stared off for a moment then slowly inclined his head in agreement. He straightened and looked directly at James. "That's when I left Malcolm— or some other unnamed part of him. The wind had intensified as we'd been outside. Dark storm clouds rolled toward us from the east. I wanted to return to the inn before the worst of the weather descended upon us. And I wanted time to think about what he'd told me. I promised I would make some inquiries and be back to him, or whoever was available, the next afternoon."

"You left him outside?" James asked.

"Yes. He said he liked storms and wished to savor it when it began, all new and wild. I told him not to catch his death of cold. He laughed at me and said for that would serve all our purposes. I reprimanded him. He sobered and told me not to worry. As I rode across the bridge that accessed the sanatorium island and looked back. I saw him still standing there, watching me leave. I raised my hand to wave at him. He waved back. That was the last time I saw him."

James's brows furrowed. "Did anyone see you return to the inn?"

"Yes, I spoke to the proprietor to request dinner."

"Did you make it back to the inn before the rain came?"

He laughed. "Barely, but yes. We joked about it at the inn."

"So, your clothes were dry?"

"Yes, why do you ask?"

"Wondering if a person could drown another person without getting wet themselves."

Soothcoor perked up at that observation.

"When were you arrested?" James continued.

"The next morning, while I was having breakfast at the inn."

James frowned. "That was quick. What had them decide you were the murderer so swiftly?"

Soothcoor shook his head. "I have no idea, and no one would answer my questions."

"I will have to speak to the magistrate," James mused.

"Good luck. I will tell you that Boyd Ratcliffe was there when I was arrested."

James frowned. "I need to understand why the magistrate seems to believe waiting for the assizes is merely a formality and had you put directly into the general prison population."

Soothcoor nodded. "I think that was Boyd Ratcliffe's influence. he kept going on and on about the perfidy of murdering an ill man."

James harrumphed but continued, "Can you remember who else was staying at the inn?"

He shook his head. "I kept to myself; I didn't feel like conversing with others..." He tilted his head to the side. "The register. There were two names before mine on the register. I don't know if they were still residing at the inn, only that they'd been there before me. Baron Stackpoole and another scrawl of a name that looked like Cameron Ramsay. I dismissed the notion the second name was Ramsay as there was no reason for Mr. Ramsay to be in the area. He fluttered about Mrs. Montgomery, not quite a suitor, but always irritatingly around, and I assumed I had his name on my mind for that reason.

"We knew Stackpoole had been at the inn as he had left a pot of honey for his son when he last visited. Young Stackpoole regularly goes to see his mother and, according to him, he has a love of honey."

Soothcoor frowned and looked intently at James. "Baron Stackpoole left a pot of honey for his son?"

"Yes. Mr. Stackpoole thought it a peace offering from his father."

Soothcoor compressed his lips. "That does not sound like something the baron would do as a peace offering. Strange. And from what Mr. Stackpoole told us in London, it did not sound as if his father visited his mother. You said Mr. Stackpoole has taken ill?"

"Yes. Mr. Stackpoole has had violent stomach and bowel issues. Cecilia is now concerned as Mr. Stackpoole traveled with us. She is resting today, else would have contrived to coerce me to allow her to accompany me here."

Soothcoor laughed. "I'm sure she would have. So, you managed to convince her to stay at the hotel. Well done!"

Sir James smirked. "It wasn't as hard as it might be at other times. Cecilia is just recovering from a spring influenza that laid her quite low, and she doesn't want to take any chances as she is enceinte."

"Enceinte! Congratulations."

"Thank you."

He looked down at his hands. "So is Mrs. Montgomery," he said quietly.

James stared at Alastair for a moment. "I don't know whether to congratulate you or swear like a sailor."

Alastair's lips lifted slightly at the side.

"I know. And when that becomes known, it will be another reason I will be judged guilty of murder."

CHAPTER 10

THE LINEN DRAPERS

An ornate black wrought iron stanchion held up the *Magnum and Sons Linen Drapers'* white sign with its simple black lettering. The building was a neat Georgian brick structure with a slate roof, no doubt built during the flurry of canal building at the end of the last century. As she looked down the road, Cecilia noted several more modern businesses interspersed with older Tudor buildings. There were numerous people walking about the town from various classes, including a woman who appeared to wear an elaborate white wig from the previous century.

She walked alone, with a vigorous stride, into the linen drapers. Cecilia and Sarah were not far behind her. Before entering the charming shop, Cecilia cautioned herself to maintain an invalidish manner. What had once been an easy manner to adopt, she'd found it getting increasingly difficult to maintain. James didn't like it when she fell back into the weak, fainting, naïve-woman role. She was none of those things and James reminded her he remained enamored of the clever, slyly humorous, and laughing woman he'd married.

Cecilia knew her short, slender stature did much to give people she met the impression she was an invalidish female before she'd ever spoke to them! Today, the addition of a little ash on her face would heighten the effect.

She stopped just inside the door. There were a dozen women in the mercantile, gathered together in clumps loudly chatting—not at all shopping for fabric or assorted fripperies. She heard the door open behind her and quickly stepped aside to allow another woman to enter. Cecilia nodded apologetically to the newcomer for blocking her entrance, then looked down and made her way to a long counter with baskets of ribbons and bows.

"Oh, look, my lady, at this ribbon!" Sarah said, picking up a wood spool of blue ribbon. "It matches your eyes! Sir James would certainly notice that ribbon threaded through your hair."

Cecilia smiled wanly. "Yes, I suppose...," she said faintly, passing the ribbon through her gloved fingers.

"I believe we have a couple ells of fabric in that same shade that my lady might be interested to see," said a man from across the counter.

Cecilia looked up into the eyes of a chubby, balding young gentleman. She felt him look her over, calculating her worth.

"Perfect amount and weight for a spencer," the man continued, smiling in quite an ingratiating manner.

"Perhaps...," Cecilia said faintly, her eyes wandering away as another surge of coughing gripped her. She noted several women looking at her curiously. She smiled in what she hoped was an appropriate shy manner as she recovered her composure. There was generally one woman in a crowd of women like this who gravitated to the shy ones.

"Might there be a chair where my lady might sit for a moment?" Sarah asked the clerk. "She is still recovering from a long illness and the walk here has brought on renewed coughing and fatigue. Perhaps she might like to look at the fabric then," Sarah told him, her voice pitched for others to hear.

Cecilia kept her eyes downcast, forcing a smile away. In the year since she'd married James, Sarah had become the foil for Cecilia's fragile-woman persona, a role her Aunt Jessamine played when Cecilia sought her first husband's murderer. Cecilia thought Sarah enjoyed her little bits of invalid playacting and her role as Cecilia's caregiver. Unfortunately, at the moment, her coughing was all too real.

"Yes, of course," the clerk said. "Right this way." He led her to a chair near a large coal stove.

"Thank you," she said softly. She looked about while the man went to find the fabric. Cecilia humorously thought she'd be obliged to purchase the fabric, no matter what it looked like.

A tall angular woman walked up to Cecilia. "Are you quite all right? That cough sounded nasty, and you do look a bit peaked."

Cecilia looked at the woman and smiled. "Yes, thank you. I'm recovering from being sick. Unfortunately, this plaguey cough lingers and I tire easily," she said. "My doctor said walking would be good for me."

"You might need both rest and walking. I am Mrs. Tiptree." She sat down on the chair on the other side of the coal stove.

"Lady Branstoke," Cecilia said in return.

"What brings you to Camdenton Village?" she asked.

"My doctor has suggested a short stay at a sanatorium where I should not have to worry about any household matters. A friend suggested Camden House."

"And a good suggestion it is too. That is Mrs. Worcham over there," she said, pointing to the woman with the last-century wig."

"Oh!"

Mrs. Tiptree laughed. "Don't mind Emily Worcham and her wigs. The poor dear has a skin condition that has caused most of her hair to fall out, so she has taken to wearing wigs. All nature of wigs. It is her bit of humor. Today, a full white wig. Tomorrow, it could be a wig of dark red curls."

Cecilia looked over at the bewigged woman.

"I know her wig choices might make her appear to be one with the patients. She says living in a quiet sanatorium, as she does, can be overwhelming. She feels for her own sanity she needs to liven her life up occasionally," Mrs. Tiptree said with a laugh.

"How does Dr. Worcham feel about his wife's habit?"

"He does not have an objection, for you see, all the patients love her. She helps them see they need not feel so tightly bound to convention. Let me introduce her to you. You will love her, too.—Mrs. Worcham—Emily!" Mrs. Tiptree called out. She rose from the chair and crossed the space to the other side of the room where Mrs. Worcham talked animatedly with three other women. A moment later she returned to Cecilia's side, accompanied by Mrs. Worcham.

Mrs. Worcham was Cecilia's height, and with her bright, smiling dark eyes, she resembled an alert sparrow. One look at this woman and Cecilia knew this woman would see through her charade, if she were not careful. She had that keen observation eye that missed nothing.

"Mrs. Worcham, this is Lady Branstoke. She's going to Camden House this afternoon to see about a short stay. Lady Branstoke, this is our favorite Camden House resident, Emily Worcham, Dr. Worcham's wife."

The two women acknowledged the introduction, and then Mrs. Worcham sat down on the seat Mrs.

Tiptree had been sitting in. "And why is it you wish to come to Camden House," Mrs. Worcham inquired.

Cecilia drew her handkerchief from the cuff of her jacket where she had placed it for easy access. She sniffed lightly and blotted at the end of her nose. "Forgive me for admitting it is not my notion. I was very sick not a sennight ago. I contracted a terrible influenza. I was confined to my bed for two weeks. Now that the illness has passed, a cough remains, and I am slow to regain my strength. My dear husband is concerned as I am with child. He doesn't believe I am resting enough. He thinks I am trying to do too much too fast, so he suggested a sanatorium stay for a time to ensure I get the proper rest and care I need to fully recover." She smiled weakly, waving the handkerchief before her. "I protested but the dratted man found a medical man to support his concerns and his suggested solution."

Mrs. Worcham leaned forward to pat her hand resting in her lap. "If that is your situation then Camden House is the perfect place for you to rest and recover. I dare swear that after just a couple of weeks, you will feel rested and ready for what life has for you."

"But, but...I heard—they said at the inn, that a man was murdered there," she said softly, keeping her eyes wide and fearful.

Mrs. Worcham closed her eyes briefly, then opened them again, their bright bird light dimmed. "Yes. Mr. Montgomery. We really don't know what happened," she said, frowning.

"Didn't they arrest someone?" Mrs. Tiptree asked.

Mrs. Worcham looked up at her where she stood near Cecilia. "Yes, yes they did," she said, her voice turning brisk. She looked back at Cecila. "So, you have no worries, my dear. I look forward to seeing you at Camden House." She rose and smoothed the fabric of her skirt down. "And I really did intend to buy a length of lace today. I heard from Mrs. Shepley they've received a new shipment."

What just happened? Cecilia wondered.

She looked over her shoulder where Sarah stood behind her. Her maid ever so slightly shook her head. Mrs. Worcham's demeanor changed abruptly when Mrs. Tiptree asked for confirmation that someone had been arrested. Why would that be?

She had just said they didn't know what happened and, practically in the next breath, briskly agreed a person had been arrested. Cecilia stared after the woman, now fingering lace on the other side of the store. Cecilia had the feeling Mrs. Worcham did not think the Earl of Soothcoor was the murderer. That was the only cause she could reason for her abrupt change in demeanor. What did she know? And how did she know it? It was fortuitous to meet her before she must go to Camden House. She turned back to Mrs. Tiptree who'd resumed her seat opposite Cecilia.

"Can you tell me about this murder? And," she added softly, conspiratorially, "you would be doing me a favor to remain engaged with me lest that clerk come back with fabric he intends for me to purchase."

Mr. Tiptree laughed. "Yes, that is young Mr. Jenkins. He tries very hard to prove himself to Mr. Magnum, the owner of the shop, as he would like to court Mr. Magnum's elder daughter, Iris. Frankly, I think his efforts are wasted on that Miss. She aspires to a higher status, which I doubt she could acquire. However, it is sometimes amusing to observe the antics of the young in their mating dances. I shall do all I can to keep him away from your purse."

Cecilia extended a shy smile to her. "Thank you. And the murder victim?" she reminded her.

"Oh, bless you, yes. It was Mr. Montgomery. He had

been a longtime resident of Camden House. They don't have many longtime residents there as Dr. Worcham does not want his sanatorium to be little better than a prison. There are other institutions for the severely ill."

"But murder," Cecilia said softly, opening her eyes wide, hoping to draw the woman out more.

Mrs. Tiptree nodded. Then her brow furrowed. "But the location and manner of death was quite similar to an earlier death at Camden House."

"An earlier death?" Cecilia parroted.

"Yes, indeed. It happened ten months ago, and that death was judged a suicide. I do not know what the difference between the two deaths might be. They were both found face down in the canal rushes near the northeast corner of the house. Why one is considered murder and the other suicide, I don't know." She shook her head, then stopped and shook her finger in Lady Cecilia's direction. "They are being quiet up at the big house, that is for sure. And the magistrate made a surprisingly quick arrest. Too quick, to my mind," she said flatly.

Cecilia coughed and nodded vaguely. "Do you know the man arrested?"

Mrs. Tiptree compressed her lips as she shook her head. "Some peer, I heard. Seems strange. Never came here before, as far as I've heard, and up and murders Mr. Montgomery."

"Did you ever meet this Mr. Montgomery?"

"No, no. Those of us in the village rarely see the patients. But I felt like I knew him Emily—I mean Mrs. Worcham—talked about him a lot, how sad it was that his affliction kept him in a sanatorium. She's a very caring, tender-hearted soul."

"I see. Thank you. I should be returning to The New Bell Inn now. My husband will likely be returning from his errand and wondering where we are! Thank you for introducing me to Mrs. Worcham. Meeting her has alleviated many of my concerns," she admitted. "I'm sorry that we will not likely meet again, that there is no mixing between the sanatorium and the village."

"I'm delighted, my dear, that I've had the chance to meet you, too. You will enjoy it at Camden House."

Cecilia reached across the space between them and patted Mrs. Tiptree's arm. "Thank you, again." Cecilia rose from the chair and turned. "—Sarah?" Cecilia said.

"Right here, my lady."

"Excellent. Good day to you," Cecilia said to Mrs. Tiptree, bestowing a warm smile in her direction as she turned to leave the store.

JAMES ARRIVED BACK at The New Bell Inn scarcely fifteen minutes after Cecilia and Sarah returned. Cecilia took to her bed, letting Mrs. Price know she was tired after her excursion and requested a light nuncheon. She sent Sarah to find out how the two ill people were doing, so James caught her quite alone.

Without the need for playacting, Cecilia jumped out of bed and hurdled herself into James's arms.

He laughed as he caught her. He nuzzled the side of her neck. "So, what have you been up to today, my love," he asked as he set her back into the circle of his arms.

Her exuberance caused another cough to grip her. She cleared her throat afterward. "Sarah and I walked to the Linen Draper's today. It wasn't far, and I believe supported Dr. Nowlton's suggestion to walk and get outside."

"Yes, if it truly isn't far, it would," he said doubtfully, after hearing her cough again. He stroked her back.

"It isn't. And it is the hub of local female society. It

was quite crowded. Guess who I fortuitously met there!" she said, bouncing on the balls of her feet.

"I'm not even going to guess," he said as he held her still. "You have a habit of meeting the correct people."

She laughed; James thought it sounded like the tinkling of bells.

"Mrs. Worcham!" she said.

"The good doctor's wife?" James asked, his eyebrows rising. Once again, she had managed to surprise him.

"Yes! I told her my circumstance—the story as we agreed upon—and she thought Camden House would be the perfect place for me to continue my recuperation," she said impishly.

James laughed. "I do not know how you do it. You are my most resourceful wife."

"I am your only wife so be careful what you say," she said with mock severity.

James laughed more and hugged her to him. "But, in all seriousness, have you heard anything of Mr. Stackpoole?"

"Yes, he is not better and even had a setback of symptoms again today. And another person has exhibited the same signs of illness!"

"Who?"

"A maid here. Her name is Susan Divers. She told Sarah she didn't feel well this morning; but thought it just the matter of a sore throat, then it seemed to consume her entire body and she went on to exhibit the same loss of bowel control and stomach contents. Nasty. Miss Hammond is tending to her and Mr. Stackpoole."

He shook his head as he compressed his lips briefly. "We need to remove you from this inn as soon as possible. I do not wish to see you sick again."

"I agree." She tugged on the lapels of his jacket. "—But tell me of Soothcoor."

"A moment, let me order the carriage." James left the room to call down to one of the inn staff to have his carriage brought around. Another illness was more than unsettling. He wanted Cecilia out of the inn as soon as possible.

"How is Soothcoor?" Cecilia demanded when he'd returned and closed the door behind him. "What did he have to say about Mr. Montgomery and his death?"

He ran a hand through his hair. "Not much more than we already knew. Mr. Montgomery was alive when he left him, standing outside near the edge of the canal. He'd told Alastair he'd requested his Scottish solicitor to take divorce papers to Scotland to file."

"Getting a divorce will take time; however, it is doable, especially under the circumstances, I would assume," Cecilia said.

"Yes. He did tell me one crucial detail that Mrs. Montgomery failed to relate to us."

Cecilia's head tilted to the side. "What is that?"

"Mrs. Montgomery is enceinte."

"What? Oh, dear." She sat abruptly on the edge of the bed, her thoughts racing through all the ramifications of that information.

"While only circumstantial evidence exists to suggest Soothcoor murdered Mr. Montgomery, her condition does point to a clear motive."

"Yes, I see that," Cecilia said. *Oh no, oh, no!* she thought. She rose from the bed to pace the small bedroom while wringing her hands. "I must get into Camden House as soon possible."

"Agreed. After I get you settled there, I want to seek out the magistrate and see why he focused on Soothcoor as the murderer so swiftly. While I am not in favor of you becoming a patient at the sanatorium, it might be the healthiest place for you to be," he said grimly. "Are you packed and ready?"

"Almost. I have just a few more things to gather. Can I ask you to call Sarah?"

"I'd rather you did not," he said.

"Why?"

"She has been in other parts of the inn that have contagion. We should limit the risks to you."

Cecilia rolled her eyes, but she agreed. "I'll gather everything together."

"I'll help. The sooner I have out of here the better."

"Oh, James! You are being melodramatic."

"Maybe." He crossed to the wardrobe in the corner of the room and pulled out her portmanteau and her cloak from where it hung. He checked a drawer in the bottom and discovered her bonnet and pulled that out along with a stack of lace-edged handkerchiefs. He held those up.

"I can see you are well prepared for the role," he said with a small smile.

"I always carry a stack. They have come in so handy," she said, taking the stack from him. She tucked a clean one up the sleeve of the dull-green gown she wore. She rearranged her fichu higher around her neck, draped her shawl over her shoulders, pulling in close, then put on her cloak over the shawl and clasped it at her neck.

"I should be bundled well enough for the weather," she said as she tied her bonnet on, glancing at a mirror hung on the wall.

James nodded approval at her bundled appearance, then picked up her portmanteau and escorted her out of the room and down the stairs while Cecilia kept her features wan and weak.

Mr. Price saw them and scurried over to them.

"Are you leaving?" he asked, worry edging his tone.

"I am taking Lady Branstoke to Camden House."

"But we have prepared a luncheon for you," the man protested.

"Allow Miss Hammond and my servants to enjoy the food," James said. "With illness here, I want my wife out of here as soon as possible."

"Of course, Sir James," the innkeeper said, bowing his head.

James led Cecilia outside as George Romley pulled the carriage around to the front of the inn.

The sky turned dark gray as the carriage progressed up the road, even though it wasn't a long drive from the inn and through the village to Camden House. It was just a matter of turning a corner and the scene that stretched before them looked desolate, matching the gray skies encroaching upon them. The road, built as part of a dike for a canal, ran three feet above the surrounding countryside with scarcely a tree in sight. Up ahead, on an island rising above the surrounding landscape, stood a rambling gray stone and brick mansion with chimneys stuck up on various slate roof levels in seemingly random, gothic fashion.

Unlike the surrounding landscape, trees and shrubs filled the property. Leaves fluttered and plants swayed in a wind that threatened to bring rain clouds over the area. There was only one approach to the mansion, a newer-looking brick bridge over the straight canal that ran beside the road.

"Are you certain you wish to become a patient here?" James asked Cecilia as the carriage turned to cross the bridge, the horses' hooves clapped loud on the brick surface.

"Yes, more than ever, now that we know of Mrs. Montgomery's condition."

The corner of James's mouth quirked up in a smile. "Alastair deserves his happiness for all he does for people. Though knowing Alastair, it wouldn't matter to him if the child were born out of wedlock."

"I'd have to agree. But think, James, what should occur if Soothcoor were found guilty? His title and properties could be stripped away. That should have far-reaching effects on all of his charities."

He nodded. "They would evaporate in an instant and the ghouls of society would be only too happy to make up stories to pervert everything good he has done to evil."

Cecilia put her hand on his. "We shall not let that happen."

The carriage drew up before the grand dark oak door to the mansion as clumps of patients, with their matrons and orderlies, made their way into the house ahead of the coming rainstorm.

A broad-shouldered man came to meet their carriage, one hand on his head to hold his hat in place in the increasing wind. He handed Cecilia out of the carriage and took the portmanteau from James, gesturing them up the stairs before shouting instructions to Romley to drive the carriage to the back of the building to the stable yard. He then hurried up the stairs to join the Branstokes in the entrance hall.

"That storm came up quite rapidly," Cecilia observed. She shivered and clutched her cape around her as a crack of thunder shook the windows. She looked up as if to see the roof come crashing down on them.

"Yes, they have been doing so this season," the man said. "Sir James and Lady Branstoke, I presume?" he said. "This way please." His arm extended toward a small room to the left, no doubt formerly a cloakroom.

Cecilia glanced about the grand hall with its high, arched ceiling braced with ornately carved oak ceiling beams. It was a long room with a stone floor. Chairs—mainly Tudor in style—dotted the room in small groupings. Beyond the little room where the man directed them was a pair of large wrought iron gates that could shut off the entrance to the rest of the mansion. At that moment, they stood open, and patients and their guardians walked through them deeper into the mansion. Cecilia caught the glances of those who passed her along with their whispered words, no doubt wondering about her identity.

"Before you meet Dr. Worcham, I will introduce you to Mr. Turnbull-Minchin, our superintendent. He will ask you some questions and then take you to meet Dr. Worcham. Is that agreeable?"

Cecilia nodded faintly while James responded with unusual vigor, "Yes, of course. Let's get on with it."

Looking down, Cecilia held back a smirk at James's manner, so unlike him. What was his intention?

"Sir James and Lady Branstoke, this is Superintendent Mr. Turnbull-Minchin. Sir James and Lady Branstoke, sir, to see Dr. Worcham," the majordomo said as he bowed himself out of the room. The frizzled-haired, middle-aged man behind the desk rose on hearing their rank.

"Sir James, Lady Branstoke, please come in," he said. He gestured to the two chairs in front of his desk.

"We've come to see Dr. Worcham," James said, ignoring the chair and standing behind Cecilia. He placed a hand on her shoulder.

"Yes, yes, and you will. Just a few questions, please, for registration purposes." The man tried to smile pleasantly. He dipped his quill in ink. "Now, full name and direction, please."

"Cecilia Houghton Haukstrom Branstoke," Cecilia said softly.

"Lady Cecilia Houghton Haukstrom Branstoke," put in James, "granddaughter of the Duke of Cheney."

The man's eyebrows rose. "I see," he said. "Age?"

"Six and twenty."

"Home?"

Cecilia looked up at her husband.

"Summerworth Park, in Kent, outside the village of Ingleston," Sir James supplied.

"You have come quite a distance," Mr. Turnbull-Minchin said.

"Your sanatorium has been highly recommended."

"Oh? By whom?"

"Mr. Stackpoole."

"Stackpoole!" The man leaned back in his chair as he looked at them. "How do you know him?"

"We have several mutual friends in London. Stackpoole says his mother has been here for several years and he has been satisfied with her care. Said she is calm and happy here."

"Yes, yes, she has been." His brows knitted together. "Have you spoken to Mr. Stackpoole recently?" he asked.

James shook his head. "Not recently. He has been ill."

"Oh, I'm sorry to hear that. One last question, then I'll take you to Dr. Worcham. It's a delicate issue, and I apologize. We require your yearly income—"

"I beg your pardon. You treat patients differently based on income?"

"No, no, not in terms of medical care. I assure you Dr. Worcham treats all of his patients equally and makes no difference. It is only my poor lot to assign patients to their lodgings and any extras in keeping with what they may be accustomed to having. Size of rooms, types of meals, assistance with dressing and care. These are the services that don't relate to their health and speak more to what they are accustomed to receiving. Dr. Worcham believes we need to keep our patients comfortable to aid in their recovery and provide for them that to which they are accustomed. I ask for income so I can determine if they truly can afford what they would like or if, ultimately, they cannot pay. That can prove to be too embarrassing for all. I do not like to distress Dr. Worcham with such mundane matters or move patients from a large single room to shared accommodations. That does not help their treatment."

Reluctantly James nodded. "I can see your concern. Trust that I am able to pay your fees," he said severely.

"Yes, yes, of course," he said quickly. "Now may I ask the nature of your wife's illness?"

"No, you may not," James said, staring him down.

"I see. Well then, let me advise you of a few of the rules. Visitors are only allowed visitation in the great hall, where you first entered, or outside. We do encourage our patients to walk the grounds and visitors are welcome to join them.

"Dr. Worcham believes a good diet is important for the health of the body. We serve three meals a day at Camden House: Breakfast, a hearty meal to get the body alert, a lunch at 1 p.m., offering lighter fare designed to bridge the body's needs until dinner which is at 5 p.m. The meals are simple fare, shunning heavy sauces. Dr. Worcham believes heavy sauces weigh one's stomach down robbing one of energy.

"We do make attempts to satisfy all food favorites with one exception. Food items made or flavored with sugar or honey are forbidden. Dr. Worcham believes sweets can be detrimental to our equilibrium. I always advise this on registration, so spouses or relatives of patients know not to bring in sweet treats. They will be confiscated. Dr. Worcham wants everyone to know that on entry so there are no hard feelings later. Is this acceptable to you?" Mr. Turnbull-Minchin asked with steely professionalism.

It was clear to James and Cecilia the man did not like his financial requests being ignored and had dropped his overt friendliness. However, he was professional, and they had no trouble agreeing to the rules he laid out.

"Good," Mr. Turnbull-Minchin said with a stiff nod. "Let me conduct you, then, to Dr. Worcham. He is generally in the library at this time of day, doing observations." He stood up. "If you will follow me?"

CHAPTER 11

CAMDEN HOUSE SANATORIUM

*H*e led them out of the small anteroom and through the decorative wrought iron gates to the passage Cecilia had seen the patients who came from outside go through. He opened the doors to a room on the left. Cecilia couldn't help but smile when she looked about her. It was a room lined with white-washed bookshelves. A library. There were two large windows at the far end of the room and with the whitewashed shelves and trim the room had a lighter, brighter feel. Around the room were various tables and chairs where patients played games, read together, or just sat and talked quietly. Armchairs and couches grouped near the fireplace were covered in a floral jacquard fabric. A grass-green carpet covered the floor. The room felt warm and intimate despite its large size.

Mr. Turnbull-Minchin led them to one of the seating arrangements near the fireplace. "Dr. Worcham, pardon the interruption," he said with great deference at odds with his manner to James and Cecilia in his office, "Sir James and Lady Branstoke to see you."

The doctor rose from his chair, excusing himself to those he had been speaking to when they approached. Though gray threaded his curly brown hair, Cecilia judged him to be some years younger than the woman she'd met that morning at the linen drapers. And she was surprised to hear a Scottish burr in his voice. When he turned to them, he spread out his arms then drew them together in almost a prayer position. "Welcome to Camden House Sanatorium. Come, let's find a quieter spot where we might get to know one another," he said. "I don't believe the small parlor is booked right now. We can go there," he said, leading to a door in the middle of a wall of bookshelves. "This building is a warren of rooms," he said as they entered a straw, brown-and-pale-rose-colored room.

The room was at once both more austere and formal than the library, the furniture severely angular without pillows or other softening elements.

"Now, tell me about yourself, Lady Branstoke," he said as he settled her on a sofa and took a chair at right angles to her. He sat on the edge of his chair, clasping her hands in his.

"Even through yer gloves, I can feel the cold in yer fingers. Are ye frightened to be here? There is no need I assure ye. I know from Sir James's letter that ye have been ill. Can ye tell me more?"

"Yes. We have been staying down in Kent, at our main estate this season, as I am expecting our first child."

"I thought ye might be, looking at ye. Pregnant women have a certain look about them," he said encouragingly. "But surely ye are not here because ye are enceinte?"

"No, no," she said. "Over three weeks ago I came down with the influenza that has visited so many others in our region. It was particularly severe all around."

"We lost a tenant farmer's wife and a couple of village people to this illness," James somberly explained.

Cecilia looked up at James where he stood behind the sofa and nodded at his words. She looked back at Dr. Worcham. "I immediately took to my bed and didn't rise again for ten long days—I still cough and wheeze a little bit," she admitted.

"A lot," corrected James, looking down at her.

Cecilia shrugged in wry agreement. "To my mind, worse than the cough and breathy voice is my fatigue. I can't seem to shake this awful fatigue. It's like a weight upon my chest. It is all I can do to get dressed in the morning."

"My wife is someone who always wants to be doing things. As she is now, doing anything fatigues her. It was suggested to me I take her to a sanatorium for complete rest. So long as she is in our home, she wants to be up and doing, and that just makes it worse," he said, looking down at her severely.

Cecilia smiled weakly. "I can be stubborn."

"That does not even go far enough to describe your persistence to be up and doing."

Dr. Worcham laughed. "I understand. So why are you here, at Camden House? You are far away from where you live and there are sanatoriums being opened all over England and Scotland."

"Your Camden House Sanatorium was recommended to us by Mr. Stackpoole. He said his mother is happy here."

Dr. Worcham leaned back. "Ah, you know young Mr. Stackpoole?"

"Yes."

He nodded. "He is an excellent son to his mother, very caring and concerned. It is a pity that she feels so strongly that it is not safe for her in her own home. I know the baron and do not get the impression he would do any harm to his wife; but, what goes on between husband and wife is often unknown. I've seen severely beaten women whose husbands were scions of society and appeared to be the mildest mannered of gentlemen."

"We have not met the baron," Sir James said. "I understand the baron is not in favor of Mr. Stackpoole's chosen bride. Since we are friends of the fiancée's family, that colors our impression of the baron."

"While my wife is here for her health, I am here for another reason as well," James told him, "which brings me to the second reason I am here. Mr. Stackpoole's fiancée's mother requested me to come here."

Dr. Worcham looked at him curiously. "His fiancée's mother?"

"Yes, Mrs. Lilias Montgomery," James said.

"Montgomery?" questioned Dr. Worcham.

"She said her husband was a resident patient here and had died. She asked me to come here to discover more."

"I don't understand," Dr. Worcham said. "You said fiancée's mother and that implies children."

James nodded.

"I was aware Mr. Montgomery had been married, though he requested that knowledge be kept secret here, but nothing was ever said to me about children by Mr. Montgomery or his cousin," Dr. Worcham said.

"Boyd Ratcliffe?"

"Yes."

Cecilia kept her eyes down. She and James had agreed she was not to appear to know much. Hiding her surprise at Dr. Worcham's lack of knowledge was difficult.

"Might we not get my wife settled into a room before we continue this conversation? She needs to rest," James said.

"Yes, of course. We have a room available just down the hall from Lady Stackpoole. It is not as large as you might prefer Ladies who have stayed there in the past have found it quite comfortable. I'll send for Matron," Dr. Worcham said, pulling on the bell rope.

Cecilia nodded. "Thank you," she whispered.

"You will not be able to accompany your wife upstairs, Sir James," Dr. Worcham told him. "Guests are not allowed in the patients' living areas to preserve respect for others staying on the same floor."

A woman in a starched white cap and a starched white full apron worn over an ash gray dress entered the room. "You rang for me, Dr. Worcham?"

"Yes, Mildred. This is Lady Branstoke come to stay with us for a bit. Please make her comfortable in Room 5, if you will. She is recovering from an illness, and she is expecting her first child. She is quite worn out."

"Of course, Doctor. If you will accompany me, my lady," the austere woman said.

James brushed a kiss against her head as he helped her to rise. She would be on her own now. He knew that the cough and fatigue were real. Being sick could mean a clouded thought process. And the actual murderer could even yet be staying in Camden House. If she asked the wrong question of the wrong person, she could jeopardize her life. He did not like this plan but didn't know another way to investigate inside the sanatorium.

"Sir James," Dr. Worcham said, recalling his attention.

James turned back to face the doctor. "I beg your pardon. I do not like being apart from my wife, even if I know it is for her health."

"You are to be commended. I can't tell you how many husbands I've seen remark that it will be a respite for them for their wives be here for a time."

James frowned. "Are most of your patients quarreling spouses?"

The doctor laughed. "It's cyclical. Right now, only the Stackpooles, but when the baron gets to waxing eloquently to his club, we might get a spate again." He shrugged. "They pay enough that I can then afford to take some charity cases."

James looked intently at Dr. Worcham. "Understand Dr. Worcham, my wife has been extremely ill, and though she wishes to deny it, she needs care to recover her strength for herself and our unborn child."

Dr. Worcham sobered. "I understand, and we will do all we can to provide for her the environment she requires."

"Thank you for your care of my wife. Now I must be off. Mr. Stackpoole took ill at The New Bell Inn. I need to check up on him and see if he needs anything. He did tell us about his mother and your sanatorium. That is not a story." He rose to his feet.

Dr, Worcham rose as well and walked him to the door that led back to the main hall. James was surprised to find this connection. Dr. Worcham laughed a bit as James looked around, noting their new location. "As I said, this is a warren."

James nodded. "I will return tomorrow to check on my wife."

"We shall be happy to receive you," Dr. Worcham said.

James left the doctor, and the majordomo handed him his hat and gloves, then opened the door to let him out of the building.

"When I saw the door to the parlor open, I sent a runner to tell your coachman to bring your carriage around. You are welcome to wait in here until he comes around," the man offered.

James looked up at the sky. It was a solid gray; however, it did not look as if it would rain. "I'll wait out here, thank you."

"As you wish sir," the man said, bowing James out the door.

James stepped out onto the wide stone front porch and walked slowly down the steps. He took the time to study the landscape. Walking paths of crushed gray stone wound through neatly tended grass and around bushes and trees within thirty to forty feet of the building, the winding path dotted with benches for patients to rest and enjoy the outdoors. Beyond, where the ground began to slope down toward the canal, natural grasses, rushes, and nettles were allowed to grow tall, no doubt to discourage patients from walking too near the canal. Across the canal, the fens stretched flat, a green and brown expanse heavy with the scent of wet earth and more rain to come. Lonely looking. James wondered why monks would have built a monastery in this desolate landscape four hundred years ago. It was only if one looked to the south did one get a sense of the village in the distance where trees massed, and spirals of white smoke rose above them. The village was less than one hundred years old, coming into being with the building of the canals that drained much of the ground around, making it available for farming. Yet it didn't appear as if the land to the west of Camden House was farmed. He wondered why.

CHAPTER 12

LADY STACKPOOLE

ecilia found she was tired when the matron showed her to her room. She didn't like that the fatigue was real. The walk she and Sarsh had taken to the linen drapers that morning, while healthy, sapped her energy.

The room assigned to her was small but well-appointed, decorated in shades of blue, burgundy, and cream. It looked as if it might have at one time been part of a larger room divided in half. The drapery and bed curtains were in shades of blue, the walls covered in wallpaper with a subtle floral print. The furniture was red mahogany, its burgundy tone carried forward in the rug on the floor, the tufted velvet headboard, and with burgundy color brushed across the raised designs of the cornice pieces otherwise painted in a cream tone as was the door. She looked at the narrow bed and sighed ruefully. She hadn't slept in a narrow single bed since she'd been a child. She would miss James in the night.

"I trust this will suit you, Lady Branstoke," said the matron. "Should you need anything, you have only to pull this bell pull and either I, or one of the floor maids will answer."

"Everything looks lovely, thank you."

"Dinner is served in the grand dining hall at five. I shall return to show you the way. You are looking fatigued. I suggest you rest until then. Time enough for meeting others later," the matron said. She walked toward the door. "Is there anything else you need now?"

"No, not at all," Cecilia said. "I plan to do as you suggested and lay down for a rest."

"Very good, ma'am," the matron said as she closed the door behind her.

Cecilia sat down at the edge of the bed. She saw her portmanteau had preceded her into the room and was sitting on a bureau. She removed her shoes and laid back against two pillows.

Cecilia didn't know how long she slept until a faint scuffling close by woke her. She carefully opened her eyes without moving. Over by the bureau, she saw a young girl stealthily attempting to open her portmanteau. She watched her. The child looked about eight to ten years old. Her brown hair was pulled back away from her face and fell in ringlets down her back. She wore a plain cream-colored dress with one deep flounce at the hem. On her feet were serviceable black boots.

The child glanced toward her as she silently opened the case and saw Cecilia watching her. She squealed and jumped away from the bureau.

"I...I..." she floundered, then turned and ran from the room, throwing the door to Cecilia's room open with a loud bang.

"Stop!" Cecilia called after her. From out in the hall somewhere she heard a woman's voice call out, "Liddy! What have you been up to?"

Cecilia swung her feet to the floor and put her shoes on, then walked to the door and looked down the hall. A woman stood in the middle of the hall, turned away from Cecilia, looking in the direction the young girl fled. She hitched her shawl up her shoulder and shook her head. She turned in Cecilia's direction.

"Who was that girl?" Cecilia asked the woman as she walked out into the hall.

"Miss Lydia, or as we here call her, Liddy," the woman replied.

"She lives here?"

"Unfortunately, yes."

"I woke up to see her in my room trying to get into my portmanteau."

"I'm sorry to hear that." The woman walked up to Cecilia. "I'm Lady Stackpoole, but please call me Julia. Many of us are quite informal here."

"Benjamin Stackpoole's mother!" Cecilia exclaimed.

"Yes. How do you know my son?"

"I beg your pardon. I am Lady Branstoke, you can call me Cecilia. We met your son on our way here. He had suffered a carriage accident."

"Accident? Was he all right? Where was this?" Julia wrung her hands. "That is what I do dislike about being here, missing my son," she lamented.

"He survived the accident with just a sprained wrist. He'd been on his way to see you."

"To see me? It isn't time for his quarterly visit. Why would he be coming to see me now?"

"Because of Mr. Montgomery."

"Malcolm Montgomery from here? His death you mean? But why would Mr. Montgomery be of interest to Benjamin?—No, wait," she said, looking around the hall. "Let's go into my room to talk," she said looking around the broad hall. "More private. In our small piece of the world, everyone is curious about everything around us, and poor Mr. Montgomery's death has been on all tongues since it happened." She led Cecilia into her small room and carefully shut the door after them.

Lady Stackpoole's room appeared as a mirror of Cecilia's, save for the coloring. Whereas Cecila's room was blue with cream and burgundy, Lady Stackpoole's was shades of green, cream, and burgundy. There were several large planters in her room as well, filled with ferns and small palms. They reminded Cecilia of the plants in Soothcoor's stepmother's conservatory at Appleton—without the poisonous *Gloriosa Superba* plants she'd discovered there. A small painting of a younger Benjamin Stackpoole stood on the fireplace mantle.

Cecilia crossed to the fireplace to look at the picture closely. "When was this painted? He looks much older now."

Julia joined Cecilia by the mantle. She smiled in affectionate memory. "He is. He was seventeen in that picture before he went to university. Now he wants to travel the world while serving his country on diplomatic missions," she said with pride.

"Which, I gather from Mr. Stackpoole, his father opposes."

Julia's face fell. "Yes, this is true. Be assured, Benjamin will not bow to his father's edicts. It has become a subject of estrangement between my husband and Benjamin."

"Are you aware Mr. Stackpoole has a fiancée?"

"A fiancée! Last time he was here, he said there was a young lady he was courting but wouldn't say anything more until he'd asked for her hand. I take it he has asked and she said yes? Is that why he was coming to see me?" Excitement crept back into Julia's voice.

"I am probably speaking out of turn as this is your son's tale to relate; however, I will admit Baron Stackpoole opposed the match initially because the young lady is Scottish."

"Scottish?!"

"Yes. I do not know Aileen—that is her name—or her siblings. I only know her mother, Mrs. Montgomery."

"Montgomery?" Julia stared at her.

"Yes,"

Julia worried the fingertips of her left hand together. "Do you know if my Benjamin's fiancée's family has any relation to our Mr. Malcolm Montgomery?" she asked hesitantly.

"Yes. Aileen Montgomery is his daughter."

Julia sat abruptly down on the foot of her bed. Her brows drew together, and she shook her head as she considered what Cecilia told her. "It was our understanding," she said slowly and carefully, "that Mr. Montgomery was single, that he'd never married."

Cecilia sat down by the window in the room's lone chair. "The story is more convoluted than that."

"If you mean about the multiple people he believed himself to be? Most everyone here knew about them and indulged him."

"Is that how you saw them, as people he believed himself to be?"

"Yes, a way for him to express his emotions. When he was angry, he believed himself to be someone named Archie, a most vile person who gave him liberty to act outrageously. I told him on several occasions that pretending to be another person does not absolve him from his behavior and he should be ashamed of himself."

"What was his reaction to your scolding?" Cecilia asked.

She laughed abruptly. "He'd merely bow his head and say, of course, I was right, and apologize—not that that ever stopped him from pretending to be Archie!"

"Did you ever say anything to Dr. Worcham about this inappropriate behavior?" Cecilia asked carefully.

"Several times! Dr. Worcham said that was part of Mr. Montgomery's affliction, the inability to control himself. He encouraged all of us to endeavor to see we did nothing to cause Mr. Montgomery to take up that character. We didn't mind Gregory when we met him. He was a polite sort, acting like a butler, or majordomo, doing for others in a subservient manner."

Cecilia nodded, now wondering, *what was the truth?* When she thought of Mrs. Montgomery relating to her and James the night he found himself lusting for his own daughter, she feared the 'others' residing within him was more likely the truth of his illness.

A knock at the door interrupted them.

"Come in!" called out Julia.

"Lady Stackpoole, have you seen...Oh! Lady Branstoke, here you are," said Mildred, the matron who'd showed Cecilia to her room earlier. "I came to wake you for dinner and show you to the dining hall. I was rite concerned when I couldn't find ya and your door bein' open."

"My apologies, Mildred. I woke and walked out into the hall where I met Lady Stackpoole. We just started talking and came in here," Cecilia said.

"All right then. Would you like me to take you to the dining hall to get you oriented?"

"I'll do that, Mildred," Julia offered. "Imagine! She has met my son, so we have had a comfortable coze discussing him."

"I guess that's all right then," the matron said slowly, frowning.

Cecilia cocked her head to the side. "Why wouldn't it be?" she asked.

"Mr. Turnbull-Minchin doesn't like patients in other patient's rooms, is all."

"Since when has that rule come about?" Julia asked. "On this floor, we have always visited each other, and I have visited the north dormitory to see Miss Dorn on several occasions."

The matron shook her head. "That may be in the past; but, in the future he says as how as we are to discourage such visits. Visitin' only to happen in common areas. But seenin' as Lady Branstoke is new, it will be all right for now."

Julia compressed her lips. "We shall see," was all she said. She looked over at Cecilia. "Let's go down to dinner. There are a couple of people I would like to introduce you to."

"Dr. Worcham has ordered a light dinner for you, milady," the matron told Cecilia. "Said yur to go straight to bed after dinner, too. Doesn't want too much excitement for ya yur first night here. I'll see that it's brought to where ya sit with Lady Stackpoole."

"Thank you," Cecilia said.

The dining hall surprised Cecilia. It was one half of the former monastery chapel, a wall dividing it down the middle through where the altar would have been. It made for a pleasant dining room as the wide, tall chapel windows were not all stained glass. At their arched peaks were stained-glass biblical stories while the rest of the window glass was beveled clear glass that let in light and provided a view of the east Camden House grounds and, further, over the canal to the fens beyond.

"This is a pleasant room for a dining hall," Cecilia observed.

Julia agreed. "In the morning," she said, "the stained glass that's at the top of the window arches can glow with the morning light, if it is sunny, and reflect color on the opposite side of the room. A very nice breakfast and wake-up room. But not so much," she added with a laugh, "if it is a gloomy day."

"What's in the other half of the chapel," Cecilia asked as they took a seat.

"The chapel dormitory. It's a men's dormitory," Julia said. "Don't get used to this service," she added as women came around with plates of food to serve all. "Mr. Turnbull-Minchin says this is a luxury that other sanatoriums don't have. As of next week, our food service will be buffet style."

"I understand from things Mr. Stackpoole told my husband and me, and from what you have said, that Mr. Turnbull-Minchin has made many changes since he arrived here."

She nodded. "Many," she said, her voice heavy with displeased meaning. "Ah, here come some of my friends, and Liddy is with them so you can meet the miscreant who invaded your room," she finished, her voice changing to indulgent pleasure.

"The older woman majestically leading the way is Mrs. Vance. Hilda Vance. Mrs. Vance's family claims she has dementia. She doesn't, but she likes it here, so doesn't fight them about it. Yet, now they want to take charge of all her money and control everything. She is preparing for that fight by revealing secrets about them. In other words, she is planning to resort to blackmail to get them to leave her alone."

Cecilia suppressed a laugh and decided she was going to like Mrs. Vance.

"The gentleman escorting her is Mr. Quetal. Mr. Quetal had a nervous breakdown six months ago. He was the estate agent for an impecunious new heir to a peerage. The heir harangued and pressured him to make the young man's new estate solvent, but the heir kept spending money the estate didn't have. Mr. Quetal tried desperately to do a good job. He cracked under the pressure—especially when threatened with the loss of his job without a referral."

Cecilia studied the man. About thirty, she thought, a little too thin, but not worrisomely so. His brown hair thinned at the top of his head. What was nice to see was how he didn't stoop. He walked with his shoulders back, and the manner of his attire was conservative but neat.

On the man's other arm, he escorted Miss Liddy. The young girl had obviously changed clothes and had her hair attended to. She aped Mrs. Vance in her posture, looking over at her from time to time. What Cecilia hadn't seen before was the port wine stain birthmark that wrapped halfway around her left eye and came down in an arc across her cheek to just below her ear.

"Can you believe little Liddy is here because her mother can't stand to look at her?" Julia whispered.

Cecilia's head turned sharply to look at Julia in shock then back to the threesome approaching the table. Behind them were two others, a frazzled strawberry blonde in a plain brown gown and a beautiful young man—there could be no other words to describe him—in an elegantly tailored suit of a rich blue over a waistcoat of figured pale-blue silk.

Julia introduced Cecilia to Mrs. Vance, Mr. Quetal, and Liddy. As they were taking seats, she introduced her to Miss Dorn and Mr. Hobart.

Cecilia nodded to them, then hurried to grab her handkerchief out of the long sleeve of her dress. She could feel the pressure of another cough coming. And she'd had so few this day. She turned her head and coughed into her handkerchief, then turned back to the others at the table.

"My apologies!" she said, her voice hoarse, another cough threatening. "I promise you my illness is past."

"Yet the cough won't say goodbye, so naughty," said Mrs. Vance. "I have experienced the same."

"Thank you for understanding," Cecilia said. "I just can't seem to recover completely. That's why I'm here."

"It's always nice to meet new people; however, I hope for your sake it is a short acquaintance," Mrs. Vance said, reaching across to pat her hand.

"You're too kind," Cecilia said meekly.

"And what she is not telling you is she is enceinte as well," Julia said.

Next to Mrs. Vance, Miss Dorn let out a yowl of anguish and began to cry. She stumbled out of her chair, knocking it over as she turned to run from the room. All eyes followed her exit except for Mrs. Vance's. She looked up and rolled her pale-gray eyes, then looked over at Julia.

"Julia, my dear, that was ill-done."

Julia had the grace to look contrite. "It was not done out of malice, and it is true. Miss Dorn needs to learn not to react so strongly," she said.

"Excuse me, what happened? Why did Miss Dorn start to cry and run from the room?" Cecilia asked. She noted the men looked studiously down.

"She lost her baby, now she cries when she hears of another woman having a baby," little Liddy said shrugging, her young, singsong voice carrying across the room. She took a bite of buttered bread as all eyes in the room turned from following Miss Dorn out of the room to Liddy's pronouncement.

"Hush, child," Mrs. Vance gently reprimanded.

"Why?" Liddy asked, her voice softer. Her head tilted to the side. "It's true. And she's always wanting a baby or saying she's going to have a baby when she's not."

"We know, dear, she's just having a difficult time right now," Mrs. Vance said.

Liddy shrugged. "She even asked Mr. Montgomery if he would give her a baby. He said no and told her he'd report her to Dr. Worcham if she kept bothering him."

"Quite right of Mr. Montgomery," said Julia with a definitive nod. "He had standards too high to deal with the likes of her," she finished.

Liddy looked at Julia, a sly expression on her face. "Then she said she bet Archie would."

"What!" Julia exclaimed. Both Mr. Quetal and Mr. Hobart looked aside to hide a laugh. Mrs. Vance closed her eyes and shook her head.

"When did this occur?" Cecilia asked softly.

"A couple of days before he died…I miss him," Liddy said, slumping in her chair.

Cecilia's thoughts went into a whirl. While the other men might find the idea of Mr. Montgomery's playacting persona allowing this woman to believe his *character* would bed her, Cecilia knew the Archie inside Mr. Montgomery could well act upon baser instincts. None of these people knew Mr. Montgomery's true turmoil. They would likely think of him as some monster if they did know. What had been Miss Dorn's experience with Archie? And if she couldn't get Archie to come out, could she have killed him in a fit of anger? She was a sturdily built woman. Did she have the physicality to do that? Or could she have acquired another lover—a jealous lover—here at the sanatorium? Cecilia didn't know, but she would like to talk to Miss Dorn about Mr. Montgomery and Archie. Did she see him again after their discussion? Did she see or hear anything that could provide clues as to how he died?

"Did you see Mr. Montgomery often, Liddy?" Cecilia asked, her voice cracking around another threatening cough.

"Oh, yes! He was teaching me maths. I saw him every day in the library or outside if the weather was nice—unless he had appointments with Dr. Worcham."

Another paroxysm of coughing gripped Cecilia, try as she might to hold it back. Matron Mildred heard her and came over.

"Lady Branstoke, I am concerned to hear you cough so. Too much excitement for your first day. I heard from Mrs. Worcham how you were in the village today, too. Best you return to your room now and have an early night. That is why you are here, after all. Lots of rest. I'll have a floor maid bring you a tisane to help you sleep."

The others at the table chorused in solicitous comments, encouraging her to retire. Cecilia had no choice but to acquiesce. She had so many questions to ask about Mr. Montgomery and who he associated with! But she acknowledged she was tired, and her chest and throat hurt from her coughing. She really thought she had been getting better. Perhaps an early sleep would help her. She could be of no help to Soothcoor if her sickness relapsed. Time for bed. She rose from her chair and bid the others good night.

CHAPTER 13

THE MAGISTRATE

*J*ames had left Cecilia at Camden House with misgivings. He trusted Cecilia to be circumspect in her investigation. What he wasn't certain about was her strength, and would she do too much, ignoring any signs of weakness her body put forth in her enthusiasm to discover the truth of Mr. Montgomery's death? He'd said nearly as much to Dr. Worcham before he left—leaving out the investigation into Mr. Montgomery—and the man said he understood. The good doctor had no knowledge of Cecilia's tenacious manner, he thought, smiling to himself.

His beautiful wife had certainly changed him in the year they'd been married. He'd always been considered a rather phlegmatic man within society, languid, reserved, and bored with everything. A mere observer of society and its machinations. His observation habit was what had drawn him to Cecilia to begin with, and his appreciation for her tenacious manner. He doubted she would have survived that first investigation she undertook if he hadn't played curious bodyguard to what she'd been doing.

And he'd feared for her life during her recent influenza. Now the lingering cough she endured chilled him whenever he heard it. He loved her to distraction and couldn't imagine being with any other woman.

He inhaled deeply as he considered his next move in the investigation. He needed to meet the local magistrate and find out how he came to quickly determine Soothcoor to be the murderer. Something—or someone—had to have pushed him in that direction for the arrest to have happened as swiftly as Alastair said it had. Before breakfast yet! That screamed suspicion.

He'd learned the magistrate's direction before leaving the inn. It was three miles further on toward Stamford. He'd sent along a letter of introduction and hoped he'd worded it noncommittally enough to convey an open attitude. The magistrate was the local gentry, Squire Eccleston. Mr. Price said he was a fair man though a bit touchy about his position in society. James would have to ensure his London manners were tucked discreetly out of sight for this visit. Many people outside of London frowned on Londoners—not that James considered himself a Londoner though another might.

Squire Eccleston's white-washed Georgian-style manor house looked austere, rising up as it did from the flat landscape around it. More land recovered from drainage, James assumed. Sheep grazed in the distant fields, and nearby fields were planted, though whatever grew there appeared to struggle to gain growth just as they did near Summerworth Park due to the cold weather.

The squire came out to meet him as he drove up.

"Sir James," he greeted as James stepped out of the carriage.

"Magistrate," James responded.

"Come in, come in," he said, leading the way inside. "You said in your note that Mrs. Montgomery sent you up here."

James nodded, "She requested I investigate her husband's death," he said. "Were you aware that Mrs. Montgomery believed her husband to be dead these two years past?"

The magistrate frowned as he pushed open the door to his office on the ground floor of the manor. "No, I wasn't. Strange. Why was that?"

"It is my understanding that it was at Mr. Montgomery's request. Are you aware of the nature of Mr. Montgomery's illness that had him residing at Camden House?"

"I was told something about a spontaneous violent nature," he said, waving at him to take a seat across from his desk.

"Mrs. Montgomery told me he had at least three different personalities," James said, leaning forward, resting his elbows on his chair arms, "one of whom she said was violent. He was called 'Archie' and is the reason Mr. Montgomery had himself committed, first in Scotland and later here at Camden House. He arranged to have himself declared dead with only his father, his cousin, the family vicar, Dr. Worcham, and Mrs. Montgomery's father knowing this was not true."

Squire Eccleston frowned. "I think there is something illegal about all that. I shall have to consult a barrister."

James's hands shrugged. "For the most part, the estate trustee—his cousin—has treated her fairly, keeping the property for her son. What all parties failed to consider was whether Mrs. Montgomery should choose to remarry. My wife is of the opinion this is a typical gentleman's failure to consider their wives," he said with a small smile.

Squire Eccleston smiled slightly in return. "In my time as a magistrate, I have seen other instances of wives not being properly accounted for in wills, assuming the executors would do the right thing, causing all manner of grief for families."

"Yes. In this instance, there was no thought to Mrs. Montgomery wishing to remarry and now she does."

Eccleston frowned. "And so, the gentleman she wished to marry traveled here and killed Mr. Montgomery."

"Did he? Did someone see it happen? That's what Mrs. Montgomery wishes to know. What exactly happened?"

Eccleston leaned back in his chair, interlacing his lands together where they rested on his stomach. "Stands to reason what happened. In a fit of anger, her lover fought with Mr. Montgomery and held him underwater until he drowned."

"Held him underwater."

"Yes. According to Dr. Worcham, drowning was the cause of death."

"What do you know of the gentleman you have arrested?"

"The Earl of Soothcoor?"

"Yes."

He pursed his lips as he shrugged. "Mr. Ratcliffe told me he was acquainted with Mr. Montgomery and Mrs. Montgomery from their childhood in Scotland. That he had, twenty years ago, asked for Mrs. Montgomery's hand in marriage and had been refused because she was to marry Mr. Montgomery. Now that he thought she was free he determined to marry her and when he found she was still married, traveled here to kill Mr. Montgomery."

"This you got from Mr. Boyd Ratcliffe."

"Yes. And the staff at Camden House confirmed he arrived first the previous day to talk to Mr. Montgomery, then returned late in the next day to see Mr. Montgomery when he was at dinner. After dinner the two of them went outside to talk and walk the grounds. Mr. Montgomery's body was discovered in the canal early the next morning."

"So why the quick arrest of the Earl of Soothcoor?"

"I'm a busy man, Sir James, besides being the local magistrate, I am a property owner, and this has been a hard year for property owners, freeholders, and tenant farmers alike. Everything Mr. Ratcliffe said fit the facts. The earl had plenty of motive and time. He was the only one there. Who else could or would have done it?"

"So, without proof, you arrested him." James saw the magistrate growing frustrated and angry with his questioning.

"Yes! If there is doubt, it is a matter for the court. I did my job!"

"Including treating a well-respected member of the aristocracy, well-known for championing the weak, the innocent, and the ill, like a common murderer and having him thrown into the general prison population?"

"The warden wasn't there, and Mr. Ratcliffe said it would be fitting for the night to have him in the general prison for what he did to his cousin," he explained, with some discomfort in his voice.

"Do you know he was injured in that violent population? Instead of using what money he had to have a surgeon see to his wounds he had the warden buy decent blankets for everyone there?"

"No, and I don't see what that has to do with the matter of his guilt."

"And you have never gone to see him since you arrested him, to ask him for more information about that night, have you?"

"I told you I am a busy man. He was arrested and put where he needed to be."

James rose from his chair. "I do not argue that this is

a particularly hard year for all rural property owners. I am one myself. I understand the time required to fight against nature. Nonetheless, a magistrate for an area is an important position. If you do not have the time to be a magistrate, then let someone else have the position."

The magistrate rose as well, anger quivering in his body. "And what makes you so sure this Earl of Soothcoor did not kill Mr. Montgomery?"

James ticked off the reasons on his fingers. "I know more of Mr. Montgomery's illness, I know more of their childhood history, I know the earl, and lastly, I know when he arrived back at the inn he had dry clothes on. How do you drown someone without getting wet? Now, excuse me if I leave you to your property woes while I investigate who really killed Mr. Montgomery."

CHAPTER 14

MR. MONTGOMERY AT CAMDEN HOUSE

"I wonder why Mr. Montgomery claimed he was not married?" Julia mused the next morning as she and Cecilia walked along one of the winding paths around Camden House. It was not a sunny day but a far more pleasant day than the others Cecilia had felt since she came up north.

"Two years ago, Mrs. Montgomery was told he died, that he had committed suicide," Cecilia offered.

"Suicide!" exclaimed Julia. She shook her head. "That does not sound like the Mr. Montgomery I knew! I'm sure I do not understand." Her brow furrowed a moment as she stopped on the path. "I do recall," she said slowly, "he was very ill at one time—over two years ago now," she said. She started walking again on a path that took them around the bushes toward the back of Camden House. "He did come close to dying, then; however, Dr. Worcham and the staff here took excellent care of him, and he recovered, for which he was *not* grateful."

"Not grateful?" parroted Cecilia.

Julia shook her head. "I overhead one outburst, some months later, when he played Archie, and quite dramatically told Dr. Worcham he should have let him die."

Cecilia stopped in the shade of a large tree as she looked out over the canal to the fens. "I wonder why Dr. Worcham went along with the death tale? According to Mrs. Montgomery, Mr. Montgomery's father, his cousin, her father, and their vicar were all aware he lived. They were the ones to spread it about that he had died. The rest of the family went into full morning. It is only in the past year that Mrs. Montgomery has put the past behind her and found a new love. She tells us she was happy, giddy even, to find love again and wrote to family members to share her news. That is when Mr. Montgomery's cousin wrote to her and told her she could not marry again as Mr. Montgomery was not dead."

Julia shook her head. "Poor woman," she said. She linked arms with Cecilia as they walked on down the path. "And is it this woman's daughter whom my Benjamin wishes to marry?" she asked.

"Yes. And Baron Stackpoole forbids the marriage because of Mr. Montgomery's illness. He says they can't know that Aileen hasn't inherited the same mental health condition."

Julia snorted quite inelegantly. "Excuse my vulgarity, that sounds like something my husband would try to do. He would be against her just because she is Scottish with the added mental health issues, he would be beside himself." She suddenly laughed. "I can almost visualize him quivering with anger. He has no control over Benjamin—certainly no financial control. My Benjamin is his own man. He needs nothing from his father."

"Did you know Baron Stackpoole came up here when it was first discovered Mr. Montgomery was alive?"

"No! He certainly didn't come to see me. What did he want? What did he do?"

"I don't know," Cecilia admitted. "Perhaps to ask Dr. Worcham about Mr. Montgomery's health? Truthfully, I don't know if he actually came to Camden House and visited with Mr. Montgomery or Dr. Worcham. Is there a guest registry?"

"Yes, there is, but it would be difficult for us to see it...I can casually ask some of the staff that I am friendly with—though Mr. Turnbull-Minchin now frowns on us *fraternizing*, as he calls it." She fingered the petal of a flower that had managed to bloom under the protected branches of the trees. "What about the man that killed Malcolm? Do we know why he did it?"

Cecilia looked at Julia seriously. "The magistrate arrested the wrong man."

She dropped the flower and looked at Cecilia. "What do you mean?" she asked.

Cecilia took a big breath then let it out slowly as she looked across the canal. She looked back at Julia. "I am not typically a gambling woman; however, I will take a gamble with you."

"What do you mean."

"I will tell you what I know but you cannot share it with others."

Julia's features pulled together in a deep frown. She cocked her head to the side as she considered Cecilia. "All right," she said slowly.

"Come, let's turn around and begin our walk back. I find I am tiring and will need to lay down for a while.— The Earl of Soothcoor, the man arrested, was Mr. Montgomery's childhood friend."

"The Earl of Soothcoor? That's who was arrested?" Julia exclaimed.

"Yes."

"They never told us, just that the murderer had been

apprehended. I've heard of him. My Benjamin has spoken of him. They call him *'The Dour Earl'.*"

Cecilia laughed. "Yes, they do."

"He was the visitor who came to see Mr. Montgomery that day?"

"Yes."

"Why?"

"To find out why he'd pretended to be dead to his wife and children and, more importantly, if he would petition for a divorce."

"This is so confusing. Did Dr. Worcham know he was married?"

"I don't know. I wonder about that. Would the doctor have allowed him to fake his death if he knew he had a wife and child?" Cecilia asked, her voice growing hoarse and tight as a cough threatened.

"I can't see Dr. Worcham allowing him to fake his death at all, no matter the circumstance! That is worrisome."

A sudden coughing fit overwhelmed Cecilia. "Oh bother, the dratted cough has been so good this morning not to plague me," she said as she held a handkerchief to her mouth. "There is a bench over there," she said, pointing to an ornate filigree metal bench underneath another tree, away from the popular walkway. "Let's sit down there for a moment before we return to the house."

Julia nodded and the women crossed to the out-of-the-way bench. Cecilia clasped her gloved hands together when she sat down. She looked at Julia sitting beside her. "I'm going to trust you," she squeaked out before she laughed again.

"I beg your pardon?"

She cleared her throat. "I came to Camden House for two reasons. The first is to investigate the death of a dead man."

"You came here to investigate Mr. Montgomery's death? You are not ill?"

She shook her head. "I am ill, or rather, I am recovering from a prolonged bout with influenza. It zapped my strength, especially the coughing. I am also with child and my husband—and me to some extent—fear for any lingering effects my illness might have had on my unborn child," she said as she unconsciously rested her hands on her rounding belly. "I do need rest, and as I said, I will lie down when we go inside. I do need, just like Dr. Worcham is prescribing, sunshine and short walks outside—though there is not much sun," she said ruefully. "My cough persists, as you've heard, and my energy flags much too easily. I do not like that. I enjoy being an active woman and it tries my soul that I can't be that woman right now." She cleared her throat again.

"I can understand that conundrum," Julia said.

"I convinced my husband if I were to check into Camden House, I could get the rest I require and at the same time, learn more about Mr. Montgomery. I suggested that asking gentle questions should not be too tasking. He didn't like the idea, but after talking to your son about Camden House, we felt it worth it to try this investigative route while my husband investigates all leads outside of Camden House."

"You referred to this as the investigation into the death of a dead man."

Cecilia nodded. "Most everyone in his family, and those within his circle of friends, already thought him a dead man. Dead more than these two years. Grief had been packaged up and set aside, life had moved on. His family were starting to find happiness—and his wife wished to marry again."

"And not having any idea he was alive, she didn't know of any impediment."

"Correct."

"And the man she would marry?" she asked,

"The Earl of Soothcoor."

Julia's eyes widened and her mouth opened into a silent 'O'.

"Please, please, keep this to yourself. That fact alone would make others certain he'd murdered Mr. Montgomery. I assure you, he did not. That is not the kind of man he is. I know people say any man or woman can commit murder if the circumstances are right. Not Soothcoor. He is the kindest man, always helping those less fortunate—though he tries not to let that be widely known."

She coughed again then cocked her head to the side as she considered Soothcoor. She looked directly at Lady Stackpoole to try to explain the man to her. "He's humble about what he does. He is invited everywhere— and not just when a hostess needs to even her numbers. He'll stand up at balls with the wallflowers. He is not in the least bit handsome. His is a long face with dark eyes that droop down in the corners. His hair is black, streaked with gray and always looks like it needs a comb," she said with a laugh.

"His lips are well defined," she continued seriously, "though the bottom lip is thin. He does not smile much, which is how he acquired the *'Dour Earl'* moniker," she said with a faint laugh. "But I have witnessed a rare moment of joy for him. It lit his face and, as I watched him, I couldn't help but smile as well," Cecilia said.

"What gave him that joy?" Julia asked.

"When he realized his nephew was safe—that Sir James and I had rescued little Christopher." Cecilia laughed suddenly. "Oh, look at me. Just remembering has my eyes tearing," she said, swiping at her cheeks with her gloved hands.

"Rescued! That sounds like a story I should like to hear!" Julia said.

Cecilia laughed again. "Another day. Right now, I do need to lie down."

"And while you rest, I will try to find out about the guest register the day Mr. Montgomery died. I'm curious to know if Jacob came to Camden House and when."

"You don't think the magistrate would have looked at it or taken it?"

"I don't know. I'll see what I can find out about that as well."

Cecila stood up and, with Julia, walked back to Camden House.

"Excuse me, Lady Branstoke, Sir James Branstoke is downstairs in the great hall. Do you feel well enough to see him?" asked Matron Mildred from the doorway of Cecilia's room.

Cecilia had been dozing again, husbanding her strength for when James came—as she knew he would —and for the meal hours where she might have more conversation with the others.

"Yes, yes, I am," Cecilia assured her as she rolled over to swing her feet to the floor. "I've been expecting him," she said.

"Very good, then I won't send him away," the matron said.

"Send him away?" Cecilia parroted. "Do you do that often?"

The matron chuckled. "More than one would think. Some are always looking to see the worst in our patients. We try to protect them. We allow them to turn down visitors and sometimes we turn down visitors if we believe it is not one of our patients' better days. We don't want their visitors to see them in anything less than perfect condition."

"Hmm, I suppose that makes sense. Lady Stackpoole and I were just having a discussion on visitations here. When we checked into The New Bell Inn, we saw Baron Stackpoole's name in the guest register from the time when Mr. Montgomery died yet, Lady Stackpoole said she never had a visit from him. We thought he must have changed his mind about visiting here. Did he come and you turn him way?" she asked as she picked up her cape from where she'd laid it earlier on a chair by the window.

"I didn't, though I might have been so inclined if I saw him. That man belittles her so when he visits—it takes two days for her to be herself again," the matron said, her arms akimbo.

Cecilia shook her head. "She seems like such a strong woman, that's hard to believe," she said as she walked out of the room. "By the way, young Miss Liddy sneaked into my room when I was sleeping yesterday. I caught her looking through my portmanteau."

The matron's expression fell. "I'm right sorry about that, milady. Poor child has been ever so mischievous since Mr. Montgomery died. We need to find her a new mentor."

"Mr. Montgomery was her mentor?" Cecilia said as they walked toward the stairs.

"Just developed that way over time and did her a world of good. Child always feels inferior due to that birthmark on her face," the woman said.

Cecilia held her handkerchief to her lips as she coughed mildly. "Lady Stackpoole told me her mother won't even look at her."

The matron compressed her lips. "That be true. Dr. Worcham says before he died, her father gave her attention and never minded the birthmark. Not the mother. Because Mr. Montgomery did pay attention to her and gave her lessons, she followed him around everywhere. Now the poor thing is lost."

Cecilia stopped at the top of the stairs. "Thank you, Matron," she said, "for telling me more about Liddy. It helps my understanding of her actions."

"You're welcome, milady," the matron said, bobbing a small curtsy, and Cecilia started down the stairs.

She found James in the grand hall, studying a large painting of Camden House before it became the sanatorium.

He turned at the sound of her footsteps.

"How did you know that was me?" she asked.

"I'm accustomed to the sound and the scent of you, my love," James said, taking both her hands in his. He brushed her cheek with a light kiss. He looked down at her, concern in his expression. "How are you feeling?"

She shrugged. "The same. I am getting more rest, and the coughing spells don't seem quite as harsh today as yesterday. I went walking this morning, then laid down. I think that was helpful."

James frowned. "Now, where can we talk that won't fatigue you."

"I think outside is best, that's why I brought my cape. There are plenty of benches outside," she said, silently holding the cape out for James to take it from her to drape about her shoulders. She smiled up at him as he did so. "Don't worry, I shall lay down again after our visit."

James tucked her arm in his and led her outside. There were others enjoying the outdoors as well. Cecilia directed him to the left path.

"If no one has yet claimed it, there is a bench in a wind-protected area this way," she said. She led him to one of the benches she and Julia stopped by that morning. She sat down and James sat down next to her, pulling her close.

"Tell me about the magistrate," Cecilia said as she pulled her cape about herself.

James sighed. "He's a man more concerned with his properties right now than with the death of a man in a sanatorium. He quickly took the suggested scenario that fit the few facts that were known, ignored others, and leaped to Soothcoor's guilt."

"What few facts?" Cecilia asked.

"That Soothcoor visited Mr. Montgomery, that he knew Mr. Montgomery, and he wanted to marry Mrs. Montgomery so he had motive and, by the fact of being on the Camden House grounds, had opportunity."

"That's it? Did he have witnesses? Does he know the cause or time of death? Or is it all circumstantial—and how did he even know that much?"

"When Dr. Worcham sent for the magistrate, he also sent for Mr. Montgomery's cousin and executor, Mr. Boyd Ratcliffe. He lives not far away, so he arrived nearly at the same time. He is the one who gave the information to Squire Eccleston and strongly suggested that of course it was Soothcoor who committed the crime, due to motive and opportunity."

"I see."

"He did tell me that Mr. Montgomery was held under water until he drowned."

Cecilia's brow furrowed. She looked over at one of the canals that made Camden House sit on an island. "There are steep sides to these canals. How does one hold someone under water here? Unless they are in the water with them. How deep are the canals?"

"I don't know. I will find out. I have already checked with Mr. Price. Soothcoor clothes were dry when he arrived back at The New Bell Inn. There were comments made of how lucky he was as it started to rain almost as soon as he walked in the door."

"Sounds like you need to visit Mr. Ratcliffe."

"That is my plan. Have you learned anything here?"

"There is a woman here, Miss Dorn, who had relations with her employer's nephew and found herself pregnant. As she was of good family, he agreed to marry her to avoid scandal. She lost the child after a few weeks, and he cried off the marriage. Now she keeps importuning men to get her pregnant again so she can claim she didn't lose the first babe. She has become quite delusional. She harassed Mr. Montgomery, trying to get him to service her. He refused."

"Are you thinking she could have killed him in a fit of rage at his refusal?"

Cecilia shrugged. "I'm not saying she did, all I'm saying is she is as likely a suspect as Soothcoor, don't you think?"

"How strong is she? Do you think she could hold him underwater?"

"I don't know. Probably not. But, it throws some doubt on the absolute conviction Soothcoor was the murderer. I will be finding out more. I have also discovered there is a young child here, a girl, who Mr. Montgomery taught. He'd taken her under his wing. The matron told me she was his shadow. I'm going to befriend her and see if she was spying on him when he was killed."

"Do you think she could have been?"

"It's possible, though I admit not probable. She has the run of the facility, it seems."

"How old is she and why is she here?"

"I think she is between eight and ten years old. She has a port wine stain birthmark on her face. I'm told her mother sent her away after her father died because she couldn't stand to see the imperfection in her child's face. It embarrasses her."

James made a sour expression.

"Yes. That is my thought as well. I need to find out who her family is. The patients and the matron on my floor just call her Miss Liddy."

"Why did Dr. Worcham allow her in the facility if she is not ill?"

"Money, most likely. Perhaps pity as well."

He shook his head. "—I need to see you back inside. I can tell your voice is getting that cloudiness it gets before you cough."

She laughed. "Yes, I can feel it coming, too," she said, pulling out her handkerchief.

He stood and pulled her to her feet and again tucked her arm in his as she walked back to the house.

"Are you going to see Mr. Ratcliffe?"

"Yes, but not today. I want to talk to Soothcoor again. I want to question his powers of observation as to what—or who—was around him as he left Camden House that day. I also want to know more about this Boyd Ratcliffe. If he is local, some people at the pub might know of him and know the tenor of the man."

Cecilia nodded. "Do you think the magistrate will be in contact with him after your visit?"

"Perhaps. He was certainly angry enough at me. I'll just have to take that chance and deal with whatever the outcome is."

"Other than resting some more, I will try to make friends with Miss Liddy...And I think I want a chat with Mrs. Worcham as well."

"Why is that?"

She shrugged. "Just a feeling. Sometimes she is a little too laughingly affable."

James raised a brow. "Whatever you deem necessary —that doesn't get you into trouble."

"Me, in trouble?" Cecilia asked archly, a teasing light in her eyes as she slid a sideways glance up at him.

James groaned.

~

THE TURNKEY immediately recognized Sir James when he rode up to the Stamford Borough Gaol—his manner deferential and eagerly accommodating.

"Warden's to lunch, sar, over ta his howse. I be sartin you can see him thar."

"I shall go to his house, then. Thank you," Sir James said, repressing a smile for the turnkey's manner.

"Ya knows where it be?"

"Yes," James said as he headed toward the back of the gaol.

The Warden was just coming out when James came around the gaol.

"Sir James! What brings you here again?"

"I have a few questions for the earl. Has the doctor been out to see him? I left you enough money, didn't I?" James asked, though he was certain he had been more than generous. "Does he have everything he needs?"

"Yes sar, and the doctor has tended to his injury."

"May I see him, please?"

"Yes, I got my keys right here," he said, unhooking a large ring from an oversized belt at his side. He jingled it as he walked over to the debtor-prison half of the building and unlocked the door.

"Has anyone been to see him?" James asked.

"Squire Eccleston came by this morning. Didn't stay long and was in a temper when he left, muttering something to himself, though I didn't catch what it be. I mentioned you'd visited his lordship. He said he knew that and said a few choice words about yourself."

Sir James laughed. "I'm sure he did," he said wryly as they stepped into the hallway.

The warden looked at him sideways. "Called him to order, eh?"

"I provided him with some observations," James said mildly.

The warden grunted deep in his chest. He pounded on the heavy wood door of the small room occupied by Soothcoor. "Company, my lord," he said as he unlocked that door. "A half- hour?" he asked Sir James.

"Yes, a half-hour is fine, thank you," James said as he passed the warden into the room.

The warden closed the door and locked him in.

Soothcoor looked better. He wore different, cleaner clothes and it appeared he'd been able to avail himself of at least a washbowl for his face and hands, and a comb for his hair. No razor for his face and Soothcoor was typically a clean-shaven man. He'd have to see what he could do about getting a barber for him.

A clean bandage wrapped his leg, and a crutch leaned against the bed.

"How's the leg," James asked. He walked up to the table and pulled the chair out to sit down.

Soothcoor shrugged. "Painful. When the worst heals, I'll need a cane."

"I see you did get a crutch."

"Yes, but since I have nowhere to go anyway, I've managed without it."

"You will need it when we get you out of here."

"Do you think I will?"

"Yes."

Soothcoor shrugged. "Magistrate came by earlier today."

"So the warden told me. What did he want?"

"Ask me some questions about my relationship with Malcolm, how long I'd known him, why did I come to see him, basically everything I knew Mr. Ratcliffe had told him the morning he arrested me."

"Trying to see if your answers matched?"

"I suppose, but nothing of substance—except for one thing. He asked me where the clothes were that I'd worn to Camden House."

"And you told him?"

"The jacket, pants, and vest were the same as I wore the day he arrested me. I put on clean linens that morning, so the previous day's linens were in my valise."

"I'll bet he didn't like the answer."

"No, he didn't seem to. Why did he ask? Do you know?"

"He believed you drowned Mr. Montgomery, which you wouldn't have been able to do unless you got in the water with him and held him underwater."

Soothcoor frowned. "That would be hard for any one person to do. Malcolm was strong. He wasn't a tall man. But he was a sturdy man, and he did know how to swim."

"I was going to ask you if he knew how to swim."

"We often swam together in the ponds and streams on my grandfather's estate."

"What do you know about Montgomery's relationship to his uncle, Boyd Ratcliffe."

"He hated him."

"Why"

"I don't know," Soothcoor said slowly, "I just believe it had to do with the time he and his mother lived with him."

James cocked his head. "Lived with him?"

"Yes. There was a fire at the Montgomery estate while his father traveled out of the country. This was long before I knew him. He and his mother lived with Ratcliffe for the year Malcolm's father was away. Malcolm could never clearly remember that time and didn't want to try. It was one of the gaps in his memory, but he knew he hated Ratcliffe. As he was growing up, if Ratcliffe came to visit, Malcolm would run away, and no punishment he might be given would stop him."

James's brow furrowed. "I can't imagine what would have caused that behavior—or perhaps I can and don't want to consider it."

"I know." Soothcoor shifted his position to ease his leg. "Such have been my thoughts, especially to know he is now married to Malcolm's mother. What perversion could he have subjected a young boy to that would lead him to splinter, like the logs he splintered with an ax and often talked of. He sympathized with splintered logs, if you can believe that. He would laugh about it, but he did sympathize. He'd run his hand along the splinters his ax caused and mouthed a silent apology. He thought I didn't notice. I did."

"Did you ever see any evidence of the persona he and others refer to as 'Archie'?"

"Strangely, no. I think I have been in the company of the one known as Gregory, back when we were children, but never an angry, violent person which I understand in Archie's role."

"Interesting that you refer to him as having a role. I tend to agree with you. I do wish Dr. Nowlton were here. I am certain he would make sense of this for us."

"That young man is intelligent and sharp. I wish I could get him to work for my charities."

"Yes, he would be an asset. But to return to Archie. If Malcolm was being threatened in any way, wouldn't Archie come to the fore to deal with the threat?"

"I would think so, but you have to remember, what we think happened to Malcolm was a perversion of the mind. I don't know that we can use logic to explain it or understand it."

James frowned and scratched the back of his head.

"As much as it goes against the norm for me, I shall have to concede I may never understand what went on in Mr. Montgomery's brain. Could he have committed suicide?"

"I have endlessly thought about that. It is possible, but I don't believe so. I still think it is more probable for him to be murdered than for him to kill himself."

The door to the cell opened.

"Your time is up, Sir James."

James rose from his chair. "Time has flitted by much too quickly. Think of anything you saw on the grounds, anything at all, and send me a note." He turned to the warden. "You will allow him access to pen and paper, won't you?"

"Yes, he has that now."

"Good. Note down everyone you met since you came up here. Friend or foe. I hope to call on you again tomorrow afternoon after what will certainly be a most enlightening meeting with Mr. Ratcliffe."

CHAPTER 15

INTERVIEWS

Though Cecilia did nap in the afternoon, she was rested and up before dinner. She chose a dark-green gown with a red shawl for dinner. She thought the red against her face would reflect more color to her wan complexion.

She left her room early and sat in one of the settees that were spaced at intervals down the wide hall of the ladies' wing, waiting for Julia and Mrs. Vance.

Mrs. Vance was the first to join her, dressed in an icy-blue formal gown. She sat down next to Cecilia and, at Cecilia's raised brows at her attire, Mrs. Vance laughed.

"Where else do I have to wear it?" she said merrily. "And it just gives my obnoxious nephews more reason to see me locked up here."

"How long have you been here?"

"Four years come September."

"Why?"

"I became extremely depressed when my daughter died, followed in less than three months by my husband. My husband was in business with his brother. Other than our daughter, Rose, we had no children, so the business went to his brother and his brother's sons,

Enoch and Jeffrey. I asked to come here. I'd heard about it and at the time I couldn't stand to be in my home where I'd lost two of my loved ones so close together. It sounded so restful, and it has been, up until now. And now I find I'm done with restful and I'm ready for adventure!" she said, rubbing her gloved hands together, her eyes twinkling.

"So why are your nephews being troublesome now?" Cecilia asked.

Mrs. Vance smiled. "They didn't know until after their father died how much of the business I own and how much money was left to me. They are my heirs as I have no one else, but they want control of my money now."

Cecilia nodded. Mrs. Vance must be one of the patients at Camden House who have been in residence since before Mr. Montgomery came. "How well did you know Mr. Montgomery?" she asked.

"Socially here at Camden House. Card playing is a regular activity in the evening in the library and he and I often played partners. Now that I think about it, that was his only social activity. Kept much to himself," Mrs. Vance said thoughtfully. "He read a lot, was friendly enough when addressed. A quiet man."

"Did he ever have visitors?" Cecilia asked.

"Not regularly, except for that cousin of his," she said.

"Mr. Ratcliffe?" Cecilia clarified.

"Him? Nasty man. Not nice at all. Leering. Haughty. Looked down on all of us. I can tell you, Mr. Montgomery certainly did not like him and strived to be least in sight when he came. He's also the banker for Camden Hall. Imagine a man like him as guardian to sweet Mr. Montgomery. Shameful.—A little over a year ago, shortly after Christmas, a nice Scotsman did come to visit him."

"Which nice Scotsman?" Cecilia asked. Then she remembered the Scotsman who'd been in London and suddenly left when Mr. Montgomery was pronounced alive. "Mr. Cameron Ramsay?" she asked.

"Yes, that was his name. Mr. Montgomery's Scottish solicitor, you know."

Cecilia blinked in surprise. Mr. Ramsay was a solicitor? "No, I didn't know," she said. She looked across the wide hall.

How did Mr. Ramsay come to know he was alive? Did Mr. Montgomery send for him? If he knew, who else knew before Mr. Montgomery died? What would his Scottish solicitor be doing visiting him at Camden Hall? Unless—

Cecilia turned back to look at Mrs. Vance. "Was Mr. Ramsay here to draw up Mr. Montgomery's will?"

"Oh yes, he was. Did it very legal, too. I was one of the witnesses."

Cecilia realized how valuable a resource Mrs. Vance could be for her investigation. "You were?" she said. "Who else?"

"Mrs. Worcham and Miss Hammond, who is not here anymore unfortunately. He would have liked Lady Stackpoole to be a witness but she had not yet returned from her yearly holiday visit to her home."

Her lips twisted into an amused smile. "—Not a gentleman amongst us. Mr. Ramsay said it would still be legal. We all met in the library, back when visitors were allowed in there before Mr. Turnbull-Minchin and his rules," she said disgustedly. "It was all formal. He also had me, and Mrs. Worcham, read the will. Miss Hammond didn't read that well, not all that legal stuff, but I did since I helped my husband with his correspondence. I read it aloud for her benefit."

"Can you tell me about the will?" Cecilia asked, her voice growing rebelliously hoarse again.

Mrs. Vance nodded. "That was the big surprise to all of us. He left everything to his wife with a man named Mr. Sedgewick as the co-executor for his estate with Mr. Ramsay, the solicitor. We had no idea he was married, and we were pledged to secret for that part. We couldn't even tell Lady Stackpoole, and she was supposed to be one of the signatories. Because she wasn't here, she couldn't know."

"Did you say Sedgewick?" Cecilia squeaked out. She grabbed her handkerchief from where she'd tucked it in her sleeve and tried to clear her throat. "Did you say Sedgewick?" she managed to ask again, before her cough came.

"Yes." Mrs. Vance tilted her head. "Do you know him? Mr. Montgomery said he was a childhood friend and he trusted him to take care of his family."

"Yes, yes, I do know him." Cecilia coughed again, this cough cleared the congestion. "Mr. Sedgewick is the man the magistrate arrested for Mr. Montgomery's murder."

"I thought they arrested a peer," Mrs. Vance said, her brow furrowing with confusion.

Cecilia nodded. "They did. Alastair Sedgewick, Earl of Soothcoor."

Mrs. Vance's confusion turned to a frown. "Hmm. He even made a statement in his will hoping this Mr. Sedgewick would marry his wife if he should die. Mrs. Worcham questioned him severely about this. She feared he was planning suicide. He had threatened that before. He laughed and assured her that the 'others' wouldn't let him."

"Do you know who the 'others' are?"

"Oh, that was just Mr. Montgomery's little joke," she said dismissively. "Those characters he played. He said by acting out through his characters he could better deal with his emotions."

"I wish it were that simple," Cecilia said with a long sigh.

"What do you mean?"

"Never mind me.—Julia!" Cecilia called out when she saw the woman come up the stairs.

Julia appeared agitated, her eyes over-bright. She walked quickly to where she and Mrs. Vance sat. "Cecilia! Your suspicions were correct. Many gentlemen came to visit Mr. Montgomery over the last couple of weeks. Including my husband!"

"Why should Baron Stackpoole wish to visit Mr. Montgomery?" Mrs. Vance asked.

"Because our son wishes to marry Mr. Montgomery's daughter," Julia explained.

Mrs. Vance laughed. "And with him not liking foreigners! I'll bet that had him knotted up."

"It did indeed. I can't think why he would want to meet Mr. Montgomery. He has no control over Benjamin, financial or otherwise. It has had him practically foaming at the mouth in frustration that Benjamin does not need to listen to his father."

"He is helpless in the face of Benjamin's independence. Worse, Benjamin tries hard not to sneer at his father's ideas. Stackpoole knows he is only trying not to laugh at him and that irritates him more. The majordomo told me he tried to give Mr. Montgomery a gift, it looked like a jar of something. Mr. Montgomery refused it. He heard him saying it wasn't allowed. He said Baron Stackpoole looked frustrated and angry that his gift had been rejected and quickly left."

Cecilia thought about what the gift could be, she wondered…"Mr. Turnbull-Minchin explained to my husband and I when we first came here that the one thing Dr. Worcham does not want the patients to have is any form of sweet. He said it causes agitations."

Mrs. Vance nodded. "I've been here long enough to have seen that happen. Julia, remember Polly Reubart?"

Julia thought for a moment. "Yes, sometimes she would pass out if she had sweets. Faint dead away. In others, it can cause agitation. And I believe Dr. Worcham even wondered if sweets had anything to do with Miss George's drowning in the canal."

"Do you think the Baron was trying to give Mr. Montgomery something sweet?" Mrs. Vance asked.

Cecilia's lips compressed, then she sighed out grimly at where her suspicious thoughts went. "Not just something. I'm thinking it was honey."

"Honey!" Julia exclaimed. "Stackpoole *hates* honey. He's hated it ever since an incident he experienced in Damascus. He refused to ever allow any honey in our house and Benjamin loves honey."

"Julia, at The New Bell Inn, I heard Mr. Price tell your son that Baron Stackpoole had left a jar of honey for him."

"What! Honey!" Julia's eyes narrowed and glinted with anger. "*Mad honey!* Why would he do that? How could he do that to his own son!"

"What, what is it?" Mrs. Vance asked.

"There is a honey found in the Middle East that contains something from a certain variety of rhododendrons that makes anyone who eats that raw honey violently sick. They call it Mad Honey. It was given to Jacob as a joke when he was there. It made him so sick he developed a keen dislike for any honey. Would not allow it in the house."

Disgust replaced anger. "Benjamin would be surprised by the gift but he would accept the honey as a gift at face value. That boy is such an optimist he'd think it a peace offering from his father."

"And, I assume, he'd share it?" Cecilia asked.

"Most likely."

"I need to send a note to James immediately to confiscate that honey. I know Mrs. Price and a maid at the inn have both succumbed to the same violent sickness Mr. Stackpoole has, and if they are drinking medicinal tisanes, they are continually staying sick if they add honey to their drink! Excuse me while I write a quick note to my husband. Do you think I can get someone to take it to The New Bell Inn today?"

"For a coin or two one of the porters will as they go home for the day," Julia said.

"I'd best hurry then."

Cecilia rushed back to her room and found a pencil and paper in her portmanteau. She quickly related what she had learned about the *Mad Honey* and how it could be the source of the illness at The New Bell. As a last thought, she told him about Mr. Ramsay being Mr. Montgomery's Scottish solicitor and the will Mr. Montgomery had drawn up a year ago that had Soothcoor as its executor with Mr. Ramsay.

She dug a couple of coins out of her reticule, then hurried back to the hall. The ladies were still there with more of the residents beginning to mill about waiting for the call to dinner.

Cecilia was breathing hard when she resumed her seat next to Mrs. Vance.

"Careful, my dear," Mrs. Vance said. "You were coughing not long ago and rushing about could bring it on again."

Cecilia nodded. "Yes," she said, her breathing raspy. She held her handkerchief up to her lips again. "Sometimes my sense of urgency gets ahead of me."

Mrs. Vance patted her hand. "Just relax now," she instructed.

Cecilia sat for a moment as her breathing calmed. She thought more about that Mad Honey.

"Julia, do you suppose that honey could be used as a poison?" Cecilia mused.

"I don't know," Julia said. "I know it makes people sick. I suppose if it were given to someone long enough...We should ask Dr. Worcham."

"Matron! Matron, dear," called out Mrs. Vance, waving at their floor matron who was just coming up the stairs.

"Yes, ma'am," the matron said as she trundled across the room to them.

"We would like to talk to Dr. Worcham. Is he available?" Mrs. Vance asked in her bird-bright voice.

"I don't rightly know," matron said, hesitantly.

"Could you go find out, please?"

"But it's time for dinner. I was just coming to tell you that," she protested.

"That's fine. Perfect, even. Wouldn't you say so, ladies?" she said to Julia and Cecilia.

They nodded.

She turned back to the matron. "If you can find him while we eat our dinners, we would so appreciate that," she said sweetly, slipping a coin into her hand.

The trio went down the stairs together as matron went off in search of Dr. Worcham. Julia introduced Cecilia to one of the young porters who was getting ready to leave for the day. He eagerly agreed to take her note to Sir James, cheerily saying it gave him an excuse —and the funds—to stop off for a pint.

As they approached the dining hall, Cecilia threaded her arm through Mrs. Vance's. "I was impressed how you handled matron. Well done!" she said.

The woman smiled impishly. "At least this way she won't be hovering over our table as she likes to do."

"Does Liddy eat with you every night?" Cecilia asked.

"Not every night," Julia said. "She makes the

rounds between several tables. She has a lot of friends here. I think she feels she needs to associate with all of them so as not to lose them as friends, seeing as how her mother does not number among the friendly faces."

"Do you know Liddy's last name?" Cecilia asked.

Julia thought a moment. "How odd, but I don't. Do you Mrs. Vance?"

"I know I have heard it. Wind, or Winter, or Wing, or something like that," she said. "I also heard her father would have been in line to a title and property if he had hadn't died. Liddy has mentioned that."

"Many times," Julia added drily. "I don't think she knows what that means. It's just something she's heard."

Cecilia frowned. "Surely a child of her age would be educated about such things."

Mrs. Vance huffed. "Liddy has scarcely been educated in anything, except for what Mr. Montgomery taught her. The sanatorium is not set up for children and their education. She should be in a school for girls, not a sanatorium," she said as they walked into the dining hall. "Ah, the gentlemen are before us, and Liddy is sitting with them."

Cecilia's brow drew together on hearing learning was not an opportunity for Liddy at the sanatorium. "Do you mind if I sit next to Liddy?" Cecilia asked. "I'd like to get to know her better."

"I have no objection," Mrs. Vance said. "It will be interesting to see if she has any objections."

"Hello, Miss Lydia. May I take this seat next to you?" Cecilia asked as she pulled out the chair next to Liddy's.

A fleeting expression of startled fear crossed Liddy's face, quickly replaced with a non-committal shrug. "I guess."

"Thank you. I wanted to apologize," Cecilia said.

"Apologize?" Liddy repeated, her face crumpled up in confusion.

"Yes, I'm sorry I was not awake when you came to visit me in my room yesterday," Cecilia said, determined not to mention she'd seen her in her portmanteaux.

"Oh."

"Mrs. Vance and Lady Stackpoole have told me you were a good friend to Mr. Montgomery."

"Yes. He teached me and listened to me."

Cecilia nodded. "It is very special to have a friend who listens to you."

"And he didn't laugh at me," she said solemnly, shaking her head.

Cecilia frowned. "I don't think anyone here laughs at you. From what I've heard, everyone likes you."

Liddy sighed dramatically. "I know. I'm not talking about this stupid purple birthmark. That's just me."

"Oh, then I confess I am confused. What do you mean?"

"I mean," she said, speaking with careful emphasis, "he never laughed at my *treasure chest*."

"Your treasure chest?"

She nodded and took a bite of food.

"Our Miss Liddy likes to collect things and store them in a box she calls her treasure chest."

"It is my treasure chest," Liddy defended fiercely.

"We," Mrs. Vance continued sadly, waving her hand to indicate everyone in the room and beyond, "have made the mistake of laughing at an item or two in her collection."

"Mr. Montgomery never thought them silly," Liddy said stoutly between bites. "He liked them all."

"What do you like to collect in your...treasure chest," Cecilia asked.

She shrugged, one thin shoulder rising nearly to her ear. "Things."

"Things you see and like?"

The child nodded as she quickly shoveled more food into her mouth. Cecilia wanted to tell her to slow down, but didn't want to risk breaking the tenuous communication she had with her.

"I did something like that at one time," Cecilia told her. "My grandparents took me to the beach, and I collected shells and bits of sea glass from the sand. I kept the shells in glass vases on a shelf in my bedroom."

"Do you still have them?"

Cecilia smiled sadly. "No, I moved away from there," she told her, thinking back to all she'd left behind in her forced arranged marriage to George Waddley so many years ago. She wondered if the shells were still there. Or if her father even owned that house any longer, or if he'd finally wagered it away like everything else he did in his life.

She pushed those thoughts away. Another time, another place, another life. Now, she had wonderful, loving James and their coming babe. She laid a hand on her growing stomach.

"Do you miss them?" a serious Liddy asked her, bringing Cecilia out of her past.

"My shells? Yes, I think I do. I hadn't realized that until you asked me," Cecilia told her.

Liddy looked at her intently. "Maybe I will show you my treasure chest. If you promise not to laugh."

"I should like that, and I make you a solemn promise not to laugh."

She nodded, then looked around. "I'm done," she proclaimed to the room, her chair scraping across the stone floor as she pushed her chair away from the table and skipped out of the room.

"You have made a conquest," Mrs. Vance observed.

"She's really a sweet child. While she hasn't been physically abused, she has none the less been abused. I feel sorry for her."

"As do we all," said Julia from across the table.

"Do either of you gentleman know the child's last name?" Cecila asked.

Mr. Quetal and Mr. Hobart shook their heads. Beyond them, Cecilia saw Matron enter the dining hall and walk toward their table.

"Ladies, Dr. Worcham says as how he will see you in the library after dinner."

"Thank you, Matron," Mrs. Vance said.

"Matron," Cecilia said before the woman turned to leave. "What is Miss Liddy's last name? She reminds me of someone, and it is teasing my mind."

"Wingate, my lady."

An explosion of surprised and shocked thoughts bashed against each other in Cecilia's mind.

"Wingate?"

Matron looked at her, a curious look on her face.

"You look as if you know that name," Julia observed.

"I do," Cecilia said. "...It is the family name of the Duke of Ellinbourne."

"I wonder where she might fit in his family," Julia mused.

"Hmm, yes, how far the branches might extend to get to Miss Liddy," Cecilia said.

"Wasn't there a painter by that name as well?" Mr. Hobart asked.

"Yes. Clarence Wingate. He was an uncle of the current duke. In fact, the current duke is as much of an accomplished artist as his uncle was. He had a painting in the Spring Royal Academy of Art show that just ended," Cecilia said.

"Do you think she could be closely enough related

to the duke for him to take an interest in the child?" Julia asked.

Cecilia shrugged, then smiled. "I don't know the duke well, nonetheless, Ellinbourne will be on the receiving end of a severe set-down from me if he doesn't," she said.

"You would do that to a duke?" squeaked Mr. Quetal.

"Immediately. A duke might have a title, but he is not a god and has a responsibility to show others the proper way to go on."

Mr. Hobart laughed. "I find that a naïve notion."

Cecilia smiled. "It depends on how one does it and in what *company*," she said with emphasis, cagily thinking of her grandfather, the Duke of Cheney. She rose from her chair. "Ladies, shall we go speak to Dr. Worcham now?"

Mrs. Vance and Julia followed her down the corridor to the library,

~

THEY FOUND Dr. Worcham sitting in an armchair near the fireplace, reading.

"Good evening, Dr. Worcham," Cecilia said.

Dr. Worcham looked up, removing his reading glasses as he did so. "I understand from Matron Mildred you wished to speak with me." He placed his book on a table next to him.

"Yes," Cecilia said. She sat in the chair opposite him. Mrs. Vance and Julia sat on the settee that completed the inviting social congregation area in front of the fire. "Have you ever heard of a substance known as *Mad Honey*?" she asked.

"Mad Honey?" He frowned. "Yes, I have. Why?"

"Is it poisonous?" Julia asked, leaning forward.

"Not to a healthy person, no. It could be detrimental to a person already weak from another illness. Nothing I have read has suggested it is inherently poisonous. And the effects can vary based on the health of the person ingesting the substance."

"Even if they had it repeatedly?" Julia insisted, her lips compressed.

"Why are you asking about Mad Honey?" he asked, a deep frown creasing his brows.

"We think Mad Honey might be responsible for the spate of illness that has been occurring at The New Bell Inn," Cecilia explained.

"How do you know about that? I only heard about it this afternoon."

"We know my son was coming to visit, and that he has taken quite violently ill repeatedly since staying at the inn."

The doctor nodded.

"From Lady Branstoke I have learned that my husband was at The New Bell Inn shortly before Mr. Montgomery died, and he left a jar of honey with the innkeeper in keeping for our son when he next came to visit. I think it was Mad Honey, and I believe the original intended recipient of the honey was Mr. Montgomery."

"Why do you think that?"

"Because he tried to give it to Mr. Montgomery, but he rejected the gift, saying sweets are not allowed."

Dr. Worcham raised his eyebrows. "That is true, and I commend Mr. Montgomery's memory that he rejected it for that reason. How do you know that?" he asked, his tone turning severe.

"Ah, well—"

"Please just accept our knowledge," Cecilia said, smiling at Julia.

Dr. Worcham frowned again. "I don't like it, but for

the moment I will. What would be Baron Stackpoole's motive?"

"I believe he didn't want Mr. Montgomery and our son to meet," Julia explained. "You see, Benjamin has recently asked Mr. Montgomery's daughter to marry him."

"Mr. Montgomery's daughter?" Dr. Worcham asked, now giving the women his full attention.

"I know Mr. Montgomery was not single," Cecilia told Dr. Worcham. "And I know you encouraged those here to believe he was single. I'm sorry if I spoke out of line to advise he was not."

He waved his hand negligently. "That was Malcolm's idea. I didn't contradict him. Yes, I knew he'd been married. How did you know he wasn't single?"

"I met Mrs. Montgomery last December at a musicale," Cecilia said. "We became friends when she was able to provide information needed to rescue a kidnapped child."

He looked at her with such intensity he made her uncomfortable. "You were in Scotland?" he finally asked.

"No, no. I met her in London. She'd brought her family to London to get them settled before the Season started."

"Harrumph," said Dr. Worcham, the frown back across his brow. He tapped his fingertips on his chair arm. "No one said anything about Malcom having a child," he said fretfully.

"Three children," Cecilia said.

"Three?"

Cecilia nodded. "Three. Aileen, Sorcha, and Hugh. And it was for Aileen's season that they are in London. Aileen seems to have caught the fancy of Lady Stackpoole's son, Benjamin."

"My husband does not approve of the match as Mr.

Montgomery is Scottish and that he resides here, at Camden House," Julia said, picking up the story.

"If Baron Stackpoole denied the match, why would he want to keep them from meeting? Wouldn't that be the end of it?" Dr. Worcham asked.

"My son is not under any control of, or obligation to, my husband. The baron could decry the match, but he could not deny it. He probably wanted to see if he could turn Mr. Montgomery against the match as well."

Dr. Worcham nodded his understanding as he again drummed his fingertips on the arm of his chair. "Badly done," he muttered. "Badly done all around."

"I beg your pardon?" said Cecilia, leaning closer.

He frowned as he shook his head. "Nothing for you ladies to be concerned about.—Lady Branstoke, have you sent word to The New Bell Inn concerning the jar of honey?"

She nodded. "I did so before dinner."

His lips pulled to one side, then exhaled sharply. He slapped his hands against the chair arms as he stood up suddenly. Cecelia wondered if that was in approval or disapproval. There was something about the doctor's manner that bothered her. And what did he mean by *Badly Done*. What was badly done?

"Dr. Worcham, why was it put about that Mr. Montgomery died two years ago?" Cecilia asked.

He shook his head "I have to go now. Did you get the information you required about Mad Honey?"

Before they could answer, he hurried out of the library. The ladies looked at each other in concern and confusion for the doctor's hasty departure.

"Is there something going on I don't know about?" Mrs. Vance asked.

"Can we tell her?" Julia asked.

"I think we should, as I believe Mr. Montgomery's will might soon become a matter of great importance,"

Cecilia said. "And I believe it is time for a chat with Mrs. Worcham, as well."

"She's probably in the strawberry parlor at this hour," Mrs. Vance said. "Let's check there."

She stood and Julia and Cecilia followed her.

"Strawberry parlor. I haven't heard of that room," Cecilia said as Mrs. Vance led them down the length of the library toward the windows. Just before they reached the windows, Mrs. Vance turned to the right and pressed a hidden latch in the shelves, releasing a door into a cozy parlor decorated with strawberry-patterned wallpaper and fabric with other pieces in solid strawberry red or leaf green.

Mrs. Vance had been correct. This was where Mrs. Worcham sat alone, working on her sewing.

"Excuse us for bothering you, Mrs. Worcham, but might we talk with you?" Cecilia asked. Behind her, Julia carefully shut the door leading back to the library.

CHAPTER 16

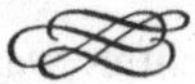

THE LADIES CHAT

Mrs. Worcham laid her embroidery work for the hem of a new gown down beside her.

"Of course. How may I help you, ladies?" Mrs. Worcham smiled happily, her cheeks like little rosy apples. Her wig was an attractive dark brunette. It looked so natural on her, Cecilia wondered if it was close to her natural hair color.

"We've come to talk to you, if we might," Cecilia answered as she and the other two ladies took seats near Mrs. Worcham.

"How luscious! But you know—or at least Mrs. Vance and Lady Stackpoole know—Mr. Turnbull-Minchin does not like me to associate with the patients."

"Why not?" Cecilia asked.

Mrs. Worcham shrugged. "Control, I suppose. Mr. Ratcliffe suggested Thaddeus hire him to help get Camden House expenses under control, but I dare swear," she said with a laugh, "sometimes he wants to control everything, not just what has a monetary impact."

"That doesn't bother you?" Cecilia asked.

"Not particularly," she said airily. "My dear Thaddeus has been so much more relaxed since he hired Mr. Turnbull-Minchin. Things were so at odds for him. His anxiety was terrible. As much as I do not care for Mr. Ratcliffe, I commend him for recommending Thaddeus hire a superintendent."

"I know Mr. Ratcliffe was Mr. Montgomery's cousin and guardian—" Cecilia began.

"I didn't know that!" Mrs. Worcham exclaimed.

"Nor I," said Mrs. Vance. Next to her Julia nodded, her expression perplexed.

"Mr. Mongomery seemed to hate the man! He always hid when Mr. Ratcliffe came to Camden House," Julia said.

Cecilia nodded. "He did that even as a child."

"How do you know that?" Mrs. Worcham said.

Cecilia bit her lip, realizing she had revealed more than she meant to. She took a deep breath in and blew it out.

"Mrs. Montgomery sent a letter to my husband asking that he and I come to London. She had just found out that her husband—whom she had supposed dead these past two years—had been killed, and that the Earl of Soothcoor had been arrested for his murder."

"The murder of a dead man," Mrs. Vance said. "How very confusing."

"Yes. And it gets worse."

"My husband told me they had arrested the man who murdered Mr. Montgomery. I didn't know who it was. I didn't think to ask," Mrs. Worcham said.

"Well, he didn't murder him. Would never murder him! You were one of the signatories to Mr. Montgomery's will."

"Yes."

"The earl is the Mr. Sedgewick named in the will."

"Mr. Montgomery spoke so fondly of him," Mrs. Worcham said.

Mrs. Vance nodded.

"It is my understanding that the cause of death has been identified as drowning because he was found in the water," Cecilia said.

"Yes, that is what I was told."

"The canals here are steep sided. How does one hold a person under the water along here without getting wet themselves? And if one is in a fight, wouldn't there be some evidence on their person of that activity?"

"What are you saying, Lady Branstoke?" Mrs. Worcham asked.

"Soothcoor came to visit Mr. Montgomery on two consecutive days. They were longtime friends and rivals for the hand of the woman who became Mrs. Montgomery. Mrs. Montgomery thought herself a widow. Now, she and the earl planned to marry. As proper, she notified Mr. Ratcliffe, who she knew as the executor of the estate, and overall guardian for her children."

"Children!" Mrs. Worcham exclaimed.

Cecilia nodded. "Two girls and a boy. I'm surprised they weren't mentioned in the will."

"He did say *family* in the will, He never specified names," Mrs. Vance said. "I suppose we should have questioned that," she said to Mrs. Worcham. She turned to Cecilia. "He did name his wife and swore us to secrecy about her. Mr. Ramsay did say family could means more than just a wife in terms of the will. We didn't think to question that."

Mrs. Worcham put her hands to her head. "I wonder if my husband knows about the children?"

"He didn't seem to know. He does now because we just talked to him about my son wanting to marry Mr. Montgomery's oldest girl, Aileen," Julia put in.

Mrs. Worcham's face crumbled. "Oh Thaddeus," she whispered. "What have you gotten yourself into?"

Cecilia reached out to gently touch her arm.

"It was Mr. Ratcliffe who wrote Mrs. Montgomery to tell her she could not marry Soothcoor because Mr. Montgomery was still alive," she told her. "Soothcoor came to see Mr. Montgomery on her behalf—and his own, too, I'm sure."

"But, to continue, Soothcoor left Mr. Montgomery standing outside as he returned to The New Bell Inn. When he returned, the rain deluge started just after he was inside the inn. It was so sudden it startled him, and he looked back at the closed door and the sound of the pounding rain outside. Those who saw him laughed that he was lucky not to get caught in that heavy rain. His clothing was dry and in excellent condition according to Mr. Price. No sign of a struggle."

"My husband said Mr. Ratcliffe told him the murderer had history with Mr. Montgomery and that with the rumble of the approaching storm negating sounds of a fight, he killed him.

"Someone may have taken advantage of the approaching storm. How would Mr. Ratcliffe know that? When was Mr. Montgomery's body found?"

"We hire a groundsman from the village to take care of the property. He comes at dawn. He saw something in the canal as he came down the canal path to the bridge and investigated. Woke Mr. Turnbull-Minchin, and he sent for the magistrate and Mr. Ratcliffe."

"How long did it take the magistrate and Mr. Ratcliffe to arrive after the discovery?"

"Mr. Ratcliffe was already here. He'd stayed with us. He'd ridden over earlier that evening and got caught in the rain. His clothing had become drenched on his way here. I invited him to stay here and ordered a maid see to his clothes," Mrs. Worcham explained.

"Why was he coming here at that time of day?"

"He often did that. Evening was a good time to discuss the business of Camden House with my husband and Mr. Turnbull-Minchin," she explained.

Cecilia cocked her head to the side. "Why did he discuss sanatorium business with Dr.Worcham? What is his relationship to the good doctor?"

"Oh! You don't know! Mr. Ratcliffe arranged for all the investors who bought shares in Camden House. He owns the biggest bank in Stamford."

"What!" Julia said, sitting straighter.

"Makes sense," Mrs. Vance said, nodding sagely. "Sanatoriums can be a lucrative business from what I've read. Wish I'd known. I'd have bought a share."

"I don't understand," Julia said.

"Camden House is a business accountable to investors for profit and loss," Cecilia explained. "Isn't that correct Mrs. Worcham?"

"Precisely, Lady Branstoke," Mrs. Worcham said. "I liked it better when we were a small, private sanatorium, not an institution driven by money," she said forlornly, dropping her cheery disposition.

She spread her hands then dropped them in her lap. "Thaddeus is not a money person. Once Mr. Ratcliffe sank his claws into him with flattery that he could have a renowned sanatorium if he expanded Camden House, he's had stars in his eyes. He does anything Mr. Ratcliffe tells him to do, promising it will build the business.—Business! A sanatorium should not be considered a business! Certainly not like a factory with investors and the like is a business."

"I think you have answered my question as to why Dr. Worcham agreed to Mr. Montgomery's fake death."

"If you mean Mr. Ratcliffe talked my husband into agreeing to the scheme, you are correct, though I argued against it. Unfortunately, my words to Thaddeus fell on deaf ears," she said sadly. She stared off across the room. "We used to be so close as a couple. Now we seem so far apart, and I think that is when it started." She looked back at the ladies. "Look at me here in this small parlor. I used to sit out in the library with Thaddeus and others in the evening, partaking in the discussions as I did a bit of needlecraft. Now I'm not allowed to sit with anyone. Nor am I allowed to chat with patients. That's Mr. Turnbull-Minchin's edict. I feel like a prisoner here. Patients have more liberties than I do. That's why I like to go to the linen drapers, where we met, Lady Branstoke. There I have people to talk to."

"Did Mr. Turnbull-Minchin say why you are not to talk to patients?"

"He gave some rambling, disjointed excuse that it set a bad precedent to be conversing with patients as if they were normal people."

"Which we are!" interjected Julia.

Mrs. Worcham nodded. "Such an attitude shows you precisely why he is unfit to be a superintendent here. He has no knowledge of the needs of our patients."

"Has anyone done anything to Mr. Montgomery's room since he passed?" Cecilia asked.

Mrs. Worcham shook her head. "No one should have. If a patient dies while they are here, we have a rule that the room remains undisturbed for a minimum of one month. If any relative is going to claim their belongings, it would be in that month, and a month allows any spirits that might be lingering to decide it is good to move on."

"Spirits?"

"We say that for the other patient's benefits. After a month the notion of a ghost fades."

"Might I have a look in his room?"

"We'd probably have to sneak in," Mrs. Worcham warned. "That won't be easy."

"Where is his room?"

"Here on the ground floor. When Mr. Montgomery was threatening suicide by jumping out of his second-floor bedroom, Thaddeus had him moved to the ground floor. It's actually a nice room. He even has a terrace door. It is kept locked as far as I know, both the inside door and the terrace door."

"Will I have to pick the lock to gain entry?" Cecilia asked.

"You know how to do that?"

"Yes. Hairpins are quite useful in that way, especially on older locks, as are on the doors here."

"Well, you won't need to do so as we have a second set of keys in our rooms," Mrs. Worcham said.

"Splendid!"

"When shall we do this?" Mrs. Vance asked.

"I didn't think we would all go," protested Mrs. Worcham.

"You'll need lookouts and backup," Mrs. Vance said, getting into the idea of an adventure.

Cecilia laughed at Mrs. Vance's attitude but didn't nay say her. If they were discovered, it would be easier to claim they were a bunch of nosey women. "Midnight, I'd say. The appropriate time after everyone has gone to sleep for there to be things heard that go bump in the night."

"Oh, please don't even suggest that," said Mrs. Worcham. "I sometimes go down to the kitchen late in the evening for warm milk. I have trouble falling asleep and that helps me. Thaddeus is used to me doing that nocturnal activity and won't think a bit about it."

"What about Matron?"

"I have some laudanum in my room. We could slip a teaspoon into her evening tea."

"How will you get that by her."

Mrs. Worcham smiled. "A little distraction and it's done," she said lightly.

"I feel a horrible coughing fit coming on," suggested Cecilia, warming to Mrs. Worcham's idea. "She is solicitous to those."

"Yes. But what—?"

The door to the little parlor opened. It was Dr. Worcham.

"Hello, my dear. When I didn't find you in our rooms, I came down here, thinking maybe you'd fallen asleep reading. Yet here you are talking to patients! You know Mr. Turnbull-Minchin doesn't like you to do so."

"I know, Thaddeus dear. But I get so lonely sometimes. And we were just chatting."

He looked at Cecilia and frowned. "And I suppose Lady Branstoke has told you Mr. Montgomery was married and had children?"

"Yes, and that Lady Stackpoole's son wants to marry his oldest daughter despite his father's objection. I find that romantic, don't you?"

"Romantic? To go against his father?" Dr. Worcham countered.

"Because she is Scottish. So—so—antediluvian, don't you think? I mean, you were born in Scotland. What if my father had the same objections when we wed?" Mrs. Worcham said.

Dr. Worcham harrumphed. "So that is what you have been discussing? This romance?"

"Women love romance, Dr. Worcham," Cecilia said, wrapping her arms around herself in a hug.

"I suppose that is an acceptable topic of conversation."

"It certainly isn't a depressing one," offered his wife.

"True. But it is late now. You ladies should be upstairs. Your absence will worry Matron."

"What time is it?" Cecilia asked, looking about the room until she saw a mantle clock. "Gracious, it is nine. We should go upstairs, Mrs. Vance, Lady Stackpoole. I sometime have such trouble falling asleep if I don't do so in a timely fashion," she told the doctor.

"Precisely why we have the retiring hour at 8:30. Early by society hours, healthy for you," he said, rocking back on his heels. "Now off with you."

"Yes, of course. And thank you, Mrs. Worcham, for allowing us to disturb your sewing," Cecilia said.

Mrs. Vance led the way out of the small parlor, through the library and out to the hall and up the grand staircase. They didn't speak amongst themselves, just hurried toward their destination, nodding to Mr. Turnbull-Minchin and the majordomo as they passed them.

In their wing, they nodded and mouthed an agreement to meet at midnight and each went into their own rooms.

CHAPTER 17

THE NEW BELL INN

James laid his quill down. Behind him, a low peat fire burned in the parlor fireplace, providing the room a comfortable warmth. Outside, a steady light rain pattered on the ground and against the inn windows. Downstairs in the main pub, voices and laughter rose and fell, punctuated with an occasional hearty hail across the large room.

He reread the letter he'd just written to Mr. Boyd Ratcliffe. He'd worked hard to make it nonjudgemental. He'd strived to present himself as merely a man sent to gather information for Mrs. Montgomery with no opinion as to the rightness or veracity of the information provided. That restraint had proved hard to do when every fiber of his being knew Soothcoor had been framed by Ratcliffe. What was the man's motive? Was he involved with Mr. Montgomery's death? There was so much he didn't know.

He folded the letter and put Mr. Ratcliffe's direction on the front. Hopefully Mr. Price had an ostler anxious to earn an extra coin who would take the letter to Mr. Ratcliffe and bring back his response. James stood up, stretching to relieve the kinks from sitting so long at the table. He decided to go downstairs to the pub to seek out Mr. Price instead of sending a servant for him.

Mr. Price knew just the man for James's task and promised the letter would be delivered. James thanked him and, as he walked into the pub, he heard a Scottish accent. He followed the sound of the voice to see a tall, well-dressed, lanky gentleman ordering a meal from the barmaid. James walked in his direction.

"Might I join you?" James asked.

The man looked up and smiled broadly. "Aye, yer might, at that, and weelcum, too," said the man. "Cameron Ramsay," he said, holding out his hand.

"Sir James Branstoke," James said, accepting the man's handshake. He pulled out the chair and sat down. "And I think you are just the man I wish to talk to."

The man sat straighter in his chair, his expression changing to suspicion. "And why be that?" he asked.

"Because you knew Malcolm Montgomery."

The man's shoulders slumped. "I did, aye. Known 'im nigh on fifteen years."

"When was the last time you saw him?" James asked.

"Ten days ago." He shook his head. "Ah told 'im he'd coom ta regret his mad decision ta fake his death, mor'n two year ago, and he had. He sent me a letter, that being why ah coom ta see 'im. Ratcliffe—the rat that he be—came to visit 'im to say his wife was lookin' to marry Soothcoor—which ah already knew as ah've been in London watchin' effter her fer Malcolm."

James laughed. "Soothcoor's nephew said you were always fluttering about her and that made them suspicious of you."

"Ah liked the people in her society. Ah got too comfortable. We had a plan if the missus wanted to marry. Ah would get divorce paperwork signed by Malcolm and take it to Scotland ta file. But ta my lastin' regret, I delayed doin' this as ah knew the earl and Mrs. Montgomery wanted ta wait until after the lass, Miss Aileen Montgomery, was properly wed before they declared themselves, so I didn't put the plan ta action when it should have happened."

He shook his head. "I thought there was plenty of time fer me ta talk ta them first. But somethin' happened ta make them change their minds and declare themselves. And then it were like a canon fired."

James nodded. "What happened was Mrs. Montgomery became pregnant," he softly told him, "and Mrs. Montgomery wrote to Mr. Ratcliffe, announcing her intentions to marry Soothcoor."

Mr. Ramsay slumped back in his chair. "Then this is all my fault. Everythin'. Malcolm would be alive today if ah'd confided in them instead of that surprise announcement coomin' froom Ratcliffe first. Ah came here ta see Malcolm as soon as ah could ta have him sign the papers and then ah set ooff ta Scotland ta file the papers fer divorce."

"Why not file the papers in England?" James asked.

"Easier and faster ta get approved in Scotland since they are both Scottish and married in Scotland."

"I don't understand Mr. Ratcliffe's role in everything. I know from the magistrate he was quick to place blame on Soothcoor. What does he gain from Mr. Montgomery's death and the earl accused of the murder? It's not like he wanted Mrs. Montgomery for himself as he is now married to Mr. Montgomery's mother. And there is an heir to the Montgomery properties. Was he embezzling?"

"Not that I have been able ta determine."

James shook his head. "I have requested a meeting with Mr. Ratcliffe tomorrow morning as Mrs. Montgomery's emissary. I am awaiting his response."

"I'd like ta go with you, if I might, as Mr. Montgomery's solicitor."

James frowned at first, then relented. "I'll admit I should like to hear any conversation you have with him, so the reverse is only fair."

"Excuse me, Sir James, this just come to you from Camden Hall."

"It's from my wife, I recognize her hand. She wouldn't write unless it were important." He opened the letter.

"E'gad! It's the honey, *it's the bloody damn honey!*" James exclaimed. "Excuse me," he said to Mr. Ramsay. I shall be back shortly." He spun out of his chair. "Price!" he called out. He spotted the barmaid. "Where's Mr. Price?"

"In the kitchen, sar, as Mrs. Price be sick."

"Where is it? Through there?" James asked, pointing to a hall off the bar.

"Yes, sar," said the maid, frightened by Sir James's manner.

James ran into the large kitchen and scullery combined.

Mr. Price was helping the staff plate food for the people in the bar.

"Sir James!"

James grabbed him by the shoulder. "Where's the honey?"

"Honey, sir?"

"The honey Baron Stackpoole left for his son! It's what is making people sick!"

"The honey! But—"

"Where is it!" James demanded, shaking him.

"On the tea tray Marly just took up to Mr. Stackpoole."

"Take me to Stackpoole's room, now."

"But, sir—"

James shook him. "Now!" he repeated.

The man nodded and led him out of the kitchen toward the stairs.

"Faster. We have to stop him from adding that to his tisane. It's what is keeping him sick and what is making others sick who he lets have some of his honey."

"My wife!"

"If she had any of his honey, then that is what has made her sick, too."

Mr. Price ran faster up the stairs. He pointed to Mr. Stackpoole's door. James rushed into the room.

"Oh, hello, Sir James," Mr. Stackpoole said cheerily as he stirred his tisane. James removed the cup from Mr. Stackpoole's hands.

"Did you just put the honey in the cup or is it in the pot as well?"

"What? Oh, just the cup.—Why did you take my cup away?"

"This is not regular honey. This is Mad Honey."

"What? No, it can't be, my father wouldn't do that to me."

"He would if he didn't want you to meet Mr. Montgomery. He tried to give it to Mr. Montgomery first, but sweets are not allowed at Camden House, so if he couldn't prevent a meeting by making Mr. Montgomery sick, he would make you sick instead."

Mr. Stackpoole blinked. "And all the other people who got sick they had some of my honey."

"Yes. Has any been removed from this jar and put into another jar?" James asked as he poured the contents of the cup into the slops pot.

"No—Yes! I gave some to Mrs. Price yesterday since it goes so well with her tisane."

James removed the honey jar from the tray. "You should get better now," he said as he left the room.

"Wait—" Mr. Stackpoole called after him. James

didn't stop. He had to get the rest of the honey from Mrs. Price.

He came down the stairs to encounter Mr. Price coming from their rooms on the ground floor; he held a jar in his hand.

"Is that the honey Stackpoole gave your wife?"

"It is."

"She didn't give any to anyone else, did she?"

"She says not. This is really the source of the sickness?" he asked as he handed the jar to James.

"Yes."

"I don't know if I'll ever have honey again," the innkeeper said.

James laughed. "You need to know your sources."

"Aye."

Mr. Ramsay watched from his position in the pub.

James carried the jars with him as he returned to the table. He briefly told Mr. Ramsay about the note from Cecilia.

"Ah wonder if Mr. Ratcliffe likes honey," Mr. Ramsay said.

James laughed. Then he sobered and looked at Mr. Ramsay intently. "My wife's note told me something else interesting. She said you were at Camden House a year ago to draw up another will for Mr. Montgomery."

He nodded. "Mr. Montgomery Senior had recently died and made Mr. Ratcliffe the estate guardian, given the supposed death of Malcolm, and Hugh's young age. It left him as executor of the estate and in control of all of Mrs. Montgomery's funds. Malcolm dinnae like that. And though he weren't ready ta coome out as alive because Ratcliffe was doin' a decent job with the estate—or had been under his father, he dinnae want him ta be the estate guardian and executor should or when he really died. He wanted a separate will that took those rights away from Mr. Ratcliffe.

He dinnae trust Ratcliffe not ta do somethin' ta the detriment of his family when he ultimately passed on."

"Did Mr. Ratcliffe know about this will?"

"Ah advised against tellin' Mr. Ratcliffe of its existence; however, ah believe Malcolm told Ratcliffe as a way ta ensure his continued good health.—And Ratcliffe's good behavior toward his family."

He paused for a moment and looked uncomfortable. Around them, the pub filled with locals here for the evening. "Can we go ta yer private parlor ta talk?" he asked.

James raised a brow but nodded. "Of course."

On the way to the stairs, James requested Scottish whisky for them from the barmaid.

"Thank you," said Mr. Ramsay with a wry half smile. "We may both need it."

James and Mr. Ramsay settled into armchairs set before the fireplace. The peat fire had been renewed, warming the room. The peat burned with an odd, attractive smell of sweet earth. Outside it continued to rain. The men did not bother with candles or lamps, so they could only see each other in the glow from the hearth before them. They didn't need to see better.

James held up his whisky glass, swirling the contents and watching the play of light on the rich golden-brown liquor. He seldom drank whisky, yet enjoyed the aroma and its strong, fortifying taste on this rainy night. It seemed to go with the smell of the burning peat.

Mr. Ramsay set his glass on the table between them and steepled his fingertips. "Malcolm was not born with his affliction," he said.

"I didn't think so."

"From what Gregory told me—"

"One of his 'others'?" James clarified.

"Aye. Malcolm split into these...these..." He shook his head.

"In speaking to Mrs. Montgomery, we determined to call them '*others.*' My wife thought it a better term than anything else that might have a negative connotation."

"Others, aye, ah like that as well. Malcolm split into these 'others' when he were about a five years old wean."

"He told Soothcoor he felt like a split log."

"Aye. That be an appropriate description, ah suppose. It was his escape, a way ta rune away."

"What was he running away from?"

"Ah don't know, but, ah have me guesses."

"I likened it to the trauma some of our soldiers had when the war ended. Some, to this day, can barely sleep for the war going on in their heads a year after the last battle at Waterloo, or they can't stand loud noise; they startle easily or can't relate to others as just some of the results of the war. How do you believe it developed for Mr. Montgomery?"

"Ah hesitate ta conjecture completely. Here are the facts ah know. Then we can discuss conjecture. In 1780, Mr. Montgomery was sent ta India with his regiment, the 73rd Foot. He were a major. They'd been sent ta India ta fight in the Mysore wars. His wife and Malcolm stayed behind at Clandora, their home.

"In 1781 there were a nasty fire that destroyed their estate. Malcolm and his mother went ta live with Mr. Boyd Ratcliffe while their house was rebuilt, and while waitin' for Major Montgomery ta return hoome. It would be nearly three more years afore Major Montgomery returned ta Scotland and sold his commission. I believe whatever happened ta Malcolm happened while he and his mother lived with Boyd Ratcliffe."

"Mr. Ratcliffe was not married at this time?"

"Nay. And if ah be followin' yer thinkin', you think Mrs. Montgomery and Mr. Ratcliffe became lovers."

"That did cross my mind."

Mr. Ramsay took a deep breath. "It were rumored in Scotland that they were."

James nodded, his lips compressed in a tight line.

"Aye. Effter Mr. Montgomery returned, those rumors are what drove Mr. Ratcliffe ta come south ta England."

"What did Mr. Montgomery think of the rumors?"

"He dinnae believe them. Said he knew his nephew too well. They were close in age, you know."

"I'd heard that."

"And his wife projected a great affront ta the suggestion. Mr. Montgomery loved her too much to disbelieve her. But it does make one wonder when after his death she quickly marries Ratcliffe, who fortuitously is a widower himself at that time."

"You are a man for innuendo."

Mr. Ramsay shrugged. "These things happened. Malcolm didn't like ta be around Ratcliffe."

"Did he never tell his father about his mother and Ratcliffe?"

"Malcolm claimed he didn't remember much of his time livin' with Mr. Ratcliffe. He were too afraid ta remember, I'm thinkin'."

"Odd. Mrs. Montgomery told us they couldn't get hm to go away to school."

"That were after Mr. Montgomery returned. Mr. Ratcliffe never said anythin' about schoolin' for Malcolm when Malcolm lived wit 'im. —No. Mr. Montgomery wanted him to go to school and tried every punishment he could think of ta get Malcolm ta do as he said. With regards ta going away from home, or his uncle visitin', nothing his father said or did had an impact on Malcolm. He was a fair man so eventually he gave up, but he dinnae like havin' his will thwarted!"

CHAPTER 18

MIDNIGHT MISADVENTURES

 ecilia carefully opened the door to her room. She hadn't noted earlier if they creaked or not when she opened the heavy oak door; she was pleased to discover it opened quietly. *Compliments to the staff for keeping doors in good working order*, she thought as she stepped out of her room and closed the door behind her. The hall was full of heavy shadows with little light extending from the small, oil night lamps hung on the wall. Two figures separated themselves from the wall across from her room—Julia and Mrs. Vance.

Mrs. Vance swished when she walked. Cecilia frowned.

"Mrs. Vance is that your dress or your petticoat making that sound?" she whispered.

Mrs. Vance pressed her fingertips against her cheeks. "Oh, I'm sorry. I'm so used to it. It is the petticoats."

Cecilia shook her head. "You can't come making that sound," she hissed.

Mrs. Vance nodded quickly. Cecilia thought she would go back to her room. Instead, Mrs. Vance reached under her skirts to release the ties of the offending garment. It pooled around her feet on the floor. She quickly stepped out of it, gathered it up, looked around, then opened an ornately carved and painted door of a sideboard in the hall and shoved the petticoat inside. She swung her hips side to side to demonstrate she no longer made a sound. Cecilia compressed her lips against a laugh.

Cecilia turned toward the main staircase to go downstairs. Julia caught her arm and pointed to the back end of the hallway.

"Servants' stairs," her voice only a breath of air.

Cecilia nodded and followed Julia and Mrs. Vance as they walked quietly to the servants' stairs. She hadn't noticed Julia carried a candlestick until the woman stopped to light a candle from one of the oil lamps before she opened the door. The stairwell was Stygian black. Julia held the candle holder high as the three carefully descended the steep staircase.

At the bottom, they listened for any sounds beyond the door before they opened it. This door squeaked a little. Cecilia grimaced. Cecilia held the door only as far as was needed for the other two women to enter the hall of the ground floor. There were lit oil lamps in this hall as there had been on their floor, but they were fewer, the hall even dimmer. Julia kept her candle as she led them to the right. Cecilia knew, from what Julia and Mrs. Vance had told her earlier, that the rooms they passed were two treatment rooms, the estate office, a trunk room, and Mr. Montgomery's room at the very end.

As they approached his room, they were surprised to find Liddy with Mrs. Worcham. Mrs. Worcham held up a finger to her lips to warn them to silence, then placed her hand behind her ear to signal them to listen.

Liddy, her hands covering her mouth, was trying not to laugh.

Cecilia, Julia, and Mrs. Vance crept closer. There

were noises coming from Mr. Montgomery's room. Whispers and moans punctuated with a female cry of *"Oh, Yes! Yes! More!"*

The three women turned back to Mrs. Worcham and Liddy. "Who?" Cecilia asked on a faint hiss of breath.

Mrs. Worcham motioned them to follow her. She led them toward the center of the mansion to the main hall and the grand staircase.

"That is Miss Dorn, isn't it," said Mrs. Vance when they stopped.

Mrs. Worcham nodded, her brows drawn together and her lips in a tight line.

"And Mr. Turnbull-Minchin!" piped in Liddy before she could say anything.

"Shh," the women warned Liddy.

Liddy scrunched her shoulders up toward her ears and mouthed, *"Sorry!"*

"What are you doing here, Liddy?" Cecilia whispered.

"I followed Miss Dorn when she snuck out of our room," she said.

Cecilia shook her head. "We'll take Liddy up with us," Cecilia whispered to Mrs. Worcham. She turned to Mrs. Vance. "I think there is an empty room next to you?"

Mrs. Vance nodded. "She can stay there tonight. We'll think of some reason for her being there later."

Mrs. Worcham nodded absently. Cecilia could tell her mind was on the couple in Mr. Montgomery's room. "What are you going to do?" she quietly asked Mrs. Worcham.

"Wake Thaddeus," the woman said, a determined light in her eyes. She left to return to her and Dr. Worcham's quarters.

"We're going to miss the fun," Mrs. Vance complained, as they climbed the stairs.

"Not entirely," Julia said. She gestured to the top of the stairway that branched to their wing.

Arms akimbo, there stood Matron Mildred in a worn blue robe and a voluminous night cap.

"Follow my lead," Cecilia whispered as the women and Liddy continued up the stairs. She took an ever-ready handkerchief from her dress's hidden pocket and dabbed at her eyes.

"I miss my husband," Cecilia wailed. "Why can't I go see him?"

"It's the middle of the night, dear," Julia said, picking up on Cecilia's ploy.

"I know, but I'm not coughing like I did. I want my husband!" she wailed again. She turned toward Liddy. She winked at the child and hoped she would understand what she said next. "You're a traitor, Liddy, for telling on me."

"Me!" protested Liddy.

Julia put her arm around the child. "You did nothing wrong, Liddy. She's just upset," Julia said. "I think there is a room open next to Mrs. Vance. Would you like to stay with us on our floor tonight?"

"But, I—" Liddy began.

Mrs. Vance got on her other side and turned her away from Matron. "Hush Liddy. This is make-believe," she whispered. "You don't need to say anything."

Liddy's eyes grew wide. "Ohh!"

"I'll take you to that room," Mrs. Vance said. "It's a very nice room. And you would have it all to yourself, not like in the dormitory you sleep in now."

Liddy nodded and went upstairs holding Mrs. Vance's hand while Julia helped a weeping Cecilia slowly climb the stairs.

"What is going on?" demanded Matron. She

squinted at Cecilia as she and Julia came up the last few steps.

A door suddenly slammed. They heard people running and Dr. Worcham shouting.

Miss Dorn came screeching down the hall in her nightgown. She ran up the staircase toward them, saw them at the top of the stairs and turned to run the other way. Cecilia dropped her plaintive pose and hurried after her. "Miss Dorn!" she called out.

Julia followed after her. Liddy pulled free of Mrs. Vance's hand to stand by the banister and look down into the hall below.

Cecilia grabbed Miss Dorn's arm, pulling her about, causing Miss Dorn to stumble and fall. Liddy cheered, clapped, and jumped up and down with Mrs. Vance smiling and clapping behind her. "Well done!" she crowed. Miss Dorn fought Cecilia, until Julia joined in, holding her. Miss Dorn collapsed and started crying.

"My word," uttered Matron. She started down the stairs.

Dr. Worcham ran into the main hall from where Cecilia and the others had been earlier. His hair stood in wild disarray, his banyan hung off one shoulder, the sleeve ripped. Mrs. Worcham ran after him.

"Thaddeus! You were wonderful!" his wife cried, her eyes shining through tears.

He ignored her as he went to recover Miss Dorn from Julia and Cecilia.

Julia and Cecilia let go of her and made a show of brushing off their dresses in attitudes of feigned nonchalance. But when they looked at each other, they couldn't help but giggle.

"Miss Dorn? What were you about?" asked Dr. Worcham gently.

Miss Dorn's crying had turned to hiccups. "I just want a ba-baby," the poor woman said.

He sighed.

Suddenly, Cecilia felt like the lowest fiend for capturing her. Miss Dorn was not well. Her obsession drove her into the arms of any man who would service her.

Matron now came rapidly down the stairs. "I'll take her to the kitchen to have some warm milk, and I'll watch after her," she said.

"Thank you, Matron," Dr. Worcham said. "I need to deal with the miscreant who thought to take advantage of a patient. I'll join you when I finish with him!"

He then turned to look between Julia, Cecilia, Mrs. Vance, and his wife. "I understand you all thought to search Mr. Montgomery's room. I'll do better than that. I'll let you all clean it in the morning. For now, return to your rooms. I need to deal with Mr. Turnbull-Minchin."

"You captured him? He didn't get away?" said Cecilia.

"How far and fast can a man with pants around his ankles run?" Dr. Worcham said sarcastically. "He's locked in a treatment room. Those are the only room for which he doesn't have keys."

"What are you going to do with him?" Julia ventured to ask.

"I don't know," he said heavily.

CECILIA CAME out of her room in the morning to find Liddy humming to herself and dancing. She still wore her nightgown as her day clothes were in her dormitory living space. Her dark hair was in a wild, tangled disarray. The child appeared so cheerful that Cecilia had to smile.

"Did you sleep well, Liddy?" Cecilia asked.

"Yes. The bed was soft like my bed back home," she said, skipping over to Cecilia. She grabbed Cecilia's hand and started to swing it.

"Tell me about your home," Cecilia prompted.

"I had a pony. I called her Bluebell. I like bluebells."

"So do I."

"Papa took me with him sometimes when he visited the home farm and tenant farms, and I did not have to wear that awful cream on my face Mama made me wear in company. Yuck."

Cecilia blinked. A home farm, tenant farms, and a child with a pony was not the description of a poor family. Why was she in the dormitory?

Mrs. Vance's door opened, and Liddy ran to see her before she could raise another question.

"Good morning, precious girl," Mrs. Vance enthused. "I see we need to get you some clothes. You are more lacking in proper attire than I am. I need to get my petticoat."

She opened the ornate cupboard where she'd shoved her petticoat the night before. As she pulled the garment out, a large leather ledger fell on the floor. "What's this?" she said as she picked it up.

"That's Mr. Montgomery's," Liddy said. "He told me to hide it."

Cecilia came forward, taking the book from Mrs. Vance. "When did he tell you that?"

"That night."

"That night? The night he died?" Cecilia asked.

Tears welled up in Liddy's eyes. "I don't think of it," she said, turning away and running across the hall to the windows on the other side of the hall.

Mrs. Vance and Cecilia exchanged startled looks, then Mrs. Vance went to console Liddy as Julia came out of her room.

"What's going on?" she asked.

"I don't know," Cecilia said. "Mr. Montgomery asked Liddy to hide this ledger and she hid it in this cupboard." She touched the cupboard behind her.

"When was this?"

"Judging by Liddy's reaction by recalling the event, it was the night he died. I'm going to hide this in my room for now. We'll need to examine it after breakfast."

Julia nodded.

When Cecilia came back into the hall, she saw Julia had joined Mrs. Vance and Liddy by the window. "Shall we go to the dormitory to find something for Liddy to wear?" she asked.

"I think that is a good idea," said Mrs. Vance. "Come Liddy, dry your eyes now. It is a new day, and you are going to spend it with me. We can read stories, go outside, and do anything you want to do today. How would you like that?"

She nodded, but without her typical exuberance. Cecilia felt her heart cry for the child.

There were four women's dormitory rooms, each with four beds. Liddy led them to her room. She stopped outside the door. "Shh," she whispered. "Mrs. Johnson is always sleeping. I have to be quiet."

She carefully opened the door and walked past the first bed where an old, frail-looking woman snored gently. At the second bed, she carefully pulled a large, flattish trunk out from under her cot. Mrs. Vance helped her change out of her nightgown into one of the three dresses in the trunk while Julia made her bed. Cecilia looked around the room with curiosity. One other bed was neatly made, the fourth had clothes stuffed under the covers to resemble a person sleeping there. In the dark, it probably did and only in the light of day could the sham be clearly seen. Miss Dorn's bed, she assumed.

Mrs. Vance tidied Liddy's hair with a brush and a

hair ribbon from the trunk. In her clean clothes and with her dark brown hair in a braid down her back, Liddy resumed her cheerful demeanor. They followed her back out of the room and headed for breakfast in the old chapel.

Though Cecilia wanted to question Liddy more, she hesitated, loath to cause the child any additional grief. Perhaps the ledger would provide answers.

<h1 style="text-align:center">CHAPTER 19</h1>

<h2 style="text-align:center">BOYD RATCLIFFE</h2>

Mr. Ratcliffe possessed a well-to-do property. The grounds were scrupulously maintained with tight edgings and conformed hedges. The house was of moderate size; no ivy was allowed to grow up the sides and the numerous windows sparkled cleanly in the morning light. All in all, it was a handsome, wealthy estate. James had learned Mr. Ratcliffe was a banker. Now he saw he was a prosperous banker.

The large entry hall had niches in the walls with statuary of male nudes; many, copies of famous Roman and Greek pieces. Lining the stairway were cupids. James exchanged glances with Mr. Ramsay as they walked across the hall.

Ratcliffe's butler showed them into a shadowed library toward the back of the house. The butler went to the long, draped windows at the far end of the room and pushed open the dark-burgundy velvet drapes to let some morning light into the room. Smaller statues stood on pedestals in all corners of the room, and a bronze statue took pride of place on the corner of the desk.

"The master will see you shortly," the butler said before bowing and closing the door behind him.

"So, the posturing begins," James said softly as they sat down in front of the desk.

Mr. Ramsay smiled and crossed one lanky leg over the other, his hands clasped about his knee.

When the door opened to admit Mr. Ratcliffe, James and Mr. Ramsay rose.

"Gentlemen," Mr. Ratcliffe said, nodding to them as he went around the desk, running a hand across the arse of the statue on the desk before he sat. "Sir James, your note yesterday said you were sent up here by Mrs. Montgomery to understand all the circumstances regarding Mr. Montgomery's death, but I see you here with Mr. Ramsay."

His tone of voice was polite yet held an edge of irritation.

"I met Mr. Ramsay for the first time last night at the inn. He informed me of his intention to visit you as well. We thought it might be more convenient for you if we came together," James explained easily.

Mr. Ratcliffe nodded. "I am a busy man, so I accept that—but, Mr. Ramsay, why are you here?" he asked.

"Fer Mr. Montgomery's will," he said. "He made a new will last year."

Mr. Ratcliffe waived a hand dismissively. "I know. Malcolm told me. Drawn up in an insane asylum. No court will honor a document with lunatics as witnesses. The document we made up when old Mr. Montgomery revised his will, will stand. Besides, it's already been executed," he said with a deprecating laugh.

"Nay, ah think not," said Mr. Ramsay. He uncrossed his legs and looked earnestly at Mr. Ratcliffe. "That's why ah come ta talk ta you. He weren't dead and we knew that. What we executed were ol' Mr. Montgomery's will. Ah checked. Malcolm's is not filed. At the time it were the same as his father so it weren't an issue. Now it is."

Ratcliffe frowned. Then he harrumphed. He leaned back in his chair. "No matter the witnesses were all lunatics."

"Nay, ya cannae say that," disagreed Mr. Ramsay. "Miss Hammond and Mrs. Worcham were amongst the witnesses."

Ratcliffe laughed. "Well, I wouldn't say Mrs. Worcham is totally sane, look at all those wigs she dons. And Miss Hammond, a servant? I don't even know if she can read!"

"Excuse me, gentlemen, for interrupting. I am confused," said James. "I am not conversant with either will. Why does it matter which version of the will? What changes did Mr. Montgomery make that would be objectionable to you, Mr. Ratcliffe? He still leaves everything to his wife and children, is that not correct?"

Mr. Ramsay turned to James. "Ye be correct, Sir James. Essentially the wills be the same. In the new will, Mrs. Montgomery has more of a say with regards to her funds, but the biggest change is in the namin' of the executor and guardian. Currently, it be Mr. Ratcliffe. In the new will, Malcom named the Earl of Soothcoor as executor and guardian. And had mi write in the will an unusual request that if the earl be unwed at the time of Mr. Montgomery's death, that he marry his widow."

"That won't save his neck from the noose!" exclaimed Mr. Ratcliffe.

"You are sure of your accusations of murder against Soothcoor?" James asked.

"He had motive and opportunity," Ratcliffe said flatly, crossing his arms over his chest.

"His motive?" queried Mr. Ramsay.

"That he wanted to marry Mrs. Montgomery, of course."

"Excuse me, Mr. Ratcliffe," Mr. Ramsay said, sitting straighter. "Before the earl arrived and met with Malcolm, ah met with Malcolm and he sent me ta Scotland with papers ta petition for a divorce. He told Soothcoor that. There goes yur motive."

James looked down at his hands, careful to keep his face neutral. Ramsay was gambling that Mr. Ratcliffe didn't know Mrs. Montgomery was enceinte.

"I understand Mr. Montgomery died by drowning," James said carefully. "Can we be certain he didn't commit suicide?"

"Impossible," snapped Ratcliffe.

"Were there any signs of struggle on him? I would have thought that the Archie personality I've heard about would have fought back,"

Ratcliffe snorted. "There are no such things as other personalities, that has always been Malcolm acting."

"How do you know that? Is that Dr. Worcham's medical diagnosis?"

"Ha! Gentlemen, I don't believe Dr. Worcham is a true medical professional. He is a scammer. He used his wife's dowry to buy Camden House then set about to make a name for himself in the sanatorium business. It's a lucrative business with the right clientele. Unfortunately, as his banker, I know he is stretched thin. He took on too many non-paying customers, like that girl who died last year. It's cheating his investors and draining him dry."

"If you thought him a charlatan, why was Mr. Montgomery staying there?" James asked.

"Don't get me wrong, Camden House has its purposes. It was—and can be again—a good investment. It's just when Dr. Worcham takes himself too seriously and gives services away, it's value decreases. That's why I arranged for Camden House to have a superintendent, someone to rein in expenses and report back to me on what happens at the sanatorium. Dr. Worcham didn't dare object."

"Are you one of the investors?"

"I put the investment package together."

"And, no doubt, recommended Camden House to Mr. Montgomery Senior when you heard Malcolm was at Autumnvale and wanted to leave that facility."

"Yes," he drawled, obviously pleased with himself. "Malcolm didn't know I lived so close when he agreed to come here. He thought Autumnvale was too close to his father and his family. He didn't want visitors."

"He wouldna come here if he knew you were close," Mr. Ramsay said dismissively.

"No doubt." Mr. Ratcliffe smirked.

The library door opened. "Boyd—Oh, excuse me, I didn't know you had company," said a short, gently graying blonde woman from the doorway.

James and Mr. Ramsay stood up.

"It's all right Karen, this is Sir James Branstoke, and you know Cameron Ramsay, don't you?" he said as he walked around the desk to his wife's side.

"Yes, I do. And nice to meet you, Sir James," the woman said briefly, scarcely sparing them a glance before turning back to her husband. "Boyd, I just wanted to tell you that the new statue you ordered has arrived and the carter wants to know where it goes," she said, apologetically.

"Excellent!" Mr. Ratcliffe said, rubbing his hands together. "We are finished here, aren't we gentlemen?" he asked, walking dismissively past them toward the door.

"Yes," James said. "Thank you for your time."

"Pleasure, pleasure. Give my best to Mrs. Montgomery. Must see to my new treasure," he said, striding out the door.

"I'm sorry gentlemen." Mrs. Ratcliffe twisted her hands together. She was an attractive, though timid older woman. "He has been waiting for this new statue for a week now," she explained. "He loves his statues. He says there is something about the feel of the smooth marble under his hand he can't get enough of. He likes to caress them while he's thinking," she said. "It helps with his concentration."

James and Mr. Ramsay collected their hats, gloves, and greatcoats from a footman in the hall. They said their adieus to the obviously nervous woman as they went out the door. Outside, they saw a coatless Mr. Ratcliffe giving orders to the carter as he uncarted the statue. As the wood enclosure, and then the canvas tarp fell away from the statue, they could see that the statue was another cupid.

Mr. Ramsay drew in a deep breath. James looked at him. The man shook his head, his lips compressed in a tight line.

They got in their coach and started back to The New Bell Inn.

"That new statue," Mr. Ramsay said after a moment. "It looks like Malcolm." He shuddered. "Malcolm as a cupid. Why?"

"I'm beginning to have an idea," James said grimly, "and it would explain a lot. We should pay a visit on the magistrate."

CHAPTER 20

AGAIN WITH THE MAGISTRATE

Magistrate Squire Eccleston's butler informed James and Mr. Ramsay the squire was out walking his fields and obligingly pointed them in the direction the squire had taken. They set off to find him. Once they were past the neat hedges and trees around the manor, it was easy to see the magistrate in the distance due to the flat nature of the former fen lands. He was in the company of two other men, walking along rows of young wheat plants, gesturing as he talked. Getting to the magistrate was not straightforward. It involved jumping newly dug drainage ditches between wheat rows. James silently commended the man for planting another harvest of winter wheat and having ditches dug to drain away excess rain. But such attention to solutions for his farm should not come at Soothcoor's expense.

One of the men the magistrate talked with saw them coming and pointed out their approach to the magistrate. Eccleston stopped and, arms akimbo, awaited them.

"Sir James," the magistrate said stiffly."

"Magistrate," James returned. "This is Mr. Ramsay, Mr. Montgomery's solicitor."

"Mr. Ramsay, this is Squire Eccleston, magistrate for the area."

Mr. Ramsay acknowledged the introduction.

"Do dead men need solicitors?" the magistrate asked caustically.

"'Tis the solicitor's obligation ta see that the terms o' the will are adhered ta," Mr. Ramsay politely said.

"I was under the understanding Mr. Montgomery didn't have a will," the magistrate said.

"Och, he did. Someone led you to think incorrectly," Mr. Ramsay said pleasantly.

"Ah. When did he draw up the will?"

"Over a year ago, February," Mr. Ramsay said.

Eccleston frowned and bit his lower lip. "While he was a patient here."

"Yes."

"Can a man suffering a mental condition legally draw up a will?" he asked.

"Dr. Worcham can attest to his mental state. Ah will say, in the discussion ah had with Dr. Worcham before we drew up the document, he considered Mr. Montgomery sane unless one of his other personalities were evident. They were not. I dealt solely with Malcolm."

"And the witnesses?"

There were three. All at Mr. Montgomery's request: Mrs. Worcham, Miss Hammond, and Mrs. Vance."

"Mrs. Worcham was a witness?"

Mr. Ramsay nodded. "The executor named in the new will is Alaister Sedgewick, the Earl of Soothcoor."

"My prisoner?"

"Yes. There is even an unusual paragraph in the will suggesting the earl marry his widow if he is not, himself, wed before Mr. Montgomery dies."

"Most unusual."

"The earl had no reason to want to kill Mr. Montgomery. And there are witnesses who will testify he returned to the inn in the same clothes he left in, and, as I told you before, they were not wet."

"You are thinking this is reason enough to let him go?" the magistrate asked.

"I do," said Sir James.

The magistrate frowned. "Possible. I say you need more than dry clothes. The first assize will occur at the beginning of next week. He can remain in jail until then, and let the judges decide if he should be freed or not—or you can identify another suspect for the murder with proof before then. Now excuse me gentlemen, I must continue the review you interrupted. I don't expect to see you again unless you have another suspect with solid evidence." He turned away from them, signaled the two men who had stood away while he talked to Sir James and Mr. Ramsay to return to his side.

"Well, that did not go as successfully as we might have wished," Mr. Ramsay said.

"No, but about what I expected after my last conversation with him. I'd like to go to Camden House and discover if Cecilia has been any more successful, however I know it is near the lunch hour for the patients. Let's return to The New Bell Inn. I can check on how the victims of Baron Stackpoole's malicious honey illness are recovering," James suggested.

Mr. Ramsay agreed.

AFTER BREAKFAST the women returned to their wing. No one had approached them at breakfast about their activities the previous night and Matron Mildred was not to be seen. Nor were there any whispered discussions concerning Miss Dorn or Mr. Turnbull-Minchin. The lack of gossip struck Cecilia as unnatural.

She said as much to Julia as she stopped before the door to her room.

"I agree. Most odd."

"I'll tell you what it means," interjected Mrs. Vance. "It means Mr. Turnbull-Minchin has not been shown the door, that's what it means. This is to be swept under the carpet like a lazy maid might do to an errant bit of mud."

Cecilia frowned. "I sincerely hope not."

"Harrumph," Mrs. Vance voiced. She turned to Liddy. "Come child, let's go to the library. I should like to hear you read."

"Can we go for a walk outside afterward?"

"If the weather stays as nice as it is now, I should think we can," Mrs. Vance assured her.

"Good. And I know just the book I shall read to you, too!" she said, skipping toward the stairs."

"Slowly, my dear. This is not the floor for hoydens," she reminded her.

"Oh, I don't know about that," said Julia softly. "We were fairly hoydenish last night."

Cecilia laughed. "Yes." She looked about the hall. "There are no staff about to see, come in my room with me and we'll look over that ledger Liddy hid." She opened the door to her room.

"Yes!" Julia agreed as she quickly followed her into the room.

Cecilia locked the door behind her, not wanting anyone to barge into the room like Matron had done the other day in Julia's room, while they studied the book.

Cecilia pulled the ledger out from beneath the bed mattress and laid it on top of the mattress. She opened the cover. "It's from the beginning of this year."

"A current ledger? I'm surprised there hasn't been a hue and cry!"

"Unless it's a duplicate," Cecilia offered.

"What do you mean? Why would there be a duplicate?"

"There can be the real books, then there can be the books for show."

"Books for show?"

"Yes, depending on the purpose for the duplicate books. My husband told me about such practices. His cousin was nearly beggared by a thieving estate steward who kept two sets of books, one showing the actual financial condition of his inheritance and one showing a fairytale of profit. His cousin has worked hard to recover the family fortunes, selling what he could and living frugally. James bought one of his unentailed properties from him because he had good memories of it as a child, and I'm glad he did. I love Summerworth Park, our home in Kent."

"But back to this book, there must be something suspicious in its pages for him to instruct Liddy to hide it. I don't think he would have put her in position to do so unless it was important."

Julia agreed. "He truly delighted in the child."

They flipped the page.

"It is a supplies and merchandise purchase ledger, the money out ledger," Cecilia said.

"What's the most recent entry?" Julia asked.

Cecilia turned several pages until she found a blank page. "Hmm, it appears to stop in March."

"Turn some more pages. Maybe they just skipped a few pages and then resumed."

Cecilia turned several more pages. "No-o—Oh, wait. There is writing further in. How odd." She looked at the entries. These were not like the earlier entries.

"Here is a recording of money coming in." She read the flowing lines of script. "I see names and then what looks like abbreviations. Can you make them out?" She pushed the book toward Julia.

"A few are repeating, like this one from Enoch Vance that repeats on the first of the month."

"Mrs. Vance's nephew?"

"Yes. It's not much, only three pounds per month. Others don't seem to have a pattern or are only once. How odd." She turned a few more pages to see if there was anything else. She found an open letter. Cecilia pulled it out of the book to read.

"It's from a Mr. Yellin."

"Mrs. Yellin is in the other ladies wing," Julia said. "I don't know her well. I believe she suffers from depression following the birth of her son."

"Mr. Yellin is complaining about a rate increase of three pounds per month and demanding to know how much longer his wife will be at Camden House and questioning if anything is being done to make her better."

"A rate increase? I have not heard of a rate increase," Julia said. "Let's page back to see if there is any indication of a payment from my husband." She quickly scanned previous pages. "Ah—Here is one with Stackpoole next to it for five pounds!"

"Is the code next to the entry the same as the code next to the entry from Enoch Vance and Mr. Yellin?" Cecilia asked.

"Let's see..." Julia compared the pages. "Identical. Why would there be separate entries for rate increase amounts?"

"I'd wager my best earrings that Dr. Worcham did not authorize an increase or know anything about these additional monies coming in."

"You think Mr. Turnbull-Minchin has been embezzling this way?"

"I do," Cecilia said. "We need to get this book to Mr.

Quetal. He should be able to tell us more about what these entries mean."

"Do you think he is stable enough to do so?"

"I do. What I think he needs is a dose of confidence. He strikes me as an intelligent young man. Giving him an analytical task like this would boost his morale, return some of his confidence."

Someone knocked on Cecilia's door. "Lady Branstoke?"

Cecilia quickly closed the ledger and stuck under the mattress again. "Yes?" she said as she ran to the door.

"Might you know where Lady Stackpoole is? Her son is here to see her."

Cecilia threw back the lock and opened the door. "She's here. We were just having a comfortable chat."

"My son is here? In the great hall?" Julia said, forgetting her conversation with Cecilia and swiftly leaving her room and following the maid who came with the news.

Cecilia didn't blame her for how she ran off. She slowly followed her down the stairs, thoughts and questions crashing about in her mind. She needed to figure out how to get the book into Mr. Quetal's hands. She finally decided she needed to find Mrs. Vance and Liddy and headed for the library. They might have ideas. She would start looking for answers by speaking with them.

There weren't many people in the library that morning. Cecilia surmised the rare sunny day drew them outside. She immediately saw Liddy and Mrs. Vance by the bank of windows at the far end of the library. Liddy had a large book clutched in both hands, but she wasn't reading. The two were earnestly talking.

"May I join you," Cecilia asked, sitting down next to Liddy.

"Please do," Mrs. Vance said. "Liddy has been telling me the most amazing things. Truly amazing, haven't you, my dear?" Mrs. Vance said.

Liddy shrugged her thin shoulders. "I was just telling her about my home. We lived with my uncle Edgar in a house bigger than Camden House. A house bigger than the castle in this story book," she said, holding up the book she held. "Bigger than anything!"

"That is big," Cecilia said. "Houses that big have names. Did your house have a name?"

Liddy nodded eagerly. "Yes. It was called Ellinbourne. Same as Uncle Edgar."

"Ellinbourne! Oh, gracious," Cecilia said, suddenly at a loss for words. Ellinbourne was the ancestral home of the Dukes of Ellinbourne. She knew the current duke—not well, but she knew him well enough to enjoy a casual conversation with the man at a ball or party. Now that she knew the closeness of his relationship to Liddy, she knew he would not send his young cousin— for that is what Cecilia now knew Liddy must be—to a sanatorium to hide her away.

"You know the name?" Mrs. Vance asked.

"Yes. Liddy, does your mother still live at Ellinbourne?"

She shook her head. "No, she didn't get on with Aunt Patience and her daughters when they moved in." Liddy made a face. "I didn't either. They were always giggling and talking about clothes. They never talked to me or wanted to play with me."

"I imagine they were older than you," Cecilia said to her sympathetically.

Liddy noddy sadly. "So, Mama took me to Bath with her. There was no one to play with there either, and Mama wouldn't let me out of the house. Then Mama got the idea she would go to London and send me here."

"That is a sad story," Cecilia said. "Don't you think so, Mrs. Vance?"

"I do."

"We need to find a way to give it a happy ending like the stories in your book," Cecilia said.

"All right," Liddy said. "Can we go outside now?"

Cecilia started to laugh at the exuberance of children, then her attention was caught on the size of the book Liddy held. It looked to be the same size as the ledger book under the mattress of her bed. "Let's take the book upstairs so we might read it later. Don't you think that's a good idea?"

"Can we?"

"I don't see why not, do you Mrs. Vance?"

"No, no I don't."

"Hold tight to the book," Cecilia said, pleased with the plan forming in her head to get the book to Mr. Quetal to examine. She stood up and took Liddy's hand. "I think we should go now, before Dr. Worcham finds us and reminds us we're supposed to be cleaning Mr. Montgomery's room."

Liddy giggled at that.

"Mrs. Vance, are you coming, too? Julia and I discovered something you might be interested in learning about, and after we put Liddy's book away safely, we'll go outside—for that is a much better location for such discussions."

Mrs. Vance perked up. "I believe I shall," she said. She joined Cecilia and Liddy threading their way through the library toward the great hall and the sun beckoning them outside.

Once outside, Liddy led them to the right around the building. Cecilia had not been that way, habitually walking around to the left. The landscaping was thicker to the right with more trees and large bushes. Liddy walked steadily on.

"You walk like a young lady with a purpose," teased Cecilia. "Where are you headed, Liddy?"

"To Mr. Montgomery's place."

"Mr. Montgomery's place? What do you mean?"

"You said you wanted to see my treasure box, didn't you?" she asked.

"Yes."

"I'll show you," she said patiently. "You, too, Mrs. Vance. Mr. Montgomery showed me his special place in case something happened to him. Now I'll show you in case something happens to me."

Cecilia drew in a sharp breath between her teeth. That this child should even consider something might happen to her, to say it so calmly, chilled her soul.

There were many people walking the grounds on this side of the property and sitting on oiled canvas cloths under the trees, chatting or sketching. "Liddy, would you stop a moment please?" Cecilia said.

Liddy stopped and looked up at Cecilia, confused. "Why?"

"There are many people about. If you are to show us a special place, perhaps that should be done when there are less people about. You don't want them to discover the special place do you?"

"I guess not, but I wanted you to see..."

"And we will," Cecilia promised.

"Then we might as well go in through Mr. Montgomery's room," Liddy said.

"What do you mean?"

"That terrace door leads into Mr. Montgomery's room," she explained.

"I heard there was a door here, but I thought it locked. You mean it is accessible?" Cecilia asked.

She nodded. "We went in and out that way all the time."

"Perhaps that is also best left to fewer people about,"

Cecilia said, exchanging a surprised look with Mr. Vance.

"And you know, Liddy, after our adventures last night, if we did more adventuring today without Lady Stackpoole, she would be sad," Mrs. Vance said.

The child sighed, shrugging her expressive shoulders again. "I guess so," she said resignedly.

"Let's see if we can find her. She probably went left around the building. There is a bench she likes to sit on over there. Her son is here, you know."

"Fine," Liddy said, turning about, tromping sullenly to the other side of the building.

They walked to Julia's favored seating place but did not see her. They decided to go back inside and see if Lady Stackpoole was there.

In the great hall, Cecilia stopped to ask the majordomo if he had seen Lady Stackpoole.

"She's in the library, my lady," that worthy said. "And she said to tell you if I saw you that she would await you there."

"Well, that was easy enough," Mrs. Vance said.

Cecilia laughed. "We haven't found her yet!"

"If that is where she said she would be, that is where she will be," Mrs. Vance responded.

As they approached the library, its door opened. To their surprise it was Mr. Turnbull-Minchin.

"Ladies," he said, nodding to them as he passed them by. And he looked quite pleased with himself, the corner of his lips quirking up in a small smile. Mrs. Vance looked ready to take him to task. Cecilia laid her hand on Mrs. Vance's arm, encouraging restraint. She looked across the room. Julia appeared as equally upset as Mrs. Vance. Cecilia led Mrs. Vance and Liddy over to her.

"What is he doing here?" she hissed when they came up to Julia.

"He has not been fired," Julia said. "He just escorted a woman and her husband in to see Dr. Worcham in the parlor. And when he came back out, he looked right at me and laughed."

"Laughed at you? Why did he laugh at you?"

"Probably because of the shocked expression on my face."

Cecilia shook her head. "Let's go to Mr. Montgomery's chamber to straighten it, as Dr. Worcham requested last night."

"I'm sure there won't be anything there to find if Mr. Turnbull-Minchin has been using the room."

"Perhaps not…He may not have known all the proper places to look. I'm sure our Liddy does."

Liddy nodded then scrunched her face up and giggled. "I'll bet he didn't find the boxes."

"Boxes?"

"Mr. Montgomery made a special place for my box, too," Liddy said proudly. "Not my treasure box, my second-best box."

"Your second-best box?"

"Uh-huh."

"That was quite kind of him," Mrs. Vance said, exchanging speaking looks with Cecilia and Julia over Liddy's head.

"Mr. Montgomery was very smart," she said.

"I just wish he had been smart enough not to get himself killed," Mrs. Vance muttered.

Cecilia frowned at her. She shrugged back.

They passed Mr. Quetal entering as they left the library. "Mr. Quetal, if anyone comes looking for us, we have gone to do the task Dr. Worcham gave us last night," Cecilia told him.

"What task? Where?"

"Clean Mr. Montgomery's room."

They went out the library, turned left, then through

the door near the end of the hall that led to the treatment rooms, the estate room, and Mr. Montgomery's room, Liddy leading the way. The gas lamps high on the walls had been turned up for daytime, yet there remained a gloomy feeling to the hall without windows, and just doors on either side, framed in dark wood. No paintings or sketches or anything hung on the walls.

Liddy reached the door to Mr. Montgomery's room and impatiently awaited them, rocking from foot to foot. She grinned as she threw open the door, her eyes dancing.

Immediately Cecilia could understand why.

Light flooded the room from a wall of nearly floor to ceiling windows. The glass was similar to the glass in the dining hall, watery diamond panes with occasional colored diamonds of glass. This clear glass appeared so watery it was difficult to see through. Near the ceiling were colorful bible stories.

At first, Cecilia did not see the door Liddy spoke of, then she discerned it from the windows on either side. The room was unlike any other Cecilia had seen at Camden House. A large wardrobe took up much of one wall and it, like the walls and all the interior woodwork, had been painted a stark white. In contrast, the cushions, the rug, the drapes that were tied back, and the bed linens, were all brightly colored. The room appeared double the size of the room Cecilia slept in. There was a desk, a card table, and a small couch.

Unfortunately, it had been, as Cecilia feared, ransacked. Bookshelves and drawers empty, the wardrobe open, one door sagging on a broken hinge, and everything knee deep on the floor.

"What!" protested Mr. Vance. She walked around tossed pillows and books. "This is outrageous!"

"That is a mild statement to how I feel," said Julia, her hands on her hips as she looked around the room.

Liddy, standing beside her, copied her stance and manner.

"Liddy, I know it is a mess in here, but is your hiding place safe?" Cecilia asked.

"I think so," she said. "But we have to move all this stuff out of the way over here first." She waved her hands toward the piles of books, statues, and cushions on the floor before the bookcase.

Cecilia studied the empty bookshelf behind the piles. She picked up a cushion and returned it to the couch. "Then let's get to it," she said, picking up a copy of Aristotle and placing it on the bookcase.

They made quick work of getting all the books put back on the shelves, though not with attention to neatness or any particular order. Julia was picking up the shards of a broken vase when there was a knock on the door.

"Excuse me," said Mr. Quetal, opening the door enough to poke his head in. "Dr. Worcham said I should find you here. I'm to tell you it is time for lunch."

"Thank you, Mr. Quetal. I'm afraid we all lost track of time. There is so much to do here." Cecilia said.

"This is the task Dr. Worcham gave you, to straighten Mr. Montgomery's room?"

"Yes. Someone has been in here in a terrible temper and thrown everything around."

"Do you think they were looking for something?" he asked

Cecilia shrugged, her eyes wide. "Possibly. Who's to say?—Oh! I have a project for you," she told him, her eyes now dancing with excitement. "We can discuss it at dinner tonight, is that amenable to you?"

He looked confused. "I—I suppose so."

"Excellent," she said. "We'll talk later then." She

turned away from him, leaving him noticeably be-fuddled.

"Come, ladies. We can return after lunch. I think we have done well. Shouldn't take much more time, I'm thinking," she said for his benefit. It was well they hadn't tried to find Mr. Montgomery's hiding places yet. They would have to devise a plan to make sure they were not disturbed—or at least have adequate warning if someone approached.

After lunch, Cecilia suggested they go outside for some fresh air before returning to Mr. Montgomery's room. "Let's go back toward Mr. Montgomery's room from the outside. "I'd like to see the room and the door from the outside."

They went around right to that side of the building. This time, not as many patient residents were in the area, as it was shadier, and therefore colder in the after-noon. The grass was not scythed as well in this area, either, and the rushes along the canal grew higher. Ce-cilia walked toward the canal that ran along the back-side of Camden House. A small thicket of trees and bracken grew at the end of the island where the canals met. It looked like it had, at one time, been as well tended as the rest of the grounds.

"This is where Ratman and Archie got in an argu-ment," Liddy said. "He told me to go back to the room. I didn't want to go. I was so scared!" she said, looking down at the ground around them. She looked up. "Then I heard Mr. Turnbull-Minchin yelling, and Dr. Worcham shouting for Mr. Montgomery. I knew the doctor would be mad if he caught me out here; it was past curfew. Archie told me to go through Mr. Mont-gomery's door."

Together, they walked toward the door to Mr. Montgomery's room. "I hid here, I couldn't see much. But I heard them."

"Heard who?" Cecilia asked casually.

"Archie, Mr. Turnbull-Minchin, Dr. Worcham, and that other man Mr. Montgomery didn't like, Ratman."

"Mr. Ratcliffe," Cecilia said.

"Yes, him. They were all yelling at each other. Dr. Worcham, trying to get them to calm down. Archie, shouting at Mr. Turnbull-Minchin and that Ratman, and them yelling at him and each other. I ran inside, because it reminded me of Mommy and Daddy yelling at each other all the time. It was awful!"

"I'm so sorry," Cecilia said, putting her arm around Liddy's shoulders.

"Why did they always have to yell at each other?"

"I don't know, sweetheart."

"Mr. Montgomery said he didn't either. He never yelled. Only Archie did. It was Archie who was fighting."

"How could you tell?" Cecilia asked.

"His voice was different."

"Oh." Cecilia didn't know what to make of that statement about one of Mr. Montgomery's 'others.'

They walked up to the door. Cecilia was surprised to notice she could not see into the room from the outside the way she'd been able to see out from the inside with the way the glass diamond panes had been cut and shaped. Perhaps if there were light emitting from the room it would be different., With light only on the outside, the inside was hard to discern.

Cecilia opened the door. "No!" Liddy protested, eyes wide.

"No, what, Liddy?"

"It should have been locked. I locked it so they couldn't get me."

"Perhaps whoever searched Mr. Montgomery's room left by way of this outside door."

"Oh-h-h. Yes, they could do that, I guess."

"How about you go in this way now so you can lock it and Julia, Mrs. Vance, and I can come through the house."

She frowned longer, her face a reflection of changing thoughts and feeling tumbling through her mind.

"What is it, Liddy?"

"I want to see if the key is still here."

"What do you mean?"

"The key Mr. Montgomery always hid outside."

Cecilia looked around. At the moment, there were no other residents in the vicinity save Julia and Mrs. Vance, and it looked like they were discouraging others from coming their way.

"All right, quick, quick, check it."

Liddy went to where the windows ended and picked up something off the ground, then she put it back down and came back to Cecilia all smiles.

"You were right. They must have come out the door. The key is still in its hiding place."

"You go in this way and lock the door after you."

"And I'll hide like I did that night, and you can see if you can find me!" she said.

"You hid in Mr. Montgomery's room the night he died?"

"I didn't know what else to do."

"Liddy, why haven't you told anyone about what happened that night?"

She squirmed a bit, shrugging her shoulders, her face again going through different expressions of guilt, sadness and confusion. Cecilia patiently waited. "I was afraid," she finally said, her voice cracking and her eyes welling with tears. "And Dr. Worcham was there."

Cecilia sighed and hugged her again. "You probably did right. I understand. All right, you wait in here for us, and we'll come around through the house."

She nodded and sniffed.

Cecilia handed her a handkerchief.

Liddy wiped her eyes. "I don't want anyone to see me crying again."

"It's all right. I'll be back soon."

Cecilia told Julia and Mrs. Vance what she had learned from Liddy.

"Poor child," Mrs. Vance said.

"But you are gaining her trust, Cecilia, and she is telling you. This is good," Julia said.

"Probably because I wasn't here when these events happened. Did you have any problems dissuading others from coming over this way?" Cecilia asked as they walked back to the house.

Julia laughed. "No. We just stood in the middle of the path talking, and rather than pushing past us, the few that came this way took another path."

"We do have polite people here at Camden House," Mrs. Vance said.

Cecilia and Julia laughed.

They waved to Mr. Quetal and Mr. Hobart as they entered the house and continued on talking easily together. Cecilia didn't feel particularly easy, and she doubted Julia or Mrs. Vance did either. Through unspoken agreement, they maintained a worry-free demeanor for the benefit of others.

In Mr. Montgomery's room, there was no sign of Liddy.

"Do you think Liddy went upstairs," asked Mrs. Vance. "Sometimes children forget what they are supposed to be doing."

Cecilia shook her head. "No. I think she is doing exactly what she said she did the night Mr. Montgomery died. She is hiding."

"In here?" Mrs. Vance said.

Cecilia smiled. "Yes, in here. No one found her that night. I think she wants to see if we can find her."

They'd been all over the room as they'd picked up Mr. Montgomery's belongings strewn everywhere. "We are obviously missing something. It has to be a space big enough for someone her size to hide. That leaves the wardrobe, walls, or floor. Remember, this used to be a monastery."

"You're thinking there would be a priest's hole?" Julia asked.

"No, not a priest hole. I am thinking it has to be something older, like a closet of some kind where a religious house would store or hide their valuable religious goods like gold goblets and crosses, their physical wealth."

"And an inside wall," offered Julia.

"Yes. This fireplace wall is shared with the room we found Mrs. Worcham sewing, correct?"

"Yes, it has beautiful windows like these, without a door leading outside," said Mrs. Vance.

"And a fireplace in the same position," said Julia.

"What about the opposite wall. What is that wall shared with?"

Julia narrowed her eyes as she thought. "I believe that is one of the staff gathering rooms," she said slowly.

Mrs. Vance nodded. "Their dining hall, I think."

Julia agreed.

"And this wall behind us is shared with the hallway and a trunk room," Cecilia said, moving to the far corner of the room and its tall bookcase. She pushed against the bookcase. It was solidly installed. She started to examine the cornice work, wrapping against the wood in places for hollow sounds. Then they all heard a quiet, muffled giggle. Cecilia smiled and looked at Julia and Mrs. Vance.

"Maybe I'm wrong to think anything could be beyond this wall," she said loudly. "Maybe she fooled us and hid in one of the treatment rooms until we were in here and she has run up stairs to share her giggles with others."

"I wouldn't put it past the clever child," Julia said. "Let's go see if we can find her upstairs."

They all walked loudly to the door, opened it, then sharply closed it, staying by the door.

They heard another giggle, then slowly the bookcase swung away from the wall and Liddy came out.

"Found you!" declared Cecilia, coming over to Liddy and giving her a hug.

"You cheated," Liddy accused.

"No, we didn't. You giggled, and we heard you. Let me see this little space," Cecilia said, going around Liddy to peer into a long, narrow space. There were narrow shelves along one wall and, at the end, Cecilia thought there was another doorway. This one would lead to the estate room. "So, this is where you hid your treasure box?"

"Someone with heavy boots is coming down the hall!" Julia warned.

Cecilia quickly shut the passage door and pushed Liddy before her further into the room away from the bookcase door.

It was the majordomo. "Lady Branstoke, your husband is here."

"Thank you, I'll be right up," she said. She looked at the others in the room. "Do you know if we are supposed to put fresh bed linens on the bed?"

Julia and Mrs. Vance shook their heads.

"I'll ask when I'm in the great hall," she said, following the suspicious majordomo out of the room.

CHAPTER 21

JAMES MEETS THE LADIES

Cecilia saw her husband through the wrought iron gate separating the hallway and the great hall. She had to smile at her husband's curiosity. This time, he was studying the architectural elements of the room.

She pulled the gate open and hurried toward him. "James!" she said happily.

He grabbed her hands and kissed the backs of both. He smiled down at her. "I think you are looking better. Are you resting?"

She laughed. "No, not as you would wish me to," she admitted. "However, I am feeling better. I am recovering, I promise you."

"And your cough?"

"Much reduced," she promised him. "I believe I am too busy to cough and that is my secret for recovery."

"Cecilia!" James fairly growled with consternation. "You were still supposed to take the opportunity for rest."

She laughed again. "No lecturing, please," she said as she tucked her arm in his. "Let's go outside, take advantage of the rare, pleasant weather this afternoon and meander about while you tell me what has been going on beyond Camden House."

"Mr. Ramsay and I visited Mr. Ratcliffe and the magistrate this morning. The magistrate realizes he was hasty to arrest Soothcoor, and there is reasonable doubt as to his guilt, but he won't release him. Says he's leaving it in the hands of the assize, which should be next week for this area."

Cecilia compressed her lips as she nodded, a furrow between her brows.

"Our meeting with Mr. Ratcliffe was also enlightening. He's an odd one. He collects statues of nude men and boys. Primarily Greek replicas and cupids. His wife told us that running his hand across the marble is soothing to him. We witnessed him caressing the arse of a bronze statue on his desk."

Cecilia looked up at James. "Seriously?"

"Seriously. And when we left, he was taking delivery of a new cupid with the face, Mr. Ramsay assures me, of Malcolm Montgomery."

Cecilia shuddered. "I don't know how Malcolm Montgomery's mother could countenance that. She is the woman married to Mr. Ratcliffe, correct?"

"Yes. Worse, we discovered Mr. Ratcliffe controls Camden House."

Cecilia nodded. "I know."

"You know that?"

"We deduced that," she amended.

"We?" he queried.

"Lady Stackpoole, Mrs. Vance, and I, with confirmation from Mrs. Worcham. She is unhappy with the control Mr. Ratcliffe now has over her husband. And she does not like Mr. Turnbull-Minchin, the man Mr. Ratcliffe put in place as the superintendent. I will tell you; he is a caitiff. We heard him having relations in Mr. Montgomery's old room and saw it was reported to Dr. Worcham. The doctor captured him and locked him in a treatment room. We thought that would be the last of him. This morning, we find him back at his old position as if nothing had occurred—except for the smirks he sends our way."

James frowned. "He had better not lay a hand on you."

She shook her head. "He won't. It appears Mr. Montgomery was suspicious of him, too. He took a ledger from the estate room that appears to show he was billing families of patients for additional services on the side. Those amounts are not part of the sanatorium regular books and I'd wager go directly into his own pocket."

"You think he is betraying the man who put him in that position to spy and manage things for him?"

"Yes."

"That's rich and rather fitting."

"The first assize of the quarter for this area is next week."

Cecilia took in a deep breath then let it out slowly. "All right. Then it is a good thing we are near to determining his murderers."

"Murderers?"

"Possibly, I believe so. Proving guilt will be the challenge," she said, gently leading him the way Liddy had taken her that morning.

"What have you learned, Cecilia?" James asked severely.

She stopped near the wild thicket of trees and the tall rushes at the canal edge that Liddy had led her to. "Liddy told me that here is where Mr. Ratcliffe got into an argument with Mr. Montgomery. Mr. Montgomery sent her away, since it was after curfew, and to go into Camden House through his room. He had a door to the outside. Liddy did as he told her, but not before she also heard Mr. Turnbull-Minchin and Dr. Worcham join in the arguing. That scared her and she did go inside. She said she didn't see anything that subsequently happened."

"You say Dr. Worcham, Mr. Ratcliffe, and Mr. Turnbull-Minchin were all out here?"

"Yes."

James studied the area. It had been ten days since Mr. Montgomery died. Little evidence would remain of a fight in the area. It was an area that would likely not be seen as it was at an odd corner to the house. He frowned.

"Show me where Liddy went into the building."

"This way." Cecilia led him along the canal as it paralleled the far side of the building. She was careful to encourage her husband to appear nonchalant as they passed the library windows so as not to call attention to themselves. Past the library, Cecilia cut in toward the building and the bank of windows that were for Mr. Montgomery's room. She looked about then hurried her husband to the door and tapped lightly on the glass. Mrs. Vance opened the door to them.

"Welcome, Sir James, I'm Mrs. Hilda Vance," Mrs. Vance said as she shut the door behind them.

"Pleasure," he responded.

"This is Lady Julia Stackpoole," Cecilia said drawing him further into the room. "And this is Miss Lydia Wingate." Cecilia smiled at Liddy as she caressed the back of her head. "We call her Liddy. She knew Mr. Montgomery very well. We have learned a great deal from her."

"Ladies, I am happy to make your acquaintance," James said bowing to them. "This was Mr. Montgomery's room?" He looked about the room. "It appears someone was certainly looking for something in here."

"We've been tasked with straightening the room,"

Julia said, "but, all we have managed to do so far is pick the books off the floor, put them haphazardly back on the shelves, and start picking up broken glass and porcelain."

James looked at the floor. "Someone had a tantrum with the fragile objects in here."

"More like a rage," Mrs. Vance offered. "Very naughty." She bent down to pick up a broken porcelain dog.

"Oh, no!" Liddy cried, coming over to Mrs. Vance. "They broke Weston!" She took the dog from Mrs. Vance.

"Weston?" Cecilia asked.

"That was Mr. Montgomery's dog," she said, cradling the porcelain pieces in her small hands. Her lips quivered. "Why did they have to fight with Mr. Montgomery? He just did what Dr. Worcham asked him," she said, tears trailing down her cheeks.

The others in the room looked at each other, then back at Liddy.

"What do you mean, child," Mrs. Vance said gently.

"I want to look in that room myself!" they heard the loud voice of Mr. Turnbull-Minchin from out in the hall.

"The ladies are straightening it!" Dr. Worcham protested.

"More likely finding things to steal," argued Mr. Turnbull-Minchin.

Cecilia dragged her husband toward the corner of the bookcase and looked frantically for the mechanism Liddy used to open the hidden hall. Julia reached around her to press the small hidden lever. The bookcase swung open. Cecilia pushed James into the narrow space and joined him inside. Julia closed the bookcase and grabbed a book from the shelf to look like she was returning it to the shelf when the door opened.

Liddy's eyes dried and she looked ready to laugh. Mrs. Vance grabbed her thin shoulder and gave it a warning squeeze. Liddy looked up at her. Mrs. Vance nodded her head slightly.

"Did you need something, Dr. Worcham?" Julia asked as she slid the book in her hand on to the shelf in front of her.

"Mr. Turnbull-Minchin wants to search the room."

Julia laughed. "Someone already has! Is there something specific you are looking for, Mr. Turnbull-Minchin. Perhaps we have seen it."

The superintendent frowned, his lower lip thrust forward. "I'm missing a ledger book."

"As you can see," Julia said, waving a hand at the bookshelf, "Mr. Montgomery had many books. I have not seen a ledger book in any of the books I have picked up off the floor and put back. It's possible we will find more books under all that tossed bedding. Perhaps you have already reviewed that area?" she asked archly.

"You and Miss Dorn were in this room at least once before we came this morning," Mrs. Vance said with her bird-bright manner. "Have you asked Miss Dorn?"

"Ladies," said Dr. Worcham repressively.

Beside him, Mr. Turnbull-Minchin looked like he was ready to explode.

"Are you quite all right?" Mrs. Vance asked. She kept Liddy pinned to her side.

"Where is Lady Branstoke?" he asked suddenly, looking about.

"Her husband came to visit. She is with him," Julia said.

"*Harrumph.* If you find a ledger book, bring it to my office," he ground out.

Mr. Turnbull-Minchin stomped out of the room. Dr. Worcham turned to follow him but stopped at the door. "This room is in a worse condition than I thought it was," he observed.

"Someone was not happy with Mr. Montgomery," said Julia.

"If you find any estate books, bring them to me first," he instructed.

Julia smiled. "Of course."

He closed the door behind himself as he left. Mrs. Vance went to the door to ensure she heard him walking away then waved a hand at Julia to open the hidden door.

"Could you hear?" Julia asked as Cecilia and James came back into the room.

"Yes," James said. "That space is lined with narrow shelves and old ledger books. I noticed a sliver of light at the other end. Is that an entry into the estate office?"

Liddy nodded.

"Does Mr. Turnbull-Minchin know about that door?"

"Mr. Montgomery said no," Liddy said.

"Does Dr. Worcham know?" he asked.

"Yes! He showed Mr. Montgomery."

"When did he do that, do you know?"

She thought. "About Easter?" she said. "He asked Mr. Montgomery to check the books. Mr. Montgomery was very smart with the maths. He was teaching me."

"Yes, that is what Lady Branstoke told me. That was kind of him."

She nodded enthusiastically then turned sad. "I miss him."

"I'm sure you do. Were you with him the night he died?"

"Yes, until he sent me away."

"Can you tell us about that night? Everything about that night?"

She nodded.

"You were outside with Mr. Montgomery?"

She nodded again. "Then the curfew bell rang just as Ratman came down the path, yelling for Mr. Montgomery."

"Ratman?" James repeated.

"That's what Liddy calls Mr. Ratcliffe," Cecilia explained.

Liddy nodded. "I don't like him and neither did Mr. Montgomery. He's a Ratman. I started to run back to the house, but Mr. Montgomery grabbed my hand and told me to go through his room instead."

"Why did he do that?" James crouched down in front of Liddy, gently taking her hands in his.

"So no one would know I was still outside when I wasn't supposed to be."

"That was kind of Mr. Montgomery."

She nodded. "He was like that. Then I heard Mr. Turnbull-Minchin and Dr. Worcham yelling for Mr. Montgomery. They sounded angry. I hid behind the bushes, right there," she said, pointing right outside the door.

"So, you didn't come in immediately like Mr. Montgomery told you to?" James asked.

She hung her head. "No."

"It's all right. I'm sure Mr. Montgomery would forgive you. What happened then?"

"Mr. Turnbull-Minchin said he wanted his book back. Said he knew Mr. Montgomery took it, but Mr. Montgomery wasn't there then. Archie was there and he lied and said no, he didn't have it."

"Mr. Montgomery didn't have it outside, did he?"

She tilted her head to the side. "No-o-o." she said slowly, drawing the word out.

"Then he didn't lie; he didn't have it with him." James advised somberly.

Liddy perked up at that and smiled. "Yes!" She sobered again. "Then Ratman told Mr. Turnbull-

Minchin to go away. That he needed to speak to his cousin. Mr. Turnbull-Minchin didn't listen, he came up to them and punched Mr. Montgomery."

"Mr. Turnbull-Minchin punched Mr. Montgomery?"

She nodded. "Well, it wasn't Mr. Montgomery it was Archie. He shouldn't have done that. It made Archie mad."

"What happened then?"

"Archie hit and hit Mr. Turnbull-Minchin. Ratman and Dr. Worcham tried to stop them. I got really scared then and ran into Mr. Montgomery's room. I saw the book on the bed. I didn't want Mr. Montgomery to get into any more trouble so I took it."

"And you put it in the cupboard in our hall," said Julia. "Why there?"

"Mr. Montgomery never went to your hall. Mr. Turnbull-Minchin wouldn't think to look for it there," she said simply with a small shrug.

"That was very clever, Liddy!" said Cecilia.

She grinned.

"It doesn't sound like anyone deliberately set out to murder Mr. Montgomery," Julia said.

"I don't know," said Mrs. Vance. "He was found in the canal in the morning. How did he get there?"

James and Cecilia acknowledged Mrs. Vance's observation. "As far as Liddy knew before she ran away, all four men were involved," Cecilia clarified.

"Possibly manslaughter," James said. "Or this Mr. Turnbull-Minchin could have killed him because of the ledger. I don't think Mr. Ratcliffe would have wanted Mr. Montgomery dead."

"Why do you say that?"

"Because of the will with the new executor?" Mrs. Vance suggested.

"Yes," James agreed. "According to Mrs. Montgomery and Soothcoor, Mr. Ratcliffe has been handling the estate properly."

"As far as they knew," said Cecilia.

"Yes, as far as they knew," James conceded. "Mr. Ramsay will need to review everything to determine if that is true or not."

"There is probably an executor's fee associated with the estate," Mrs. Vance said.

"Yes, but I can't see that being a big enough reason to frame a man for murder," James said.

"Would Mr. Ratcliffe stay the executor if Soothcoor was found guilty?" Cecilia asked.

"I could see the courts doing that," James said.

"I wonder if he's leveraged the Montgomery estate in an investment scheme?" Mrs. Vance said slowly. "My husband almost lost everything in investments outside of the cent per cents twenty years ago."

James stared at Mrs. Vance. "Mrs. Vance, you are a genius. I would wager that is precisely what he has done and why he can't afford to allow the estate to go into another's hands!"

"And Camden House Sanatorium is the investment, which isn't doing as well as he'd thought it would because Dr. Worcham does charity work—" Cecilia said.

"—And his superintendent is embezzling," Julia added.

"He can't let the estate go out of his control, at least not until he can stop the investment failing," Cecilia said.

"But he doesn't know about Mr. Turnbull-Minchin's activities," Julia said.

"Not yet, he doesn't know. He soon will," James said.

~

AFTER JAMES LEFT, the women made short work of finishing Mr. Montgomery's room, except for the bed linens as they hadn't received instructions on the bed linens as yet. They did remove all the bed linens for laundry, carefully inspecting every piece for a hidden note or item. They found nothing.

Liddy had become engrossed in arranging the broken pieces of porcelain statues, carefully trying to put them back together. Julia knelt next to her. "Maybe I can ask my son to get us some glue to repair these. Would you like that?"

Liddy shrugged. "It won't be the same. It will never be the same," she said sadly.

"No, they won't; however, they will be gentle reminders of Mr. Montgomery for you and your treasure box. Where is your treasure box? I thought it was in the hidden room."

Liddy shook her head. "No. It's outside. In a safe place with Mr. Montgomery's," she said with a smile as she moved pieces of a statue together for the best fit.

Cecilia and Julia looked at each other. Cecilia knelt on the other side of Liddy. The child ignored her, continuing to arrange the broken pieces. She hummed as she played with the pieces.

"Liddy can you show us where Mr. Montgomery's treasure box is? It might have important papers in it."

"Maybe," Liddy said, and went back to humming.

Cecilia inhaled deeply. Cecilia thought Liddy was in her world of memory, a safe place in her unsafe world. She didn't blame her. She remembered times she'd spent hours with her good memories, blocking out her reality.

"Liddy, I have one more thing to do before dinner and I'd like your help," Cecilia told the child. "It is something that will help Mr. Montgomery tell the truth about Mr. Turnbull-Minchin. Can you help me?"

Liddy stopped humming. Her hands stilled. Her eyes filled with tears, and her lip quivered.

"Liddy! What is it? I didn't mean to make you cry! Oh, come here!" Cecilia pulled Liddy into her arms.

Mrs. Vance rested her hand on Liddy's shoulder and Julia edged closer as she handed her a handkerchief. "Liddy!" she said.

Liddy's tears suddenly became a torrent, and sobs wracked her thin body.

Cecilia rocked her gently. "It's all right, little one," she said. "We're here for you. We care about you. *Sh-h-h.* Whatever it is, we are here for you."

Liddy sniffed. "But he's gone and he's never coming back!" she wailed.

"Oh," Mrs. Vance said. "She's mourning…Finally." She dropped to her knees beside them.

The three women wrapped their arms around Liddy, tears streaming down their cheeks for Liddy and Mr. Montgomery.

CHAPTER 22

PLANS IN MOTION

On his return to The New Bell Inn, Sir James invited Mr. Ramsay and Mr. Stackpoole to dine with him in his private parlor.

"Mr. Stackpoole, I'm pleased to see you recovered," James said as Young Stackpoole eased into a chair at the table.

"As am I!" he responded. "I cannot believe my father would do such a thing to keep me from meeting Mr. Montgomery. He is violently opinionated; however, I never would have thought he would have gone to such extremes as to make me sick. I have lost my father and that saddens me."

"I believe it would sadden anyone," James solemnly acknowledged.

Mr. Ramsay nodded. He took a sip of ale. "Ah gather from this invitation this evening you have some news to share, Sir James?"

"I do. There was a witness to some of the events that occurred after Lord Soothcoor left Camden Hall."

"A witness?" Mr. Ramsay repeated.

"A child who I believe is ten, from what I remember of her family."

"There is a child patient at Camden Hall? That isn't right," Mr. Stackpoole said.

"No, it's not right, but she is there. Her name is Lydia Wingate."

"What is wrong with her that she is at Camden Hall?"

"A mentally ill person will be a suspect witness afore a judge," Mr. Ramsay warned. He crossed his arms over his chest, a frown pulling his features together.

"She is not—in any way—mentally ill. She has a prominent wine-colored birthmark on her face that her mother does not like to look at and—as she is looking for a new husband—does not like others to see she birthed a child with such a deformity."

"Would that be Lady Millicent Wingate? The widow of Lord Edmund Wingate?" Mr. Stackpoole asked.

James nodded. "The child is bright. If Lady Millicent didn't want to see her, she should have put the girl in a school."

"Except that such a school sends their students home during the summer term."

"And that would not have suited Lady Millicent," James acknowledged.

"I think I read in the society papers that she has followed Prinny's entourage to Brighton for the summer," Mr. Stackpoole said.

"I'm sure the child's father's cousin, the Duke of Ellinbourne, will take her in. What we need to concern ourselves with is what she saw." James told them about the argument she heard.

Mr. Ramsay leaned back in his chair. "The magistrate should take her statement."

"There is a woman at Camden House, a Mrs. Vance—"

"Ah remember Mrs. Vance. She signed Mr. Montgomery's will. Smart woman, that one," Mr. Ramsay said.

"Yes. She suggested Mr. Ratcliffe invested the Montgomery estate in Camden House."

"If he did that, he would not want the executorship to go to another person."

"No. If Soothcoor were found guilty he could argue he should remain the executor."

"Yes, that is what the ladies think."

"You are thinking we should notify Squire Eccleston that there is a witness?"

"I am."

"Given his attitude this morning, do you think he'd do anything?"

"I think we give this over to the ladies to handle."

"The ladies?"

"Yes. Mr. Ramsay, you will write to Mrs. Vance, Mr. Stackpoole, you will write to your mother, and I shall write to my wife."

"To what purpose?"

"To suggest the interview at Camden House."

"Why three letters?"

"So, between them, they can decide whose letter may be discovered.—Or if more than one should be."

"Discovered, why?"

"To ensure the attendance of all parties."

"Might this put the child in danger?"

"We will be there, too."

"They won't let us in."

"No, they won't. We can sneak in through Mr. Montgomery's room."

"Isn't that kept locked?"

"Yes, but Liddy showed my wife where an extra key is hidden. We can take advantage of that knowledge."

Mr. Stackpoole quickly stood up. "I'll get paper, ink, and quills from Mr. Price!" he said.

"Request some Scotch whisky, too" Mr. Ramsay called after him. "We need somethin' stronger to toast with," he said.

Mr. Stackpoole laughed and agreed as he went out the door.

~

CECILIA WAS LAUGHING and trying to hold back a cough when the majordomo approached them in the library after dinner. They were having a light, herbal tisane that was Camden House's specialty for an evening beverage, before curfew called all the residents to go to their beds. He had letters for Julia, Mrs. Vance, and two for her. They looked at each other in questioning surprise, but eagerly opened their letters.

Mrs. Vance finished first. A deep frown pulled her brows together. She sat straighter in her chair as she carefully refolded her letter and held it in her lap.

After reading her first letter, Cecilia set it aside. James, in his letter to her, said all letters the ladies received conveyed the same information. Obviously, Mrs. Vance did not like the suggestion proposed. Cecilia picked up her second letter and slid her finger under the seal. This letter was shorter, and she was the only woman to receive a second letter. Cecilia read it carefully.

My dear delight,

By now I hope all have read their letters. Our messages are alike, each in our own voice. My request now is for either Lady Stackpoole or Mrs. Vance to accidently leave their letter behind to be found. As stated in our letters to you, we are requesting the magistrate come to Camden House tomorrow morning to examine Miss Lydia Wingate. How much he will believe her is unknown and might be inconsequential. Mr. Ratcliffe, Mr. Turnbull-Minchin, and Dr. Worcham will have no way of knowing how much she heard or saw the night Mr. Montgomery died. We know, we know what she knows is enough to counter their words that he died at the hands of Soothcoor.

We will not be leaving you to face the villains alone. We will come to Camden House and enter through Mr. Montgomery's room. If you might convince them to have the examination done in either the parlor where we met with Dr. Worcham, or in the library, we can be waiting outside the door to lend support when it is required, as I'm sure it will be.

James

"Gracious," Cecilia said. She handed the second letter from James to Mrs. Vance to read.

"Ah, now I understand," said Mrs. Vance. She handed the letter to Julia. "I will leave my letter behind. Such a forgetful old woman I am." She smiled conspiratorially.

"We will need to tell Liddy what is going on and what is expected of her," Cecilia said.

"How are we to ensure they allow us in the room with Liddy when she is questioned?" Julia asked.

Cecilia's lips compressed. "I think we just enter. We remind the men Liddy is a child and children are easily frightened. She needs the support of those she knows if she is to feel confident to tell the truth."

"If we tell Liddy to have a nasty child's tantrum if we are not allowed in, she will do so with great noise," Mrs. Vance said.

Cecilia smiled. "I suppose she would."

"I don't like this," Julia said. "That is a great deal of

pressure to put on a young child who has been abandoned."

"What Liddy has in her favor is she knows what love is, she experienced it with her father, even if her mother could not have it for her, and she knows we love her. That gives a child resiliency. And she is very smart."

"I suppose," said Julia, continuing to be troubled.

"And I've spoken to Mr. Quetal about the book we want him to examine," Cecilia said.

The curfew bell rang. Those in the room with them began putting away books and games. Mrs. Vance made a show of busily gathering up her shawl and reticule, which she carried everywhere with her. The reticule slipped out of her grasp and as she bent to retrieve it, she dropped her letter on the chair seat as she pulled her shawl back up over her shoulder. "I don't know why I carry my reticule with me everywhere, I am forever dropping it," she said aloud as she turned away from her chair.

Cecilia saw the letter on the chair. She took Mrs. Vance's arm in hers and walked slowly to the library door. "You don't need to carry one here, but I admit your reticules match your dresses so well, don't you agree, Julia?" Cecilia prattled.

"La! Mrs. Vance has been stunningly well coordinated in her attire ever since I've known her," Julia enthused.

Mrs. Vance preened at the compliments until she saw Liddy still at the puzzle table. "Liddy, child, it is time for bed. You can finish your puzzle tomorrow. Come away now."

"Yes, Mrs. Vance," Liddy said regretfully.

"No one will touch it," Mrs. Vance assured her.

"Yes, miss," agreed the young maid who entered the library. "Matron told me to fetch you."

"Bother," Liddy grumbled, though she went with the maid.

"Good," said Cecilia softly. "At least we will know where she will be." She stared after her. "I think we should fetch her early."

Mrs. Vance nodded. "I wake early. I will do so. No one should think anything of me doing so."

"Thank you."

The ladies were the last to leave the library. "I'll need to bring the storybook back here early," Cecilia said quietly.

"The storybook?" Julia asked.

"Yes, Mrs. Vance would say I was quite naughty," she said with a smile.

"Cecilia, what have you done?" Mrs. Vance asked with mock severity.

"Let's just say the storybook now tells a different tale, a tale I'm hoping Mr. Quetal can read."

CHAPTER 23

LIDDY

"How beautiful you look this morning, Liddy," Cecilia said when she came into breakfast the next morning. "Quite grown-up I'd have to say."

Holding her head up high, Liddy bobbed her head regally and smiled happily. She pulled the skirt of her dark-blue dress to the side, twisting her wrist to show off the deep flounce at the hem. Then she patted her matching hair bow. "Mrs. Vance helped me," she said with a hint of smug satisfaction that had the ladies repressing laughter.

"I agree with Cecilia," said Julia. "Did Mrs. Vance tell you what might happen today?"

Liddy nodded.

"And are you ready?"

Her brows pulled together and her lips tightened for a moment. "Yes!" she finally said, nodding decisively. Then her face shifted, and she looked at them with trepidation. "You will be with me, won't you?"

"Yes, sweetheart. Now let's eat so you can have your strength to answer honestly and clearly any questions that come to you."

"Gentlemen," said Julia, addressing Mr. Quetal and

Mr. Hobart. "I see the curiosity on your faces. Our Miss Lydia was a witness to some of the activity the night Mr. Montgomery died. It has been requested that she provide an accounting of what she saw to the magistrate."

"Our Liddy?" Mr. Hobart said.

"Yes, she was out past curfew with Mr. Montgomery. He ordered her back in the house. Liddy being Liddy, dallied and heard some things the magistrate should know."

"You poor child," Mr. Hobart said. His voice sounded flat, his eyes darting around. His manner troubled Cecilia. Quite at odds with how he'd been on previous occasions. He did not strike her as the least sympathetic and more like someone who wished to run off to tell what he'd heard. She had not thought that of him. She turned to the former estate agent. Now she could not afford to be as straight forward with him as she had intended. She considered her words carefully.

"Mr. Quetal, remember I told you I had a book for you to examine? Can you come with me after breakfast to look at it? I think it needs repair and you strike me as someone who could do the job," Cecilia said.

"I'd be delighted to, Lady Branstoke."

"Thank you," she said with a broad smile. "The library is such an important part of Camden House, I would not like the materials to begin to fall apart," she said.

Julia looked at Cecilia with a question in her eyes. She nodded back at her faintly.

"Mr. Hobart, have you ever been in Mr. Montgomery's room?" Cecilia asked, turning back to him. From his last statement and manner, her trust in the handsome fribble waned.

"No, I can't say as I have, Lady Branstoke. Why do

you ask?" he asked smoothly, dabbing at the corners of his mouth with his serviette.

She waved a hand airily. "I just thought the décor is something you might appreciate."

"Mr. Montgomery loved color," Mr. Hobart said.

"Yes, he did. A rich tapestry of colors—Romney influenced, perhaps?"

He laughed. "A good description."

"But you said you'd never been in his room."

"I—I haven't. He described it to me," he said.

"Of course," Cecilia said, nodding gently. Under the table she kicked Julia, though she smiled benignly.

Julia scowled at Mr. Hobart then looked back at Cecilia. "I must admit to being disappointed."

"Disappointed at what?" Mr. Hobart asked.

Julia laughed. "Nothing to concern you, Mr. Hobart. Just women talk. I'm sorry we changed the subject on you so abruptly. I was referring to something Lady Branstoke and I were discussing as we came downstairs. So silly.—Do you think, Mr. Hobart, that you could sit for me outside after breakfast? I should like to catch your likeness in charcoal," she said.

Cecilia smiled at her and nodded. Julia would get Mr. Hobart out of the way while Mr. Quetal examined the book.

"I used to draw all the time and confess I am woefully out of practice," Julia continued. "I think your features are a good reason to pick up my charcoal again. Can we meet on the terrace after breakfast, do you suppose?"

"I should be honored, Lady Stackpoole. I do have one little errand I should like to take care of first."

"Oh, but the light is so perfect right now! It should not hold you back long. Please, can we do it immediately?" she asked.

"I'll fetch your charcoal and paper for you, Julia,

while you get him posed as you should like. That will save some time," Cecilia suggested, delighting in Julia's ruse to get Mr. Hobart out of the way.

"Oh, would you indeed? That would be oh so helpful."

"Of course."

Mrs. Vance walked away with Liddy and Mr. Quetal. Mr. Hobart looked as if he should like to follow them, but ever the gentleman, he stayed by Julia's side.

Cecilia smiled. She went upstairs to get Julia's drawing things, then came directly back downstairs.

"Here, Julia. I'll be with Mrs. Vance and Liddy if you need me," she said. She hurried back into the house before Mr. Hobart could say anything. She hoped she was incorrect in her sudden concerns with Mr. Hobart. Better to apologize later than to take chances now.

In the library, at a far corner card table, she found Mr. Quetal with Mrs. Vance and Liddy examining a book on the table. Ostensibly, it was Liddy's story book. The previous day she'd cut out the story book pages and placed the account book pages in their place. She'd hated to cut the beautiful story book, but it was the perfect size to disguise the account book. She would arrange for the book's repair when she left Camden House.

She looked over Mr. Quetal's shoulder as he studied the book.

Liddy pointed to the entries Cecilia and Julia had noted of additional funds coming in from the families of patients. "Mr. Montgomery said this was bad doings," Liddy whispered.

Mr. Quetal frowned. He ran his finger down the list of entries, then turned the page, his finger hovering over Enoch Vance.

"Gracious," Mrs. Vance whispered. "He even got Enoch to pay something."

"I understand your concern, Lady Branstoke. I'd have to study the other books. However, this strongly smells of theft. I don't know what you would call it if the money never made it into the master books. It appears our superintendent is also buying cheaper goods and marking them as higher priced items and charging others additionally. He is probably pulling in tidy sums for himself. No wonder the sanatorium has not recovered in the way Mr. Ratcliffe had anticipated."

"He chose the wrong confederate," Cecilia said. "I—"

From outside the library, they heard several loud male voices. "Quick, close the book—Liddy, you hold the story book close to you and make sure the account pages inside do not fall out." Cecilia sat in the open chair at the other side of the table.

"What is this about a witness?" Mr. Ratcliffe shouted as the library door opened. "That's the most ridiculous thing I've heard of. It was pitch black at night—"

"There was a full moon—" countered Dr. Worcham.

"Too cloudy! Did you forget the thunder and rain that night? I tell you, I don't."

"The storm came up fast. There was moonlight after sunset," Dr. Worcham ventured.

"Where is this obnoxious child who is telling tales and causing Squire Eccleston to come here?"

Liddy huddled in her chair, trying to look small and invisible.

"And why would he want to listen to anyone from here? They're all a bunch of lunatics."

Behind him, Mr. Turnbull-Minchin laughed.

"Now Mr. Ratcliffe, you know that is not so," protested Dr. Worcham. He began worrying his hands together.

A handful of patients who'd been in the library slunk out the door around the men. Mr. Ratcliffe looked around the room and saw them in their corner. His eyes narrowed.

"You!" he said, pointing at Liddy. "Come here, you bloody lying street brat. The rest of you get out."

"No!" Liddy shouted back at him.

"And you are?" Cecilia asked, standing up. "Dr. Worcham, I didn't think visitors were allowed in here. Is this man a visitor or a new patient?"

Liddy lifted her head above the top of the chair back. "That's Ratman," she spat out, then ducked down again.

"Why you little—"

"Mr. Ratcliffe, please!" implored Dr. Worcham.

"Ah, Mr. Montgomery's cousin. Mr. Ratcliffe, please calm yourself. Camden House does not allow wild emotional displays. Have you had some sugar this morning? Is that the cause of this emotion?" Cecilia asked.

Mrs. Vance raised a hand to her lips to cover a laugh.

"Who the bloody hell are you?" Mr. Ratcliffe demanded.

"This is Lady Branstoke," Dr. Worcham said. "And she is correct. We do not allow emotional displays here. Please lower your voice, sir."

"Branstoke! Now I understand," sneered Mr. Ratcliffe. He turned to Dr. Worcham. "She and that husband of hers are just trying to find someone else to accuse of Malcolm's death."

"We are trying to discover the true order of events," Cecilia said, "for whomever is the guilty party. Miss Lydia Wingate was with Mr. Montgomery when the curfew bell rang the night Mr. Montgomery died. That was well after the Earl of Soothcoor had left. And that is all we, or she, will say until the magistrate arrives. However, I will tell you, Mr. Ratcliffe, that far from being *a street brat*, as you called her, if Liddy's father had not died, he would have been the Duke of Ellinbourne. And no, before you even suggest it—for I see how your mind works—she was not born on the wrong side of the blanket."

She sat back down and smiled reassuringly at Liddy. Then she looked up at Dr. Worcham. "With all the emotions flying around, might we not have some of Camden House's wonderful tisane to settle us as we await the magistrate?"

"Yes, Lady Branstoke. I'll send for it," he said. "Mr. Ratclife, Mr. Turnbull-Minchin, please have a seat over here. I think this area by the windows would be best for Squire Eccleston's questions for Miss Wingate." Dr. Worcham looked a little less frazzled and more in control when he took the gentlemen to the other side of the room. Cecilia was glad to see that. She did wonder how long the magistrate would be. Mr. Ratcliffe was volatile, and she feared he would not tolerate waiting long.

Shortly after the tea was served, Mrs. Worcham came to the library door. "Squire Eccleston has arrived," she said. She took a quick look about the room before she stepped back to allow the magistrate to enter. She followed him in.

"Emily, Lady Branstoke, Mr. Quetal, Mrs. Vance, we will be getting underway now. You may leave," Dr. Worcham said.

"No, that we can't," said Lady Branstoke. "You are interrogating a child. That isn't like interrogating an adult. She needs support. We have heard what she has to say, we are her support to ensure she isn't pressured into saying something that is not true."

"I have no objection to them staying so long as they remain quiet and we can get this over with as quickly as possible," the magistrate said. "This whole affair has taken up too much of my time. We should have a coroner in our district to handle deaths. I will be putting it forth that the position be filled as soon as possible. It has been vacant too long," he complained. He looked across the room at Liddy. "Child—what did you say her name was?" he asked Dr. Worcham.

"Miss Lydia Wingate," Dr. Worcham supplied.

"Yes. Miss Wingate. Come here, please," the magistrate ordered.

Cecilia stood up and came around the table to Liddy's side. "Pass your book to Mrs. Vance and I'll come with you," she told her softly. She laid her arm over Liddy's shoulder as she guided her to their make-shift examination area. Julia slipped into the room as they crossed the floor. Clouds moved across the sky outside, stealing the sunshine that had spilled through the windows, casting it in shadows. Cecilia hoped Dr. Worcham called for the gas lamps to be lit to ease the sudden gloom.

Liddy looked up fearfully at Cecilia when Dr. Worcham indicated the chair she should sit in.

"It's okay," Cecilia promised her. "I will not leave your side."

"Thank you for escorting the child to me. You can return to your place," the magistrate said dismissively.

"This is my place. I will remain here," Cecilia said calmly.

"You are as contrary as your husband," he complained.

"Thank you," Cecilia said, acknowledging his words with a tip of her head. "Most of the time, I am worse."

The magistrate scowled as he turned his attention to Liddy. "Miss Wingate, I received word last night that you were with Mr. Montgomery the night he died."

"Yes," she said.

"What were you doing?"

"Listening."

"What were you listening to?"

Liddy spread her arms wide. "Everything!" she said. "All the birds and insects and animals that are out at night. You hear them if you be still. That's what Mr. Montgomery said. And I did! Especially when there is a full moon, he said. We go inside," she rocked one way, "they come out," she rocked the other way.

The magistrate frowned. "So, you say you were outside to listen to nature?"

She nodded. "'Cause I did good on my maths that afternoon."

The magistrate looked confused.

"If I might explain," Cecilia said.

"Please do or I'm afraid this interview will go on far too long."

"Mr. Montgomery acted as her tutor, as Camden House is not set up for the care and education of children, is that not correct, Dr. Worcham?" Cecilia said.

Dr. Worcham cleared his throat with a reluctant, "Yes."

"What's wrong with her? Why is she here?"

"That's not relevant to your line of questions," Dr. Worcham broke in.

Squire Eccleston looked back at him, then at Liddy. "When did you leave Mr. Montgomery's side."

"We heard Ratman yelling for him."

"Who is this Ratman?" the magistrate interrupted.

Liddy huffed but pointed at Mr. Ratcliffe. "Him," she said and continued. "And then curfew bell rang. Mr. Montgomery told me to go back to the house through his room."

"His room?" questioned the magistrate, turning to Dr. Worcham.

"Mr. Montgomery had a ground-floor room that

has a door directly to the outside," Dr. Worcham explained.

The magistrate nodded then looked back at Liddy. "Why did he tell you to go that way?"

"So I wouldn't get in trouble for being out so late," Liddy said in an exasperated tone.

Cecilia repressed a laugh at Liddy's attitude for what she thought was an obvious reason.

"Then I heard Ratman yell again," she said, "and he sounded mad. I knew that would make Archie come out. I ran and hid behind the bushes outside Mr. Montgomery's room."

"Who is Archie?" Squire Eccleston asked, turning toward the other men.

Mr. Ratcliffe laughed. "My cousin's play acting."

"Is not," Liddy said hotly. "He lived in Mr. Montgomery. He and Gregory. They took care of him."

"What?" the magistrate asked, looking to the gentlemen beside him.

"All a farce," Mr. Ratcliffe insisted.

"No-o-o," Dr. Worcham said slowly. "They were all manifestation of Malcolm. Each handled different stresses in his life. They were why he felt safer living here. He could not control them and so felt better in a structured living situation."

"He'd get delusional, that's all," Mr. Ratcliffe said.

"He was also a thief," Mr. Turnbull-Minchin said.

"How so, sir?" the magistrate asked, his brow furrowed.

"He kept coming into the estate office and stealing things like records and account books, things he couldn't possibly understand."

"Why do you say that, Mr. Turnbull-Minchin?" Dr. Worcham asked.

"Stands to reason. Never looked you in the eye and creeping about quiet like. One day I found him in the estate office, pawing through old records. Nothing of interest in an old account book but records of a previous year's activity. He was a crazy man, and that is why he was here."

"Whether he was crazy or not, is not the issue here," the magistrate said repressively. "Miss Wingate, please continue telling us what happened."

"I heard Dr. Worcham and Mr. Turnbull-Minchin call for both Mr. Montgomery and Mr. Ratcliffe. Mr. Ratcliffe swung at Mr. Montgomery, and he fell down. When Mr. Montgomery got up it wasn't Mr. Montgomery, it was Archie. He was hitting and hitting Mr. Ratcliffe. Mr. Worcham tried to get Archie to stop, pulling at him. Then I heard Mr. Montgomery cry out. That scared me so I ran inside."

"You said you heard Mr. Turnbull-Minchin. Did you see him?"

Liddy shook her head. "No. The moon disappeared."

"Did you hear or see anything else?"

She shook her head again. "Thunder and wind?" she offered hopefully.

"I meant of the men or the fight."

"No. I got really scared. I ran up the servant stairs."

The magistrate frowned. "Is that all you can tell me of that night?"

"You should tell him what you took with you," Cecilia told her, gently squeezing her shoulder.

"You mean about the numbers book?" Liddy asked, looking up at Cecilia.

"Yes, dear."

"Numbers book!" blurted out Mr. Turnbull-Minchin. "You little thief! Where's my account book?" he demanded, lunging toward her.

The room burst into an uproar of people screaming, shouting and knocking over chairs to stop the superintendent. Cecilia whisked Liddy out of the chair and behind her as James, Mr. Ramsay, and Mr. Stackpoole burst into the room from the doctor's interview room.

James, anticipating the superintendent's actions, was the first one to reach him and delivered an uppercut that floored the man. He landed amid the chairs, nursing his chin. James stood over him, waiting to see if he would get up and charge him, but the man just glared at him. Mr. Ratcliffe and the magistrate helped him to his feet.

Once the room had settled down again, Cecilia sat Liddy in a chair farther away from the magistrate.

"This book, how did you get it?" the magistrate asked Liddy.

"I took it from Mr. Montgomery's room."

"Why did you take it?"

"Mr. Montgomery said it had bad maths in it."

"Bad maths?"

She nodded.

"Ridiculous!" protested the superintendent from where he sat nursing his jaw.

The magistrate glared at Mr. Turnbull-Minchin then turned back to Liddy. "What did you do with the book?"

"I hid it."

"Where did you hide it?"

"In a cupboard in the ladies hall," she said simply.

The superintendent jumped out of his chair.

"Sit down!" ordered the magistrate.

"But—" protested Mr. Turnbull-Minchin.

"I said, sit down. I doubt the book is there any longer." The magistrate looked up at Cecilia, "Am I correct, Lady Branstoke?"

"You are, Magistrate."

"What is so special about this account book that has Mr. Turnbull-Minchin so easily roused?"

"I can tell you that," Mr. Quetal said calmly, rising

from his chair at the table across the room. He held the storybook with the hidden account book between its covers.

"And who are you?"

"Quetal, magistrate. Jeremiah Quetal. I am an estate agent—or was an estate agent by trade until my breakdown. Lady Branstoke asked me to look at the account book Liddy had hidden. I have done so this morning."

"And?"

"Among other things, it reveals additional charges made to relations of those staying here. The charges vary but are monthly. They appear to be based on the financial capabilities of the patients' families."

"He did ask me for details on our financials when I brought my wife here," James said.

"There is a letter slipped in the pages of the book from a Mr. Yellin, protesting an additional charge and demanding to know when his wife would be well enough to come home," Mr. Quetal added.

Cecilia watched Mr. Ratcliffe's face as the truth about the account book came out. It went from confused curiosity to outrage.

"You killed him! You wanted my cousin dead!" Ratcliffe proclaimed.

All eyes turned to Mr. Ratcliffe. He rose from his chair. "You said you threw that rock just to break his attention from fighting me, and that hitting him was an accident. But it wasn't, was it? You meant to hit him in the head."

"Even if I did, that didn't mean it was going to kill him."

"And it didn't then, did it? While Worcham took me into the house to attend to my injuries, you were supposed to help Malcolm. And you did. You helped him to his death!"

"I didn't put him in the water," Mr. Turnbull-Minchin protested.

"No, you didn't," said Mrs. Worcham from where she stood by Mrs. Vance. "I did," she said softly.

"Emily!" protested Dr. Worcham.

"I saw Mr. Turnbull-Minchin come in after you took Mr. Ratcliffe to a treatment room. He was alone. I wondered where Mr. Montgomery was. I had heard you all yelling minutes earlier so I went outside to see if I could help him. He was alive and conscious. Barely. He grabbed my hand. I tried yelling for someone to come help, there was another flash of lightning and clash of thunder nearly on top of each other. No one could hear me, but he wanted to say something to me. I leaned close to him. He said—and I swear there was a smile on his face—he said a woman's name, something like Lily or Lila—"

"Lilias," supplied Cecilia.

Mrs. Worcham looked over at her. "Yes, that was it. He said *Lilias can wed Alastair, as she should have.* Then he squeezed my hand tighter for a moment and died. I felt a peace in his body. I sat there beside him, crying in the rain. He was a nice man. I figured he would under-stand my actions. I rolled him into the canal and came back into the house."

"Why did you roll him into the canal?" her husband asked.

"I didn't know what had gone on. I didn't know who was responsible. I knew you would be devastated at any damage to Camden House's reputation. I thought if he was in the canal it could look like a suicide drown-ing, like that Miss George.

"Oh, Emily," her husband said.

"Well, Squire Eccleston, will you release Soothcoor from jail?" James asked.

The magistrates' mouth quirked sideways, and his

thumbs circled each other. "Damn you, Branstoke," he muttered. Finally, he stood up. "Dr. Worcham, Mr. Ratcliffe, Mr. Turnbull-Minchin, you are all under arrest for falsifying the events surrounding Mr. Montgomery's death and accusing an innocent man. More charges to follow," he ground out at the end.

Cecilia hugged Liddy. "You were magnificent!" she whispered.

Liddy giggled and hugged her back.

EPILOGUE

SUMMERWORTH PARK, AUGUST 1816

ecilia watched James snake a ribbon out to Randy for the cat to attack. The cat didn't disappoint. He reared up, tossing his head from side to side before leaping on the moving ribbon. James laughed, pulled the ribbon out from under the cat and snaked it out again.

"I thought you didn't like cats, that you tolerated Randy for my sake," she said in a teasing tone.

"I don't, on the whole. I prefer dogs., This cat is different. This cat has a personality."

"You don't think other cats do?"

"Not that I've seen, no," he said, snaking out the ribbon again. This time Randy was expecting his action and attacked his hand before he pulled it back. "Ouch! He got me!" James said half annoyed, half amused.

"Part of his personality," Cecilia said drily as she leaned back into her nest of pillows on the blue sofa. She rested a hand on her growing stomach where sometimes she felt a fluttering kick.

"Excuse me, Sir James, Lady Branstoke, correspondence has arrived for you," their butler Cranston said from the morning room doorway.

James straightened. "I'll take it," he said, extending

his arm over the back of the sofa to take it from the butler. "Ah, it's from Soothcoor with an update on Camden House," he said. He settled into his corner of the sofa, crossing one leg over the other.

My dear James and Cecilia,

As you know from my last correspondence, following my marriage to Lilias, knowledge of Mr. Ratcliffe's attempt to frame me for Malcolm's murder resulted in a sentence to a prison hulk ship for five years.

Since then, there was a run on his bank which subsequently collapsed. I arranged to purchase his estate, and his shares in Camden House, at a deep discount, on the condition the funds were given to his wife, Mr. Montgomery's mother. She has retired to Bath.

Mr. Turnbull-Minchin could not be tried for murder as there was no proof he did more than throw a rock at him; however, for his role in the evening's events and the embezzling of Camden House monies, he was sent to a penal colony.

Dr. Worcham was absolved of his role in attempting to frame me as he was judged intimidated and threatened by Mr. Ratcliffe.

I am typically a forgiving man. I do not forgive him for the pain and anguish he caused my darling wife Lilias in agreeing to fake Mr. Montgomery's death two years ago. I purchased his shares in Camden House. He and Mrs. Worcham have gone to Scotland to live.

Squire Eccleston has resigned his magistrate position. Dr. Denning, my old friend, has agreed to take over Camden House as a sanatorium and to become the coroner for the area. Mr. Quetal—upon Lady Branstoke's suggestion—I have made steward.

Mrs. Vance approached me and requested to be named the housekeeper, a role I understand, they had not had. I agreed with great alacrity. She is a sharp woman. I think she and Mr. Quetal will do well together.

Lastly, Lydia is enjoying herself while numerous family members are debating who shall have the pleasure of her company on a permanent basis. She is a delight. I wish I could keep her.

My best to you and Cecilia. I hope to see you in the new year after we both have expanded our families.

Yours,
Soothcoor

CECILIA SMILED and sighed contentedly when James finished reading. "Finally, Soothcoor has the happily ever after he deserves."

"Yes. And so do we," James said.

Cecilia slid her eyes toward him. "Until our next mystery."

THE END

AFTERWORD

Malcolm Montgomery suffered from Dissociative Identity Disorder (DID), formerly known as Multiple Personality Disorder.

Many books, TV shows, and movies that have characters with DID have one of the identities, known as alters, as "the villain," the one who committed the crime. I wanted to present a more sympathetic look at this mental illness.

I know about DID as my late ex-husband suffered from this condition. I don't know what triggered my husband's "splits"; however, like Sir James, I have my suspicions.

Giving a character this illness has been cathartic for me. Like Malcolm, my late ex-husband was a good man. He has been gone almost twenty years. May he forever rest in peace.

—Holly Newman

Gentleman's Trade

Reckless Hearts

A Lady Follows

The Rocking Horse (novella)

Perchance to Dream (short story)

ABOUT HOLLY NEWMAN

I decided to be a writer when I was in the fifth grade. I filled notebooks with stories—until a mean-spirited high school teacher told me I had no talent for writing. Crushed, for several years I stopped writing, but writing was an itch that wouldn't go away.

My interest in the Regency period came while in high school when I volunteered to re-shelve returned books at the community library. Every week there were Georgette Heyer novels to be shelved. I finally checked one out and became immersed in the world of the Regency.

Fast forward ten years. When attending Science Fiction Conventions, I met people who read science fiction, but also enjoyed the works of Jane Austen and Georgette Heyer, just as I did! They liked these books so much that they wore Regency costumes at the science fiction conventions. They even had Regency era dancing on the convention program. These science fiction readers and writers knew a lot about the Regency era. Intrigued, I did research on the era and quickly went from casual Regency reader to a Regency history buff. Woo-hoo!

After that, with encouragement from science fiction authors, it was just a small step to writing Regencies.

After living thirty years in the Arizona desert, I now live in Florida, seven miles from the Gulf Coast, with my husband, Ken, and our *clowder* of cats. (I don't dare say a number of cats. My husband has developed a habit of collecting strays.)

Subscribe to my newsletter to learn about books and other writings I'm working on. You can sign up here to subscribe and get *Perchance to Dream*, a Georgian fantasy short story.

And be sure to follow me on Bookbub, to be notified about new books and book sales.

Here are other ways to connect!

Website
Facebook
Pinterest
Goodreads
Etsy

www.ingramcontent.com/pod-product-compliance
Lightning Source LLC
Chambersburg PA
CBHW011915130726
47903CB00016B/3040